Fantasy's Bar & Grill
TRILOGY

Michelle Hughes

Tears of Crimson Publishing

Tears of Crimson Publishing
27687 AL Hwy 22
Verbena, AL 36091
www.tearsofcrimson.com

Publisher's Note: This is a work of fiction. Names, characters, places, and incidents are a product of the author's imagination. Locales and public names are sometimes used for atmospheric purposes. Any resemblance to actual people, living or dead, or to businesses, companies, events, institutions, or locales is completely coincidental.

Book Layout ©2014 BookDesignTemplates.com

Fantasy's Bar & Grill Trilogy/ Michelle Hughes. -- 1st ed.
ISBN-13: 978-1499112139
ISBN-10: 1499112130

Seduced

Fantasy's Bar and Grill – Book 1

Michelle Hughes

Tears of Crimson Publishing

CHAPTER ONE

Interview

"Stop fidgeting, Zoey. You look great, and Mr. Harold isn't 'that' bad."

I tugged at the hem of the short leather mini-skirt again, subconsciously hoping it would magically grow a few inches in length if I continued pulling. "This is the same man that threated to fire your ass on the spot for playing with a customer." I refused to mention that she'd given vivid detail about laying over said customer's knee while he spanked her.

"I was on the clock and left the bar unattended. Unless you plan on getting a little action you'll be fine." Rachel grinned wickedly and waggled her eyebrows. "I'd actually pay to see you let go that way."

I shivered unintentionally at that thought. All I wanted was a paycheck and since jobs were getting harder to come by these days, this was a position I needed as much I would hate getting. For not the first time this month I regretted not filing sexual harassment charges against my last boss since he was the reason I was currently unemployed.

"Let's get this over with before I remember all the reasons I'm an idiot for allowing you to set up this interview." I'd applied for at least twelve other jobs in the last four weeks at different law firms but my ex-boss had sabotaged each interview. The little prick had told me in no uncertain terms I'd have to crawl back to him if I planned on working in this city again. If it hadn't been for Rachel I probably would have because my bank account was running dangerously low of funds.

"Just remember to address him as sir, be respectful and you'll have no problems. I think you're just meeting him today, but the same rule goes for the other partners."

Grabbing my clutch purse off the island bar I felt my stomach clench. If you lived in New York you'd at least heard about the owners of Fantasy's Bar and Grill. They were known as the billionaire bad boys, or so the local papers labeled them, and for good reason. Each owner was a notorious billionaire playboy and they all had stories that the paparazzi loved breaking to juice up the headlines.

I followed Rachel to the elevator and continued to tell myself that I could handle this job. Even my normally loud mouth friend wouldn't tell me what really went on behind closed doors, but unless they were somehow breaking the law I'd find a way to deal with whatever they threw at me. Knowing I'd have to sign a contract to keep whatever happened at the bar confidential, if I was hired, only made me more curious about what type of establishment I was walking into.

Rachel waved down a cab when we made it outside and I felt my nerves run full throttle as we drove toward Fantasy's. The city was full of life as rush hour closed in and I let the insanity surrounding me consume my thoughts so I didn't overthink this interview. Worst case scenario is I don't get the job. I'm not qualified to be a waitress so at least if I fail at this it's of my own doing and not because I refused to sleep with my boss.

Two years of paralegal training down the drain. You'd think lawyers would have ethics and not be swayed by a sleazy little weasels word, but if I've learned anything it's that money is power, and since I'm basically broke I'm the one left to suffer. We pull up to the building and I gasp.

Fantasy's is housed in a majestic brick building that boasts at least five stories. Logically I know they are just renting space here but it made the bar look more impressive to be surrounded by all the extra room. Stepping out of the cab, I pull down on the irritating skirt hoping my ass isn't hanging out. It was Rachel's idea that I wear the most revealing outfit in her closet, and I'm hoping her intuition is right. At the moment I feel like a high-priced call girl.

Following her through the rotating glass door, I notice she enters a code on the next door we reach. It's a little ironic that such a security measure is taken at a bar, but I don't comment on it. All I can concentrate on is not busting my ass in the four inch heels that Rachel encouraged me to wear. Since I'm only five feet tall they give me a little more confidence except I'm not very steady on my feet walking in stilts.

"Just remember what I said. Make sure you call him sir and be polite." Why does she seem nervous all of a sudden? Just when I have my breathing back on an even keel she's got me worried.

At first glance, Fantasy's looks like every other upscale club in the city. Rachel has taken me to so many I know this for fact. The floor is a polished hardwood that matches the bar, and dark burgundy. Rounded booths accompanied by two small tables each in the center line the walls. It's almost cozy and I'd expected something much larger.

Rachel walks behind the bar and picks up a phone. "I have Zoey with me, where would you like me to bring her, Sir?" I watch as she nods and hangs up the receiver. "We're going to the offices."

I glance around as I follow her lead toward the back and take in a few more of the amenities. Swiveled bar stools with high backs, shimmering wine glasses hanging from an overhead rack, it really is tasteful as far as a bar goes. We continue walking through a door and I'm taken down a long hall. A set of elevators meets my eyes and she pushes a button.

Maybe I'd been wrong about my assumption that they rented space in the building. After going up to the top floor, I'm almost certain I had. We walk out onto the floor and it's plain to see this is office space. A large greeting desk is unmanned and Rachel walks around it. I can tell she's been up here many times before by the ease in which she navigates us to the back. She knocks on a set of double doors and a deep masculine voice encourages us to enter.

We're in a boardroom and I discover quickly I'm not meeting with just one of the owners but all of them. I know each of them by name, like I said they are pretty notorious in the papers. "Ms. Summers, please take a seat, Rachel you can wait outside."

I don't want her to leave and that's not like me because I've always stood on my own two feet. Being in the presence of these four enigmatic men makes me extremely nervous though. It doesn't help that they all look like they stepped off the cover of GQ. I give her the look of panic I feel but she still follows his command.

"You can relax Ms. Summers, we don't normally attack potential employees during an interview." Samson Harold is chuckling deeply and I find that sound goes straight to my sex. I'm amazed I make it to the chair at the end of the long desk since my legs start to tremble.

Trying to keep my head in the game I force myself to meet his dark grey eyes. "That's a relief, I've already lost one job over something similar." I honestly didn't mean to let that spill out of my mouth. One of my bad habits was to say exactly what I felt and it landed me in trouble more than once. Owning my mistake I took a deep breath thinking this interview couldn't start off in a worse way.

I wasn't expecting the smiles that were forwarded my way by such gorgeous men. It was my opinion that even

today, men didn't appreciate a woman who truly spoke
her mind, no matter what year we were living in.

"We've heard about your troubles with Baxter
Kingston, the third." This came from Miles Dresdon, the
man Forbes had dubbed the redheaded wonder of Wall
Street. It was rumored that his Irish heritage had
bought him a ticket into financial stardom since his
father owned a seat on the New York Stock exchange.

"Perhaps we should wipe that off the table first
thing." Leon Alexander was the son of fashion model,
Ella Alexander, who still at sixty was sought after for
her expertise in the industry. "Why don't you tell us
what happened to cause your unemployment."

I knew this was coming, but I still hated recanting
the history. "It's pretty simple really, Baxter wanted to
have sex and I told him to go stick it up his own... um
backside." Just remembering the grief that slimly little
toad caused me, pissed in my cornflakes.

"So he fired you?" Leif Barret, a.k,a the sexy boy
wonder of real estate, seemed to find the story comical
since he was biting back a laugh.

"Actually not the first time. When he corned me in
his office and tried to 'persuade' me to give in, I kicked
him in the balls and broke his nose. Then he fired me."
I was really not making a good impression. With a deep
sigh I sat back in my chair. "Just so you know I don't
normally go around doing that." My anger at recalling
that scenario deflated and left me discouraged. I
seriously needed to learn to gain a mouth filter.

"I'm curious. Why didn't you file charges against
him?" Lifting my eyes to Samson's gorgeous face I tried

to reign in the first words that came to mind, which weren't very respectful.

"I liked Deidre," that was Baxter's wife, "as much as I wanted to bring the little worm to his knees I knew it would hurt her." Call me a sentimental fool, but hurting a woman with four children over something like that wouldn't allow me to sleep well at night.

"I admire your restraint, but I assume that's not paying your bills. You've got a degree in paralegal studies, why aren't you searching for a career that better suits your skills?" Miles's emerald green eyes were searching my face and he looked like he wanted to laugh. I wasn't sure if that made me like or want to smack him. Nothing about this situation was funny to me.

"Believe me I've tried. Baxter has spread rumors to every employer I've attempted to hire on with that I was a prick tease and was just looking to blackmail my way up the corporate ladder." I couldn't help the sarcasm that entered my tone. I really wanted to kick the little weasel in the balls again for the lies he told.

"I think we've heard enough." Samson stood up to his impressive six foot height and walked toward me. I admit the man was walking sex personified, and yeah it did funny things to my insides. "We completed an intensive background check when Rachel suggested you to our company and I believe you're telling the truth. Be that as it may, I won't be offering you the job as a waitress."

I hoped the disappointment I felt didn't show on my face as I attempted a smile. Trying to put on a professional facade, I stood and offered my hand. "I thank you for your time." It was unfair, but life was rarely fair. I refused to let my dignity unravel before I left his room.

Samson took my hand in his much larger one and I swear I felt a bolt of electricity in his warm grasp. "I'm afraid you misunderstood." He smiled warmly and I took in a deep breath as the twinge of desire shot through my body. "Your talents would be wasted in such a position, and I believe we have one that can put your skills to better use."

He was still holding my hand and I got lost in those dark eyes of his. I couldn't force myself to utter a word as I simply stared at him. "Before I can describe the job in more detail, I'll need to assure that what we discuss doesn't leave this office." Finally he released my hand and walked back to the head of table, picking up a folder.

"You'll need to read through this and decide if you're willing to sign before we go any further." He placed the manila folder in front of me and I noticed the other men standing up. "We'll give you some time."

Without any further communication the men filed out of the room leaving me alone. Opening up the folder I stared down at the contract. Rachel had already informed me that all employees signed a confidentiality agreement before being hired so I expected this, but what I didn't know was exactly what type of position was being offered.

The form was pretty standard and I'd seen several of these cross my desk in the law office. Usually these were reserved for companies that had product and/or trade secrets, or software startups wanting protection from hackers or competition. Why a bar and grill would feel the need to possess one was a little confusing. I decided I would learn soon enough and after scouring through each line, I signed. Standing up, I walked to the doors where the men had departed and opened it.

Samson and Rachel were the only two people waiting and they seemed deep in conversation. I didn't want to be rude, but now that I had signed his agreement my curiosity was getting the best of me. "Excuse me Sir, but I'm finished." It was the first time since the interview began that I remembered to call him sir.

He held out his hand for the document and I handed it over. Watching him thumb through to the signature page I admit I was growing impatient to know why such secrecy was needed. "Rachel you can join us if you'd like." Samson walked back into the room and we both followed.

He motioned to the chair I'd sat in earlier, so I sat. Rachel sat down on my left and Samson on the right. "What I would like to offer you is the position of our paralegal here. I have an attorney on the payroll, but as I'm sure you're aware keeping him on staff full time would be costly, and you're services in this area would be just as effective."

He continued to talk, advising me of a generous salary and the benefits that went along with the position and I was admittedly stunned. The salary more than doubled what Baxter had paid and for the first time in a month I allowed myself to hope that I might come out from under the dark cloud he'd left over my life.

"Obviously I'm interested, but it might help if I knew exactly what I'll be doing for your company?" Interested was a light word, I was ready to flip cartwheels knowing that with this income I could actually afford to take night classes in law. It had always been my intention to become a lawyer.

"At Fantasy's we offer something besides the socializing opportunities afforded to a bar. We deal in pleasure, Ms. Summers. Our clients are chosen by interview and only a select few can afford the services we provide."

The first red flag went up at his words and immediately I assumed prostitution. "Is what you're doing here legal?" Please let it be legal, I thought to myself. I really needed this job but my obvious feeling was there would be no need for confidentiality if the services provided were accepted under the law.

"I can see by the look on your face what you're thinking, Ms. Summer. But you're wrong. What we offer at Fantasy's is perfectly legal and no we're not pimps." Samson chuckled warmly and I was hit with an overwhelming sense of desire that shocked me to my core.

"Then perhaps you'd explain what it is you do offer?" Dear lord, I wanted to find out if those full lips felt as good as they looked speaking. My libido was definitely out of control, a first for me. Rachel was sitting in the chair being as quiet as I'd ever seen her. Obviously she felt a little uncomfortable in his presence.

"While we do offer a version of sexual fantasy, the people that pay for our services don't pay for sex." His beautiful lips lifted in a smirk. "Of course if our clients decide to take it further, that's at their discretion and we can't be held accountable for those actions."

This was throwing up another red flag. The call girl services in town were able to fly under the radar by calling themselves a dating industry, but everyone knew what really happened behind closed doors. "Perhaps you'd explain the sexual fantasies you offer." Before I got up and walked out that door hating myself for turning down such a great financial opportunity.

"To put it bluntly, whatever fantasy the client chooses. Bondage or sadomasochism, playing out roles from a romance novel, cowboys, Harem scenes, you name it and we bring their desires to life. We have decorators that arrange the scene rooms, and I guess you could call them actors or actresses that help them live out the fantasy."

Definitely not what I'd been expecting and honestly I was intrigued. "So you're saying these fantasies don't have to contain sex? It sounds like every one of those could end up being sexual in nature." It actually sounded like something I wouldn't mind trying for myself and didn't that make me a hypocrite? Without the sex of course, but I could see myself paying to act out a scene where I got to berate my ex-boss for being the backstabbing little weasel he was.

"What I'm saying is we bring fantasies to life in whatever capacity our clients ask for, but it's not always about sexual pleasure. For instance, a recent scene was nothing more than a customer being treated like an infant while our actress mothered him. People all have different needs, Ms. Summers, at Fantasy's we offer them the opportunity to live them out. You'd be surprised how many older women just want to have some handsome young man pamper them with a day spa scenario while telling them how attractive they still are."

"So why do you need me?" I was having a hard time understanding how a paralegal could help in the creation of developing a fantasy role-play scenario.

"Actually your job will be very important. Each of our clients have certain expectations from what they want in a scene. We've discovered that having all those needs addressed in a contract beforehand makes things run more smoothly. I will say up front that this won't be like contracts you've helped prepare for clients in the past. Since there is a form of sexuality involved, each action needs to be addressed before things move forward so we don't inadvertently cross a line that would make our customers regret their decision."

"I'm curious, how much does a client pay for this service?" It really was none of my business but I was truly interested. I told myself not for personal reasons, but the scene with the ex-boss did come to mind.

"It's a flat fee of ten thousand dollars and then the yearly membership fee. Since we cater to a specific crowd a donation of twenty thousand a year covers our operational needs."

I almost fell out of my chair at the amount. "That explains how you can afford my salary." Holy shit that was a lot of money! My mouth gaped open and I hurriedly closed it.

"Employees get a discount though." He was laughing at me now and I knew he'd perceived my interest.

I had to get things back on a professional level. "I'll admit this is an interesting offer." Interesting wasn't really the word, exciting fit better. "Honestly I wouldn't have any clue on how to talk to clients about their, um, desires?"

"That's why I invited Rachel in with us." I'd forgotten she was even in the room as I watched him speak. The man really was too sensual for words. "She's been with us a few years and can give you all the background you'll need to decipher a client's needs. We've also comprised a portfolio of some of the more common fantasies and what questions need to be addressed. As always myself, or any of the other partners are available if you get stuck."

"I'll enjoy being able to discuss some of the incredible things that happen here with someone finally." Rachel was grinning at me and I knew she was just excited as I was about working together.

"As long as you remember that our clients expect complete confidentiality." Samson gave her a menacing look and I felt it roll over me even though it was directed at her.

"Of course, Sir. I would never reveal your secrets." Rachel being humble? I had to figure out how he managed that one since she outmaneuvered me on a daily basis and always seem to be one step ahead.

His expression relaxed immediately and he turned those devastating grey eyes back on me. "So Ms. Summers, will you be joining us at Fantasy's?"

How the hell did any woman say no to this man? I had the feeling most women didn't, and if the gossip rags were to be believed, he had a harem of his own willing to indulge him. "I think I will Mr. Harold." Forcing my own desires back, I knew I needed to remember this man was my boss and I couldn't allow myself to think of him that way.

"Wonderful. I have a three month back log of potential clients waiting so you can start as soon as you'd like." If circumstance had been different I would have taken more time to consider employment here. As it was I needed the income so if there was a possibility I could do this job, I had to take it.

"Thank you for the opportunity Mr. Harold. If it suits you I can start tomorrow morning?" I reached out my hand to shake, and the warmth of his gave me a rush. I refused to let myself think about the instant attraction I felt toward him.

"That sounds good. My secretary will have your employment papers waiting at the desk tomorrow morning at eight. Oh. While I appreciate Rachel's attire for her position, I think casual corporate might be more suited for your job title."

The smirk on his face made me flush and I nodded feeling a tad insecure as he glanced over my person. "I'll remember that, Sir." I wanted to explain how I normally didn't dress this way but he didn't seem like the type that accepted excuses. Instead for possibly the first time in my life, I used my mouth filter and kept silent.

"I'll walk you ladies to the elevator. Rachel make sure you give her the code to enter the building tomorrow."

We followed him out of the office and down the hall to the elevator. "Go over the type of scenarios with her tonight as well, I'll make sure a bonus appears on your check."

"Yes Sir. I think we'll have a great girl's night discussing that topic." Rachel was giggling and immediately Samson's face tensed. "With respect to the clients of course, Sir."

"Of course." Samson hit the ground floor button and silence filled the small space as we rode down. He didn't speak again until it came to a stop. "Have a nice evening Ms. Summers." With a small smile he walked off leaving Rachel to lead me out the exit.

She chatted excitedly on the way home and I was struck with how different our personalities were. Rachel and I had been best friends since high school but we were as different as night and day. While she was outgoing and a magnet for the men, I was usually more reserved and the girl who never got asked out. I lived vicariously through her during junior college and we'd moved in together after graduation.

I guess she was the yin to my yang and vice versa because while we were polar opposites, our friendship was the kind that was meant to stand the test of time. I'd only dated one guy and when he broke my heart, it was Rachel that pushed my ass out of the depression I'd let myself drown in for almost a year after the fact.

She drug me to parties on campus when I wanted to sit in my room and sulk. Finding out the only guy you'd ever loved fucked you to get initiated into a fraternity

did something to a girl. Without my best friend I would
have become like those cat ladies you hear about.

It had taken him almost six months to convince me to
give it up for him and it was the worst experience of my
life. I had to give it to Brad, he was one hell of an actor.
It took him telling me to my face that I sucked in bed
and he no longer wanted to see me after he'd won a
wager, for me to face the fact that he'd never loved me.

I didn't do relationships now. Men were great eye
candy but as far as trusting one in that capacity again?
Not in this lifetime. The way I saw it, sex wasn't worth
the price you paid and women that enjoyed it were just
lying to themselves.

"I can't believe you're working for Fantasy's!" Her
words pulled me out of the funk I always felt when I
remembered Brad. We'd just pulled up at our
apartment and Rachel paid off the fare. I hated that she
was bucking the costs for everything these days, but at
least soon I'd be able to pay her back. "I say we celebrate
and order in Chinese!"

Her excitement was contagious, and instantly I was
drawn out of my walk down memory lane. "I'm already
so in debt to you, you'll own my first paycheck."

"Hell girl, you're making more than I am now. I say
we celebrate!" Giggling as we walked into the building,
I knew this is why I loved her so much. Nothing phased
Rachel. Other than Samson. I'd noticed how her
demeanor changed instantly when he was around.

"Okay, but the minute I get paid I'm taking you out
for steaks." That had been our weekly treat to ourselves
before I was fired, and I missed that hunk of beef.

"Deal! You know I don't mind springing for that if you'd rather?" I'd stopped the weekly treat because it wasn't fair for her to fork over so much money.

"Two weeks. I think we can live without it a little longer." Grinning, I pushed the elevator button. I was really excited about the new job even though I had no idea what I was really in for. Asking me to set up contracts for a person's fantasies was like suggesting a nun become a stripper.

"We really do need to go over what happens at Fantasy's. Chinese will be better, we can talk while we wait." We got off on the second floor and walked to our apartment. For the first time in weeks I felt life wasn't spinning out of control.

"I have a feeling I'm about to get an education." Pulling the keys out of my purse, I unlocked the door and walked inside.

"You have no idea!" The way she was laughing told me I was in for an awakening.

My reserved side was cringing at the thought, but the part of me that had pushed back all thoughts of sensuality was curious. Maybe this was just what I needed to stop thinking about the turn my life had recently taken. More excited than I can remember being in forever I pulled a bottle of our favorite wine out of the fridge, poured up two glasses, and went to sit on the couch while she ordered our meal.

CHAPTER TWO

Eye Opener

One box of Moo Goo Gai Pan and half a bottle of wine later, my eyes were still wide as Rachel explained the kinky shit that went on at Fantasy's. I wasn't a mental prude, living with her had definitely opened my eyes about the world of sexuality I was missing. Still, some of the scenarios she defined blew my mind.

"So a client actually wanted to be ravished by an alien? No offense but some slimy creature with tentacles sounds more like a nightmare than a fantasy." Taking a deep gulp of my wine, I couldn't repress a shudder.

"You really should read some science fiction romance once in a while." Rachel was giggling at my expression. "There's some totally hot alien guys out there with human features and I guess you'd say interesting anatomy."

When she went into an explanation about their sexual parts I almost choked on my drink. Having some creature bigger than a horse stuffing himself inside my body just didn't appeal. "Yeah, I think I'll wait for the movie." Not!

"Okay. Okay. Maybe you're right. But you have to admit being a smorgasbord feast for hunky men, isn't bad. Just think about all those sexy men eating off you. Even you have to find that tempting."

Groaning at the disturbing thought, I shook my head. "Sorry Rachel I don't think guys using me as serving platter would be a big turn on." Obviously I had some major hang-ups because having a guy go downtown from the place where I bled? I couldn't even imagine why a man would want to or how the woman didn't worry that she smelled funny when he did it.

"You know you might as well be a virgin." Rachel rolled her eyes at me and sighed. "Having a guy eat your pussy is one of the most amazing things you'll ever feel."

"Uh. Yeah, no." I didn't even mind her bad girl talk anymore, so I had opened up a lot in the last few years, but thinking of sexuality that way? I wasn't ready for that.

"One of these days you're going to take a chance again and forget what that dickwad did to you. Sex is really enjoyable, Zoey, you don't know what you're missing." She filled our wine glasses to the brim, and gave me a look of regret.

We didn't talk about him. It was a girl code rule with us. "Don't start, Rach." I would never forget that painful night as long as I lived and any talk of it just made me remember. Standing up, I downed my glass of wine before putting away our food containers. It was already after midnight and I needed to get some rest before starting my new job.

"Damn it, Zoey! You need to talk about it. Letting that shit simmer in your brain is doing nothing but keeping you from enjoying a healthy sex life." Rachel stood up and helped me clear the table.

"I'm going to bed." I gave her a quick hug, then walked off to my bedroom. Rachel meant well, I knew she did, but there was no way she could understand what talking about that night made me feel.

Stripping down to my panties, I pulled out my oversized night shirt and slid it on. Slipping into bed I closed my eyes and was tormented with memories from the past. Such a naive fool I'd been. What had started off as a perfect evening had turned so wrong that I wasn't sure I'd ever get over the scars left behind. He hadn't raped me, but the insensitivity he'd shown in being my first lover was just as bad.

I'd said no to him so many times over our six months together that he was ecstatic that I'd finally changed my mind. I was tired of not knowing why all the women on campus were so addicted to sex. Maybe he'd been afraid I'd change my mind but he had my clothes off and was between my legs thrusting before I'd even had time to catch my breath.

The pain was excruciating. All I remember thinking at the time was let this shit end because I'd rather die than ever feel the sensation of being ripped apart again. In retrospect it didn't last that long, five minutes at the

most, but I'd learned that sex wasn't worth the effort.
The lingering effects of his 'lovemaking' had taken days
to wear off and lasted longer than it took for me to
discover he'd just been trying to do a virgin for some rite
of passage at his fraternity. More than my heart was
broken when he left.

I slept fitfully that night as the memories flashed
back and waking up the next morning to the blare of the
alarm clock had me wanting to toss the thing out the
window. I grumbled as my feet hit the floor and
staggered to the bathroom shower knowing this was
going to be the longest day in history.

The warm spray brought me back to life a little, and
I made a mental note not to drink so much wine on a
work night again. I had a job! The thought perked me
up even more than the shower did. Granted it was a job
that I had no idea how to do yet, and would demand that
I put my own feelings about sex into my subconscious
mind, but still. It was a job!

Stepping out of the shower, I wrapped myself in a
large towel then traipsed off to my bedroom closet.
Pulling out my favorite gray pantsuit, I knew this would
make me feel professional and give me the confidence I
needed for my first day. Laying it out on the bed, I went
through my drawers until I found a black, silk camisole.

I wanted to look my best today and as I dressed in my
favorite bra and panties I felt my mood brighten. The
last four weeks had been hell and I was determined to
make a great impression so that the next four would be
anything but. By the time I was dressed, I was ready to

show the guys at Fantasy's just what an asset they'd acquired in hiring me.

I wanted to wake Rachel up and get her opinion on my outfit, but I knew she had to work at the club tonight so I let her sleep. I had the code needed to enter the building, so I walked downstairs full of confidence and filled with excitement. This job was going to be challenging at the moment I felt that's exactly what I needed.

One cab ride later I was walking into my new life. The club was completely vacant at eight in the morning but the lights were on so I assumed I wasn't the first to arrive. I traced my steps from yesterday to find the elevator and arrived on the top floor within moments.

Walking to the desk I was surprised to see a woman of advanced years manning the desk. "Um. Hi, I'm Zoey Summers, I'm the new paralegal." I assumed this was the secretary that would have my paperwork.

The woman stood and held out her hand giving me the most down to earth smile. I instantly liked her. "The boys told me you were coming in this morning. I'm Geraldine, but everyone just calls me Dean. Can I get you a cup of coffee before we start on your papers?"

"Nice to meet you Dean. If you'll direct me to the coffee pot, I'll get it myself." In my opinion that was the most important thing to find with any office.

"I'll show you, but I'm your secretary now too, so in the future if you need anything, you just let me know." I guessed her age to be mid-fifties, and she dressed impeccably. I was a little shocked that the owners didn't have some young woman in this position, but I guess that was a little sexist of me.

"I'm sure they keep you busy enough, so I'll try to handle my end as much as I can." Giving a smile, I followed her back to the break area. A large table graced the center of the room as well as a stove, refrigerator, vending machines, and tons of cabinet space. Personally it seemed overkill for just the four partners and a secretary.

"Believe me I enjoy the work. Since my husband passed on working for the boys has kept me young." She opened up one of the cabinets and pulled down two coffee mugs with the Fantasy's logo imprinted on them.

"I'm sorry to hear that." I'd never been good at talking about death, so I felt a little uncomfortable. I attempted to show sympathy and hoped it didn't seem forced.

"My George lived a good life, he worked at Mr. Harold's seniors' estate for years." It was pretty obvious that Dean loved to talk and I could see she was devoted to the company. "Enough about that. You enjoy your coffee and I'll bring the forms back to you."

She didn't give me time to answer, instead she walked off. Hearing the owners being talked about as boys was somewhat comical, and I wondered how they'd feel knowing she felt so motherly. Definitely not my place to worry about it I decided and poured a cup of wake up juice.

Sitting down at the dining table I enjoyed the brew and decided instantly that someone had great taste in coffee. Dean walked in long enough to leave me with a

folder before leaving again.   A majority of the
paperwork was standard employment forms, I was a
little shocked to note I had to have a physical and submit
to blood work yearly.   Filling out my life history, I
wondered why my health information was needed.

The sound of coffee being poured pulled me out of my
intense concentration and I noticed Miles.   "Good
Morning."   Giving a polite smile that I was glad he
returned I knew I'd have to get used to working with
such handsome men.   At least the view here was great.
Definitely a perk I thought, before feeling bad for
thinking it.

"Good Morning, Ms. Summers." He sat down at the
table with me, which was shocking.   "If you have any
questions about anything, I hope you'll feel free to let me
know."

"If it's not inappropriate, please call me Zoey."   I
wasn't sure if they had some policy in place but I
preferred to be a little less rigid. "I do have a question
about the physical? Can I ask why that's necessary?"

"As long as you're comfortable with me using your
first name it's fine. Please call me Miles." He took a sip
from his cup and sighed. I have to tell you a sexy man
enjoy his coffee is really a turn on. "We fully cover all
our employees with our health insurance plan, so if there
are new or past medical issues we need to know so we
can prepare for the cost."

I was shocked. My last place of employment only paid
twenty five percent, so this was a real perk. "That's very
generous of you." I wasn't sure yet about calling him
Miles because it felt a little too familiar.

"We feel that taking care of our employees encourages them to do a better job for us." The smile he gave made my knees weak. I really had to gain some control. I'm not sure why suddenly I'm allowing myself to think about things I've kept pushed to the back of my mind for years.

"I'm impressed. Most employers are more concerned with their bottom line rather than the people working for them." Maybe I should not say exactly what I think, but that's just who I am.

His deep chuckle made me feel warm all over, and like a school girl I blushed. "I think you'll discover we're not like most employers."

Was he flirting with me? Definitely not. The man was gorgeous and that hot glint in those sexy emerald eyes was just my imagination. Glancing down at my paperwork, I forced myself to stop the thoughts I'm having. "I hope to discover that's a good thing then." Did that line even make sense? Hell if I know. I can't think straight with him looking at me.

"I'll look forward to getting your opinion in a few months." He stood up and I forced my attention back to his face. The smile he was wearing was even more sensual. "Have a good day Zoey. Be sure to let me know if you have any more questions." He winked at me before walking off.

Holy shit. Miles Dresdon, winked at me. Didn't that make me feel like an adolescent girl all over again! I finished up the rest of the papers and walked back to Dean before I could think about the reaction I had to his attention. Leon was standing at the desk in conversation with her when I arrived.

They both stopped to look at me and Leon smiled my way. What was it about these men and their devastating smiles? "Good Morning, Mr. Alexander." Have you ever tried to remain aloof when staring into a face of masculine perfection? Trust me it's not easy.

"Ms. Summers." His smiled broadened and he held out a long fingered, tanned hand to shake. My knees were shaking again. Dear Lord, being around these men could try the patience of saint.

"Zoey, please." I shook his hand and pulled back quickly because I needed to get my head out of fantasy land. He was one of my bosses not some gorgeous stud I could ogle at will. Although as far as ogling, he had the perfect physique for it. Over six feet tall, sandy-blond hair, and whiskey colored eyes? Add that to a body that would make any girl drool and it was hard not to look.

"Call me Leon, Zoey. I hope the paperwork wasn't too mundane?" His sensual lips lifted in a half-smile and it took me a minute to answer.

"Nothing I couldn't handle. That's the majority of my job title, dealing with paperwork." I felt insecure with my lack of verbiage, and wished that these men didn't have the ability to make me feel less confident.

"I'll take those forms from you dear." Dean broke into the conversation and I knew she'd just earned herself a Christmas present. How was I supposed to be the professional I was working with these guys? I handed over the folder and smiled gratefully.

"Thanks so much. If you could tell me where I'm supposed to work, I'd like to get started." Keeping a smile plastered on my face to cover my nerves, I waited expectantly.

"I'll do the honors. We have a nine o'clock meeting every morning, but you have at least half an hour to get acclimated before that begins." Leon kissed Dean's cheek and I was shocked at the sweet gesture. Almost as surprising was seeing Dean blush. I guess I wasn't the only one affected by the men.

Following Leon down the hall I was led to my new office and I almost had heart failure. The office was huge and had a great view of the city below. This was the type of room given to a senior partner, not some lowly paralegal. A huge desk with a state-of-the-art computer system rested on the heavy wood, and was accompanied by a large leather swivel chair. "This is amazing!"

"You'll be spending long hours here, so we want you to be comfortable." Leon resting on the edge of my new desk wasn't very comforting, but it was definitely alluring. He was dripping sex appeal and for a moment I wanted to be a little kitty lapping it up. I mentally slapped myself and cleared my throat.

"Mr. Harold said there was a portfolio of former contracts I could look over?" Get this on a professional level, my subconscious screamed at me.

"We'll present that to you in the boardroom during our meeting. For now just get comfortable with the office." He lifted that sexy ass off my desk and I was briefly disappointed. "I'll stop back in to pick you up

soon." He smiled before leaving me alone in my new
paradise.

I took several deep breaths before sitting behind my
new desk. This was turning into a morning I wouldn't
soon forget and keeping my head in the right frame of
mind was first priority. Turning on the computer I went
over the software installed. It was loaded with programs
that I'd only dreamed of using when I was working with
Baxter.

I was lost in the world of technology when a knock at
the door interrupted me. Forcing my eyes away from
the screen I answered it and was faced with Leif. Sure.
Why not deal with each of these gorgeous men on my
first day. I had to bite back a laugh.

"I just wanted to make sure you were getting settled
in okay." He was a beautiful man, just like the other
partners, but what made him stand out was his self-
confidence. This was a guy that knew he was sexy and
didn't need me or anyone else to convince him. He
reminded me of a surfer wearing business attire, with
those blue eyes and sun-bleached blond hair. I
wondered if he hated wearing the tie.

"Everything's perfect, sir. I really can't thank you
enough for giving me the opportunity to work here."

"We can ditch the sir, I'm Leif. I guess you'd say I'm
the laid back partner. I'd much rather be out enjoying
the sun than being in a stuffy office." It was like the man
had read my thoughts and I laughed. I instantly felt a
strange connection with him.

"Turn-about is fair play then, call me Zoey. If you
don't mind me asking, why aren't you?" It was no secret

to anyone who read the paper that he had more money than a person could spend in a lifetime. If I was rich I couldn't imagine working for a living.

"I ask myself that question every day." He grinned and the boyish look that made him one of the most sought after bachelors in the city was apparent. "I'm working on a real-estate investment to help me live out that dream."

"So you'd leave Fantasy's if that comes through?" It was none of my business, but he brought it up.

"Actually I'm thinking of expanding Fantasy's to an island. We're still working out the details though." The way his eyes lit up I could see it was an idea that really excited him.

"Fantasy Island, I think my mother used to watch that show." He was so easy to talk to that I found myself able to joke around.

"Wasn't that the one with the little midget that shouted for the plane?" We were both laughing and I felt really comfortable hanging out with him.

"That's the one. Although I think the politically correct term these days is little people." I wasn't sure that one was any less derogatory.

"Fantasy Island. I like that, maybe change it to Fantasy Isle. I like you Zoey, I think we'll have to keep you on." His gorgeous face was even more beautiful with that wide smile. I wasn't sure if I wanted to pinch his cheeks or fall in love.

"Well thank you, my bank account will appreciate it." I giggled. Seriously giggled. I can't remember the last time I felt happy enough to do that.

"And what exactly is Leif offering to fatten your bank account with?" Leon walked into the room and had he not been smirking with humor, I might have been worried.

"My gorgeous body of course, bro." Leif winked at me and then rolled his eyes at Leon. "I think she just decided the name of our Island."

"That deal is still up in the air. I know you want this, but we need to think about the bottom line." Leon's face turned serious and I could tell this was not a conversation I needed to be involved in.

"Aren't we going to be late to the meeting?" I had no idea what time it was but I didn't want to be caught in the middle of their disagreement on my first day here.

"Time is irrelative around here, but I'm sure Samson and Miles are waiting." The warm smile returned to his face and he led the way to the boardroom.

"We can talk later." Leif whispered in my ear almost like he was trying to keep it a secret and I had to bite back a grin.

"Glad you could join us." Samson didn't seem pleased so I assumed he didn't like to be kept waiting. His comment was directed to Leif and Leon, but I felt the displeasure just the same.

"Pull the corn cob out of your ass, Samson. It's just a meeting." Leif's comment shocked me and I wondered if I should wait outside. Samson didn't seem like the type of man who allowed being talked to that way.

"Fuck you. Stop acting like this is all a joke and get your head in the game." Samson was pissed. Wow. Remind me never to get on his bad side.

"I could wait outside?" It wasn't my place to say it, but these guys definitely didn't act like professionals.

"Forgive them. Sometimes the testosterone goes on overdrive when we're all together." Miles held out a chair for me and I took it, but made the decision if they started arguing again I'd walk out until tempers cooled.

"We're not always this way." Leon smiled and I felt my nervousness dissipate somewhat.

"You're so full of shit, Leon. She might as well learn how we do things upfront." Samson glared at Leon, then at Leif before sitting down. "We don't do formal in the office. "When we're downstairs, that's a different scenario. Our customers expect us to be in control, and that's exactly what we give them."

"I'm sorry, but I have no idea what you're saying." I'd expected these men to be the successful leaders they were but the way this meeting started completely shattered that illusion."

"What he means, sweetheart, is that downstairs we're very dominant men who expect complete obedience from our employees." Leif grinned. "If one of those employees enters the office you can damn sure bet they're being punished or about to lose their jobs."

"Punished? I assume you mean reprimanded?" I was obviously confused at his wording because punishing was something done to children not adult employees.

"No what we mean is punished. Unless you're in one of the positions that doesn't involve interaction with our customers these employees are submissive to us. So break a rule, your ass gets tanned, keep doing it, you find a new line of work." Samson was giving me a look that dared me to question his statement. He didn't know me well.

"That's ludicrous." What the hell kind of business did I just agree to work for? "I hope you didn't assume I'd be on my knees just because you sign my paycheck. I'd sooner cold-cock your ass." My days of being pushed around were long over and I'd walk out of here right now if that fact wasn't made clear.

"Calm down, Ms. Summers." Samson had a smirk on his face and at the moment I wanted to slap it off. "You weren't hired to please our customers and unless you like being on your knees no one in this office expects that of you."

Unless I liked being on my knees? What kind of damn statement was that? "I can assure you that no man would put me in that position. If these people working for you don't mind being subjugated that's their business, but I want to make sure right now you understand that I expect to be considered your equal." Mouth filter completely off, I realized after the words escaped. All I can say is I blame it on my past history and needed some assurance that they'd hired me for the right reasons.

Leif couldn't control his laugher. Miles had a wide smile on his face. Leon was grinning like a cat that just ate a bird. Samson on the other hand looked like he wanted to test the theory. He glared and I glared back. If he thought I was backing down he was about to get a dose of Zoey reality 101.

"Like I said before, it wasn't the position we hired you for. Now can we get this meeting underway or would you like to explain how high on the totem pole you consider yourself a little more." His eyes raked over me like no one had ever dared talk to him that way before, and I decided to cool down.

"As long as we're clear that I'm your employee and not some dog for you to order around, I believe I'm done." Definitely not the best way to start a new job, but I refused to feel bad about it. Life was all about knowing who and what you were and making boundaries that shouldn't be crossed.

The only sign that he was still angry was a small tick in his cheek. Later I'd reflect on why he hadn't fired me on the spot, but at the moment I was basking in the knowledge that I'd just stood my ground.

"Like I explained last night, we've got a waiting list of clients waiting to have their fantasy fulfilled. I'm hoping to have plans in motion for at least ten of them by the end of the week." He handed me a stack of folders and just that quickly the meeting took on a professional atmosphere.

"Leif, I have the final bid on the island, and we need to make a decision on that as soon as possible. I've researched as much of the bottom line as I can and think it would be a feasible investment. Out of pocket expenses will be astronomical but if we handle this correctly we should be able to regain our investments over the course of five years."

"Not to pry, but what exactly will you do with an island as far as Fantasy's?" Curiosity always got the best of me and even though it wasn't my concern, I wanted to know.

"Since you'll be handling all the contracts for that deal, it's imperative that you do know." Samson lifted a thick folder and slid it over to me. "We'll be in the planning phase for months after we win the bid, but think adult vacation with the Fantasy's theme."

I thumbed through the folder, falling in love with the tropical photos. "This is amazing!" I couldn't stop the fascination from crossing over into my voice.

"It is, isn't it?" Leif was grinning with boyish charm and I could tell he was pleased at my reaction. "Now imagine it with a full resort and a scattering of bungalows for the guests."

"Sounds like a small piece of paradise." Smiling at Leif briefly, I realized what Samson said. "You want me to draw up contracts for a real estate deal?" I wasn't sure I had the knowledge to keep them legally safe on a venture of that magnitude.

"Our lawyer will handle the property contracts, what you'll be responsible for is the fantasy aspect for the clients. I know this is a lot to throw at you at once, but something tells me you're more than capable of handling this venue and that. If however you decide it's too much, we'll make other arrangements." Samson's look of superiority seemed to dare me to take the challenge.

"I'm sure I'll manage." At the moment I was still worried about handling the ones for the club. "How far in the future are you looking to have an establishment ready for guests?"

"Now that we're in agreement that it's a viable project, we'll put in the highest bid for the property and it should be up and running within two years." This was from Miles who didn't seem particularly thrilled about the acquirement. Definitely wasn't my place to get involved with their choices. "I'll get started with the financials this morning."

He stood and walked out of the office and it was easy to see when he had a plan in mind he instantly gravitated toward it. Left with the other three men, I waited to see what other interesting conversations would be put on the table this morning.

"Like I said earlier, Ms. Summers. I need at least ten clients screened this week. Our backlog is overwhelming and I want to put a dent in it. He stood, bent over and lifted a box containing file folders. "You'll need to go through these and see which can be expedited the fastest. The portfolio I mentioned is inside and on your computer you'll find the list of actors for the fantasies. We'll need to consult with them for a time frame that works with their schedules."

I glanced at the overstuffed box and grinned. To most people being overwhelmed with an impossible task would seem daunting. For myself, a challenge like this was exactly what I loved. "I'll get on these right away, Sir." He was the only one of the brothers I didn't feel comfortable enough with to take the formality out of our relationship.

"Fine. We all break for lunch at noon, and you'll be expected to join us. Over the years we've discovered that a working lunch helps keep our business flowing more smoothly. The meetings take place each morning at nine, depending on what we're discussing, determines the length." Samson stood and walked out of the room.

"He's just a bottle of sunshine." I grumbled under my breath at the abrupt command he'd tossed out before leaving. Leon and Leif were grinning and I realized I hadn't spoken as quietly as I'd hoped.

"This was him putting on a good face for you." Leif stood and lifted the box of files for me.

That thought was more than scary because personally he'd seemed like someone I'd rather not cross and if that was his 'good face', I sure didn't want to see the bad. "Remind me to run if the other one shows."

"Don't worry, we'll protect you." Leon gestured toward the door and they both followed me back to my new office.

Leif sat the box of files down on my desk. "Are you kidding me? I'm letting her take the lead, I've never seen anyone put him in place so quickly before." His following chuckle had me feeling guilty.

"I'm surprised he didn't can my ass." Speaking like they were my best friends may have not been the smartest idea. I flushed.

"Hate to say it, Zoey, but I think you caught his interest instead. No one stands up to Samson." Leon gave me a look of pity and I knew he thought getting Samson's attention was considered a bad thing.

"Guess I'd better work my fingers to the bone to impress him then." I hoped the smile I gave was more confident than I felt because I was truly nervous now. This job was too good to give up and I needed to make a positive impression.

"We'll leave you to it then. Just let us know if you get lost." Leif winked before walking out of my office with Leon following.

They seemed like really nice guys and I was having a hard time associating them with the bad boy personas the press claimed they lived by. The only one I could see being a total jerk was Samson. I felt he'd earned his title.

CHAPTER THREE

Overwhelmed

Three hours later I'd decided I was so far in over my head I would never pull out. My deduction about the clients? These were some seriously sick fuckers. Live and let live was always my motto, but holy shit the things I read in these fantasy profiles were enough to make me cringe.

Some of the fantasies were understandable, so maybe I wasn't being completely fair. The one with the pirate and innocent maiden was sort of romantic if you were a historical romance buff, which I definitely wasn't. But at least it wasn't overly perverted. The nasty body fluid fantasy, that one was enough to make me never want to use the bathroom again. Add that to the fact I had to use the internet to even understand the terms being used and I was simply appalled.

The ten contracts I'd chosen out of the pile were probably the most basic, but I needed to get my feet wet, so to speak. That body fluid one? Yeah that was going to the bottom of the pile and would be saved until I knew what the hell I was doing.

I was shocked when Samson knocked on my door. "Bring one of your files and we'll work it together over lunch today." The man obviously didn't know how to ask for anything. Considering the way we'd started off this morning though, I decided to bite my tongue.

I gathered the pirate and maiden one because it seemed the easiest, grabbed my purse and followed behind him. We walked downstairs and he ushered me into a waiting limousine. Wasn't this the damn life, I thought to myself? The guys chatted about business and I kept silent trying to discover what made them tick.

Fifteen minutes later we pulled up at one of New York's most popular restaurants and I followed the guys inside, shocked that we had our own private dining area away from the crowd. I could definitely get used to living like this!

After enjoying appetizers and wine, I opted for a salad for a meal because I doubted I'd be able to afford much else here. The guys loaded the table with so much food I had no idea how they remained as fit as they were. As far as salads go, this was one of the best I'd ever had. I couldn't help but eye Leif's steak with longing though.

Samson caught me drooling and smirked. "You're not one of those women that stay on a diet are you?"

I was embarrassed to be caught staring, and my defenses came up. "No, but I am one who hasn't gotten her first paycheck yet and needs to be conservative." I felt like a total fool for admitting I was lacking in funds.

"Fuck. We're feeding you." He shook his head and waved over a waiter. "We need another steak over here." He turned his gray eyes to me, "how do you like it?"

If I was embarrassed before, now I was mortified. "Medium rare." I lowered my eyes to the table wishing I could hide under it. Samson gave the order to the waiter and he walked off.

"Don't pussy out on us now." My eyes flew to his at his words and I understood immediately he didn't like me hanging my head. For a man that seemed to want control he obviously expected the people he associated with to have a backbone. That was something to ponder.

"I'm not pussying out on shit, Samson, I just stated the facts." Lifting my chin, I dared him with my eyes to call me out on standing up to him. I was shocked as hell when he threw back his head and laughed. I'd also just called him by his first name without being asked. I'd say I was two seconds away from being fired.

"Good girl." With a smirk, he went back to enjoying his food and I wasn't sure it was right to be pleased I'd won his favor since he'd basically just downed me by calling me a girl. Oddly enough I liked the terminology. I was in serious trouble with these guys.

I devoured my steak when it came, and hoped I didn't look like some starved woman after I finished. Four weeks without a steak should be illegal. Wiping my mouth primly with my napkin to make up for my table manners, I looked up and noticed all the guys staring at me. "What. Do I have steak sauce on my chin?" I blotted my face again.

"I've just never seen a woman enjoy her food so much." Leon's sexy drawl sent goose bumps up my arm and I flushed.

"You go a month without steak and then we'll talk." I wasn't even embarrassed now. Something about a full belly and some of the top beef still on your palate does things to you.

"Hell I'll buy you a steak every week if you show that much pleasure in eating it." Miles winked at me and I did blush. Holy shit these guys seemed to really get off on the way I ate. How odd was that?

It was almost surreal how comfortable that lunch made me feel with them. I explained how it was mine and Rachel's thing to go out for steak before I lost my job and how much I missed it. That started a round of stories about some of their favorite things and it was really rather cozy. Of course, mountain climbing, surfing, parachuting, and skiing weren't really my idea of great hobbies, but the guys each had their own thing they loved.

I was almost regretful when the conversation turned back to business. Samson brought up the fantasy file I'd decided to work on first. "So the Pirate fantasy. Lucas would be the one I'd choose for that one. He just got back from a shoot in the Keys and has this bohemian look thing going for him."

"I'm amazed Lilith wants that one. She's a timid little thing." Leif was grinning and he seemed to have first-hand knowledge of the client referred to in the file.

"Actually I'm not surprised at all." Leon interrupted. "It's a perfect scenario for a women who wants to be ravished but doesn't have the confidence to ask for it. Darcy can decorate that one for you. She's got solid expertise in working with island settings. I think she'll be one of the first decorators we pull for the new project?" He'd been talking to me but turned to Leif for the question.

"I don't know. Her husband's doing really well with his career here and I wouldn't want to ask her to make the decision to move." He answered Leon before turning to me. "We'll have to introduce you to the entire staff. Maybe this Friday? I think we can pull together an informal meeting before the club opens."

"That's a great idea," Miles stated. "You'll be meeting them all as you arrange the contracts, but it might be nice to get to know them in an informal setting."

"I'll look into their schedules this week, but for now we need to work on the one contract so Zoey has an idea of what she's up against." Samson motioned to our server and paid off the bill. "We should take this back to the office. I know they probably have other customers waiting for this space."

I followed their lead and we drove back to the office. It was amazing how much difference an informal lunch could make. I felt like I had a much firmer grasp on the personalities I'd be working with now. We ended up back in the boardroom again and discussed the first contract.

"The most important thing in the contract is discovering what the clients truly wants to happen. Not to be sexist, but I've noticed that men usually give more details than women when it comes to their desires, so you'll have to work a little more diligently with the females." Samson sat back in the chair seeming to contemplate.

"I agree with Samson on this, whereas a man will tell you he wants a hand job while he's bound in a chair, women tend to be vaguer." Leon glanced at me and I swear my face turned bright red.

"Shit girl, are you blushing?" Leif seemed to find that hilarious and I glared at him.

"Sorry I don't normally go around talking about hand jobs." Yes it embarrassed me, but I knew it was now part of my job. "So do you want me to ask if she wants to be touched when she's tied up?" Holy hell. I can't believe I'd even said that.

"More precise, does she want her clit rubbed, his tongue on her pussy or just keep it all non-sexual." Miles said matter-of-factly making me blush even hotter.

"For a woman who can devour a steak like she's having the best orgasm of her life, you sure do get embarrassed when discussing sex." Samson chuckled and I was amazed that he seemed to be teasing me.

"I've had more experience with steak." I have no idea what made those words fall from my lips, but I felt like cutting my own tongue out at the incredulous looks they tossed my way.

"Now that's a damn shame." Miles winked at me and I knew they were all having a good laugh at my expense.

"Whatever." I was feeling defensive and needed to be in control again. "So you basically want me to lay out exactly what amount of sexuality they want infused into the scene and to have it written out in solid details?" I would find a way to do this if it killed me now. The one thing I hated most was doubting my own abilities. It was just defining sex, I could do this shit.

"That's exactly what we need. Insertion of fingers, body parts, or not. What type of emotional response is the client looking for in the scene? Fear, excitement, being overwhelmed, or just blatant passion." Samson was studying my face and I understood he was trying to get a read on my emotions.

Keeping my face schooled in a bored expression, I nodded. I couldn't imagine wanting to feel any of those things, but I wasn't the person paying for the fantasy. "I think I understand."

"Let's test the theory then. I'm Lilith, and here for my interview with you. What questions would you ask?" Leon sat up in his chair and waited for me to begin.

Crap. What questions would I ask? I closed my eyes for a second and tried to imagine I was a woman being captured by a pirate. "What is the first thing you think about when you dream about the perfect pirate fantasy?"

Leon paused for a moment before answering. "Well when I think of Pirate, I think of some big sexy man capturing me and tying me up in his room on a boat." I almost died laughing when he fluttered his eyelashes

pretending to be a women. Schooling my emotions, I
wrote down his response.

"So you're tied up in his bedroom. Does he rip your
shirt off, cut in with a knife, or does he allow you to keep
your clothes on." I was just going on gut instinct with
my ideas but I assumed that's what a woman would want
to know.

"That big bad pirate ripped it off and left my tits
hanging out." Leon sniffling was too much. I couldn't
help it I giggled.

"I can't believe you laughed at my idea. I refuse to
pay this kind of money if you're going to humiliate me."
Leon turned his face away pretending to pout, but his
point was clear. I would have to ask these questions and
keep my opinion to myself.

Controlling my humor. I continued to ask questions
in a monotone voice. Step by step I envisioned the
fantasy and asked pertinent questions. When or if you
are completely naked, where would you like or not like
to have his fingers touch you? It went on and on until I
was confident I could handle the scenario.

"Good job. I think you can call Lilith in for her
interview. If there's anything not covered after Lucas
reads it over, he'll let you know and you can call her with
follow up questions." Leon was smiling like he was
proud and it made my self-confidence go up by several
points.

"Now if you can get ten of those interviews in by
Friday, I think we'll be back on schedule again." Samson
stood up and stretched his muscular arms over his head.
"I have some other work to do, I'm sure you guys do as

well. Let's leave our Zoey to get started." The smile he gave me was a complete shock.

I walked back to my office more confident than ever that I could do this job. It didn't really matter what the fantasy was, only that what the client needed from them was outlined. This may well be the easiest job I'd ever had! By the time five o'clock rolled around I was ready to call it a night. I had the ten clients set up for interviews and was looking forward to discussing the service they were interested in.

CHAPTER FOUR

Behind the Scenes

Meeting my first client, Lilith, was a life changing event. I knew from her file that she was a forty year old woman but she was nothing like I expected a person paying for a fantasy like this would be. The woman was beautiful and I couldn't understand why a person like her would need to pay anyone for attention.

We started off the interview with questions about what she wanted to take away from the experience and I schooled my expression at her responses. Imagine a women sitting primly in front of your desk looking every inch the successful business woman giving explanations of her darkest sexual fantasies.

Lilith had no problem opening up and discussing her needs. She wanted a sexy savage pirate who made it feel like she had no choice but to surrender when he tied her up in his cabin. As far as the actual act of sex, that was a no go for her, it was about the temptation. She told me that when the scenario was finished she planned on going home and having the best sex of her life with her much older husband. Color me shocked because I was turned on by the time that interview was finished.

When I say turned on, what I mean was squirming in my chair, pressing my thighs together it turned me on so much. The other nine clients were as different as a group of people could possibly get, but their fantasies given in such detail made me understand why the club was so popular with the elite.

I discovered more about sexuality by listening to their fantasies than I had even hearing Rachel talk about her exploits with men. Even more shocking is I went home every night feeling deprived because talking with them about their needs made me understand I wasn't frigid. For the first time since that night with Brad I found myself in bed each night pleasuring my body with my fingers.

Meeting the staff that enacted the fantasies was just as surprising. These men and women had side jobs as actors, models, and other professionals who were supplementing their income with the club. Hearing them discuss their job at Fantasy's made me jealous and it was an emotion that confused my libido even more than the new awakenings I felt after listening to the clients' fantasies.

Tonight I was at the second staff party that Samson had arranged since my hiring so I could get to know the people that worked behind the Scenes. I'd learned from

Rachel that he attempted to have one of these soirees every month to keep the employees pleased with their jobs. For me it was like being brought out into a group of people that had no sexual limitations and I felt completely out of my element.

Nothing was taboo here. Liquor flowed freely, and so did the innuendos and hook ups. Hell I'd even walked into the bathroom and found two of the staff members going at it with gusto. I'd been so shocked, I stood there and watched them like some voyeur who was really enjoying the show.

Rachel joined me and my eyes were riveted to the beautiful woman bent over the sink, the handsome man behind her driving his cock inside her in tempo with her loud moans of pleasure. It wasn't until after the act that my feet could move. The couple dressed and left us behind like it was no big deal we were watching. Rachel had a great laugh at my expense.

"That's something you don't see every day." My face was so red I had to say something to stop my body from overreacting to the scene I'd just witnessed.

"It is at these parties. I've walked in on a full-fledged orgy a time or two at these events." She wrapped my arm in hers, walking me back to the full bar and I quickly ordered a drink.

The staff here was beautiful and I felt like a dowdy mouse compared to them all. Logically I knew that this was not something I'd ever want to indulge in, but my body was definitely enflamed and my curiosity aroused. "Have you ever done something like that here?" I wasn't even sure why I asked, because I didn't really know if I wanted an answer.

Rachel grinned and I knew from the look on her face that she had. I was shocked. Part of me knew I should be disgusted, but the truth was I wasn't. "Let's go mingle." She avoided my question and I allowed her to lead me around, mouth gaping at the sensual scenarios that began playing all around me almost as if I'd dreamed them up.

We were on the third floor of the building, one that was used exclusively for these staff parties. When I'd first been shown the floor, I thought it was a waste of unused space. Now I understood why they kept it free from other uses.

My eyes roamed around the room and fell on Samson resting on one of the oversized couches. A beautiful woman knelt at his feet, her face resting against his calf with a dreamy smile in place. For reasons I couldn't even begin to understand it sent a pang of jealously through my thoughts and I instantly hated her.

His eyes met mine and a small smirk fell upon his beautiful features. My core clenched and I stood mesmerized. When he motioned me over with his hand, for a moment I couldn't make my feet move. Then, as if drawn by some invisible force I walked over to him, sitting down on the side where the woman wasn't kneeling.

"Are you enjoying yourself?" His hand reached down to stroke the woman's hair and again I felt envious. The timbre of his voice pulled my attention to his eyes and I noticed his gaze was riveted on my face not the woman he was petting.

"I'm getting an education, I guess." I whispered the words, not sure why I did so when the rest of the room seemed to be overly loud.

"Not everything has to be about the job, Zoey." He smiled at me and then did the unthinkable. His long fingers moved to his belt, undoing it.

I couldn't think of one witty thing to say as he unbuttoned his pants, slid the zipper down, and then reached down to pull his cock out. For the briefest moment I panicked thinking he expected me to do something with that monstrosity he'd just unleashed, but the woman at his feet lifted and took him into her mouth.

My breath caught in my throat and I watched as she pleasured him, the sight so beautiful that I ached from just viewing it. I knew I shouldn't sit there watching my boss get sucked off. I definitely shouldn't have wished for a brief second that it was me doing that to him!

"Haven't you ever just wanted to let go and allow someone to pleasure your body for no other reason than because it pleases them?" His hand tangled in the woman's hair forcing her down on his massive length and pulling her up again. Her face was filled with ecstasy as she allowed him to fuck her mouth.

I forced my eyes back to his face. "I. Have. To. Go." Standing up quickly, I almost lost my balance. The soft chuckle forced my feet to walk away quickly and I ran back to the bathroom locking myself in one of the stalls.

He let that woman suck him in front of me! How was I supposed to deal with that?

Closing my eyes I tried to dredge up some anger that my boss had just had oral sex right in front of me. I couldn't do it. Not only could I not do it, I was so horny at the moment that all I could think about was lifting my skirt and letting my fingers bring me relief. Taking several deep breaths I refrained and felt more frustrated than I've ever felt in my life before.

I wanted to go home. These people were all just a bunch of sick perverts and working for them was screwing with my mind. Determined to do just that. I forced myself to walk out of the restroom and looked around frantically for Rachel. After several minutes of searching in panic, I ran into Miles instead.

"Everything okay honey?" His compassionate words combined with my earlier freak out left me so confused that I could only shake my head no.

"I really want to go home and I can't find Rachel." The words sounded weak and frightened and I hated allowing my insecurities to shine through to this man.

"Calm down." Miles wrapped my arm in his and pulled me out of the room that was sinking more into debauchery by the second. We walked down a hall and into a room filled with an oversized couch and table. "Wait here and I'll see if I can find her." He left me alone, giving me time to get my emotions back in order.

These were people I worked with, and seeing them so open about their sexuality had done something to me that I wasn't sure I liked. I had my life in perfect order. There was no place in it for acts of sexual depravity and

I didn't want to think about that side of my life that I'd blocked away. Well outside of my work, I relented. The truth was I was pissed that it made me feel things I didn't want to think about.

"Leif said she was, um, tied up for the next few hours." He looked uncomfortable as he joined me again and it made me feel that I wasn't the only person not at ease with what was happening here. "Would you like me to drive you home?"

"I could call a cab." I didn't want to inconvenience him, but I was ready to leave this party behind.

"I was thinking about heading out for coffee. If you don't mind joining me I could drop you off after?"

I nodded. Anything that got me out of this building faster was a good escape. Coffee would also help clear my head of the alcohol I'd imbibed. I stood and we walked back to the elevators.

I wasn't much of a car buff but the Rolls Royce suited Miles. Classic, but refined. Sliding into the passenger seat we rode in silence as he expertly maneuvered through the late night traffic. I was a little shocked when he pulled up at one of the lesser known coffee houses. It was my favorite because there was never a crowd. After ordering our drinks we sat down in a corner booth and sipped silently.

"How did you get involved with Samson? You guys seem like complete opposites." I was half way done with my coffee before I broke the silence that had seemed amicable.

"We traveled in the same social circles and to be honest we're not that different, Zoey." Relaxed back against the cushioning of the booth I wasn't sure how to explain what I meant by different.

I decided saying exactly what I meant was the only way. "I didn't see you getting off in the room for everyone to see." I really wanted to be pissed off about that but I was still dealing with my own wishes of changing places with the girl pleasing him. It really was confusing.

"Had it been a different night, you might have." He shrugged but I could tell he wasn't apologizing for Samson's behavior. "Did it really bother you so much seeing him enjoy pleasure?"

I struggled again to be honest. "You just don't do things like that in public." Maybe that made me a prude, but I couldn't accept that this was a normal thing to do.

"By whose standards? Who has the right to dictate what is right for one person and not another?" There was no anger in his tone, and I couldn't even get mad by pretending he was trying to argue.

"Society?" That was lame even to my ears. If we as women hadn't fought against rules of society I'd be barefoot and pregnant at the moment instead of working.

"Society also held the view that we should own slaves. I think you can do better than that." Miles sipped on his coffee but I could see the smile he was hiding behind the cup.

"Okay maybe that was a bad example, but there has to be some line drawn between what is accepted morally?" My argument was weak to my own ears and I hated myself for not being able to give a better one.

"In public? Maybe. But when a group of consenting adults meets in a private place what happens behind those doors is up to the individuals." He placed his cup down on the table and our eyes met.

"It's a business Miles. What makes it unacceptable for say, a guy like my ex-boss to hit on me in the work place and then it be fine for everyone to just, for lack of better words, get it on at Fantasy's?"

"Is that the real problem here? Are you worried that me or one of the other employees will come on to you and fire you if we don't get our way?" He wasn't being an ass, I could read the sincerity in those beautiful emerald eyes so I stopped to consider it.

"I don't know, maybe?" That wasn't really fair. Not once had any of the men at Fantasy's came on to me in a way that was inappropriate, I decided to say as much. "I haven't been hit on. That fear just lingers in the back of my mind, even more so now that I've seen how, um, free the staff is with sexuality."

"Well then what you're really concerned about is something that doesn't involve us. No one would be allowed to make you uncomfortable at your job. As far as the parties go, those aren't mandatory. If you don't want to be involved, don't show up honey."

How much easier could it be? He was right, not one of the bosses, or the staff members had done anything at work that would be considered inappropriate during business hours. Things were more casual in our office, but I enjoyed that aspect of my job. I took a sip of my cooling beverage and nodded.

"I will tell you that no one will offer anything unless you put it out there that you're interested first. That's a rule for all employees, including management." Miles winked at me and I felt a flutter in my chest.

What did he mean by that? Did he want me or maybe even Samson or the other men? The thought made me stop and consider that maybe they did, then I felt like an idiot. These men were beautiful. They had supermodels willing to curl up at their feet.

"I guess it doesn't matter then. From now on I'll stay away from the staff parties."

The look that came over his face seemed almost disappointed, but his lips lifted in a small smile. "If that's what you want." I had to be just dreaming that he was disappointed by my decision. Didn't I?

"I'm sorry I dragged you away tonight." Instead of asking the question that was on my mind I pushed things back toward a professional level.

"Don't be. I enjoy your company Zoey. If you ever feel like venturing out again, just let me know." With a smile he stood, walked over to pay the cashier and led me back out to his car.

I wasn't sure how to take his comment, but decided to take it in the friendly way I could accept. He was just being nice. Miles dropped me off at my apartment and I spent one of the longest nights imaginable replaying the scenes from the party through my mind.

When Monday morning rolled back around I decided to take his advice and my sanity by keeping things strictly professional with the company.

CHAPTER FIVE

Plans

The next few months at Fantasy's I avoided the staff parties and managed to come to grips with keeping my work life separated from what I knew they did behind the scenes. I'd interviewed all the backlog of clients and dealt with the Fantasy staff on the most professional level that I could bring to the meetings.

Nothing was ever mentioned about what went on there and I was proud of myself for doing the job I was hired for. Dealing with the clients became as easy as working with any other contracts at my previous law firm, it was the staff acting out the fantasies that proved a hurdle. It was time for our Friday meeting now and I was ready to unload some of my frustrations.

Lucas had become an absolute terror, and I'd wanted to backslap him after contacting several of his clients repeatedly to ask how they'd feel about changes.

Conceited ass was too nice a label for the drama king and
I wondered how any woman put up with his *I am better
than you* attitude for longer than five minutes.

Walking into the room, I flopped down into the chair
with a huge sigh. Dean brought coffee in and I was so
mentally exhausted I didn't bother to tell her I could get
my own drink. It hadn't worked since I started here so
why would today be any different. She obviously loved
pampering us all.

"Lucas should be shot in the face." I didn't mean to
unload that way, seriously I didn't. Being behind
schedule was not how I wanted to end the week and I
was feeling the pinch of the job.

Samson tossed back his head and chuckled. "If the
ladies didn't love him, I might agree. What's he done
this time?"

"Besides the fact that I've had to call dozens of clients
three times or more this week to change up stupid ass
details? Not much. We should be scheduling the scenes
with the decorators not dealing with his diva needs for
clarification." I was definitely frustrated.

"Let me guess. He needs more insight or wants to
change up every scene that's outlined? " This was from
Leon who was filled with as much humor as Samson and
starting to grate on my nerves because of it.

I'd never get anything done if this problem wasn't
fixed. Thankfully he was the only staff member who'd
given me a problem but unfortunately women tended to
request him most which meant I had four more fantasies
to deal with him on next week alone. "That's about it

and unless you want him drawn and quartered, I'd stop laughing it up Leon!"

This drew out chuckles from all the men and I allowed my head to plop down on the desk wearily. What the hell had I been thinking? This job was by no means easy! "I could use a trip to that island Leif, how soon do I get a vacation?"

"You just need something to ease the tension." Miles walked over behind my chair and started rubbing my shoulders. I might have been uncomfortable with this kind of scenario if it were anyone else, but I actually needed the release at the moment.

I moaned softly and allowed my body to completely relax. "If you stop I'm jumping out a window." There was nothing sexual about what he was doing, it just felt great.

"I'll keep that in mind." His hands continued to work their magic and the guys discussed other business of the week.

"Speaking of the island, I was think taking a trip down would be a great idea." Leif's words filtered through the bliss of Miles's hands.

"You should fly us all down, Leon. If Zoey doesn't mind roughing it for a few days, it would be a great chance to see what we'll be working with?" Samson seemed excited by the idea and stood up.

I'd discovered over the months that Leon was a pilot which I guess he'd decided to take up because of his love of parachuting. A weekend on a deserted island with four hot billionaires? That didn't sound like a terrible thing? That was relaxing massage answering, and not my common sense. "How rough are we talking?"

"We would have to set up tents. Have you ever been camping, Zoey?" Miles seemed thrilled at the idea and I knew Leif could get in some surfing too.

"Um. No. City girl here, the closest I've come to camping is spending the night on the pavement trying to get concert tickets." How bad could it be though? I really would like to see where the next phase of Fantasy's would begin.

"Actually the place was once a wildlife preserve so there is a small cabin and according to the agent it's still operational. But that's a two day flight with a stopover in Hong Kong to refuel. Instead of a few days, make it a week." Leon seemed amused that he had knowledge Samson didn't.

"We could all bring work and make a week out of it then." Miles seemed ready to jump at the opportunity but thanks to Lucas I was getting backed up with clients again. Remembering that I'd have to deal with him if we didn't do this made me rethink things though. Taking a flight and then hanging out with the guys on an island for a week? Okay I was stupid, but why not?

"I'm game if my bosses don't mind me missing work here." A vacation after less than half a year of employment? Maybe it wasn't very responsible of me, but they made the rules. Right?

"And who should we leave in charge of Fantasy's while we're away gentleman?" Samson appeared to be amused but also like he was the only person here who had any concern about running a business.

"If we only leave the downstairs bar running in our absence, Davis and Rachel should be able to handle that on their own. Or Dean can continue running the office as usual. The decorators can set up for the fantasies while we're gone and the minute we return we can move forward there." Leif seemed to have it all figured out and if it hadn't been for Samson's expression I'd have said he was pretty clever.

"Rachel's great with the waitresses, but leaving her in charge would be a disaster." Samson looked at me apologetically, but I understood why he felt that way. She was my best friend but responsibility? That definitely wasn't her strong suit.

"Davis can keep things running smoothly, he'll be in control of all the staff." Davis was the bar manager and ruled with a similar style to Samson, meaning he didn't take crap from the employees. According to Miles, he and Samson should have been born brothers they were so alike. "This is not a vacation though. We need to make some serious decisions while we're there about where to place the resort and what route will be the most comfortable for the eventual clients."

All the guys nodded but you could tell by the expressions on their faces that work was the furthest thing from their minds. I was going to Australia! Okay well not really since the island was just off the Great Barrier Reef, but close enough!

"I'll touch base with Davis, the rest of you pack for a week on the island and bring some decent walking shoes! Leon what time do you want to fly out?" Samson was all business now and I admit that my mind was on the adventure, not work.

"I should be able to get us cleared for an early morning flight." He spoke to Samson before turning to me. "Have you got a passport?"

My face fell. I'd never needed one before. "No. I could stay here and work on contracts." Never in my life had I not wanted to work more.

"Don't be ridiculous." Leif grinned with that boyish smile. "I'll take you to get that taken care of."

"Great idea." Miles grinned. "So what time should we be here in the morning?"

"Let's make it six." After Leon's comment, everyone went their separate ways and I was left with Leif. It took us less than two hours to get my passport and for him to drop me back off at the apartment.

I was grinning like a giddy school girl when I walked in and told Rachel the news. "I seriously hate you now!"

I knew she didn't mean it, so I grinned wider. "It's just work, Rach." That's what I wanted to tell myself the truth was I wasn't thinking about clients at all at the moment.

"Maybe you'll get laid while you're there." She waggled her eyebrows and just like that my gut clenched. Rachel had given me nothing but grief about missing the parties. She was pretty quick to fill me in on all the interesting scenarios I'd missed out on too.

"You don't think they'd think that do you?" For a moment I panicked. Honestly the thought hadn't crossed my mind. We'd all developed a great working relationship but as sexy as they were I didn't see them that way.

"I know if they were taking me to an island I'd be putting on some serious moves." This was why Samson couldn't leave Rachel in charge. Her mind was always in the gutter. Of course she was working at Fantasy's, so that worked in her favor until she crossed the line with a customer.

"I don't think about them that way." At her eye roll I knew I needed to get the conversation going in a different direction. "Help me pack?"

We walked back to my bedroom and Rachel pulled out my suitcase. "I'm just saying, getting a little one on one, or hell four on one action wouldn't be a bad thing." Rachel laughed at her own joke. Me doing four guys would be like her abstaining for a month. She didn't expect an answer since she began tossing things into the suitcase.

"It's a business trip." Even so I couldn't help laughing my ass off as she tossed in all my summer wear. "I don't think shorts and tanks will work."

"You're going to an island. If I know Samson, he'll make this a working deal, but you still need to be comfortable. I hear it's hot as shit down there this time of year." When I still looked ready to argue, she put her hands on her hips and glared. "Do you want to pass out from heat exhaustion or dress weather appropriately?"

"Fine, mom. Just make sure I have a few pair of jeans to cover my ass in case it gets cold at night." I packed my lingerie, footwear and socks myself, not trusting her with the underwear department.

"If it were me going, I'd hook up with one of the hunky guys and let them keep me warm, but for you I'll throw in jeans." Rachel rolled her eyes at me before walking over to the closet and pulling out my three favorite pairs.

"You're so not wearing that granny bathing suit." She snatched my one piece out of my hands as I was attempting to put it in the case. Walking off with it she came back minutes later with her tags still on, string bikini. "That's what you wear on an island!"

I eyed the pieces of fabric and guffawed. "Uh, no. That's what you wear when you're asking to get laid. I'll stick to the one piece."

"Fine. Don't blame me if you have screwed up tan lines when you get back." I was amazed she gave in that easily. Rachel was not known to back down from much. "Let's grab some dinner before you leave for an entire week!"

I slipped the one piece back in the case before zipping it up. "We doing takeout again, or do you want me to cook?" Rachel didn't cook at all, so if we ate in that chore fell to me.

"I should make you cook for me since you're going to paradise tomorrow, but let's go out? It is Friday after all." There was no way I could refuse our steak night when I was escaping to paradise tomorrow.

"Okay but if I can't fit in my bathing suit, I'm blaming you."

"Right. Because I have to twist your arm to eat." With a grin, we walked toward the front door and she stopped. "Crap, I left my wallet on your bed, I'll be right back." I knew she didn't need it, since I was buying tonight but she'd already reached the room before I could say anything.

We left out and I doubted I'd be able to eat a bite I was so excited about the trip. I quickly made a liar out of myself when we ended up at our favorite restaurant.

CHAPTER SIX

The Island

Excited didn't even begin to fit the way I felt when we boarded the company's private jet. The thing was freaking amazing and being able to sit in the cockpit while Leon navigated was something I decided I wanted to do every day for the rest of my life. It was really incredible flying through the clouds getting a front row seat.

My enthusiasm obviously humored him because he kept a smile on his face. Flying this way was amazing because it stopped all the checks you'd normally have to endure at the different airports. I had to pull myself out of the cockpit to discuss business with the other men since Samson did demand a working trip, but still it was something most people never get to experience.

We stopped overnight in Hong Kong, so the plane could get refueled and Leon could rest. Unfortunately we were all so exhausted a mutual decision was made not to explore and we ordered in room service at the hotel for the night instead. Samson did promise that he'd bring me back there someday or I may have well been heartbroken to not have taken the opportunity.

The next morning we were back on the jet and it took another twelve hours to finally reach our next to last destination, Cairns. I wasn't sure there could be a paradise to match the place. I felt like a kid. The excitement was almost overwhelming as we walked down those streets soaking up all the culture.

Leif and Miles gave me a tour while Samson and Leon secured the boat we'd be taking over to the island. It felt natural to hold both their hands as we walked into shops and bought things we'd never have any use for. We did get some peculiar looks from the natives of the city, but honestly I didn't care. Let them think I was happily fooling around with two sexy men, I knew the truth.

Leave it to Samson to not just rent a boat. When he called us down to the pier I stared in amazement at the beautiful vessel he'd acquired. It was somewhat ironic watching his attempt to explain his reasons for purchase when he normally was so reserved in his spending for the club. There was nothing reserved about this purchase.

I heard all about how Samson loved boats and already owned three from the other men. We shopped together for all the things we might need while on the island. None of us were sure what type of lodging the old cabin had, so tents, sleeping bags, and every other imaginable thing needed for a camp out was purchased. We did know there was no electricity so portable lighting devices were added into the supplies.

It would take several trips to haul this stuff in and by the time we finally set out to sea, I was exhausted. The jet lag was setting in, and the clear blue-green lull of the waters just made you want to be lazy. I gave in to that need while enjoying the sun beating down on my face as Samson took us to our destination. I was wearing a tank top and shorts, and thankful that I'd taken Rachel's advice on packing these up.

When I woke up I had a huge straw hat on my head that Leif had purchased as a joke back in town. I might have been upset about that but since I'd forgotten to put on sunscreen he saved me from a nasty burn. "Thanks a lot." Giving him a playful smirk I gasped as the island came into view.

"The pier looks pretty stable, but I'd like to check it out before we anchor off." Miles motioned toward the long wooden pier and I had no idea what would make one seem stable or not.

This was going to be the next home for Fantasy's! I couldn't believe how beautiful it was here. Long, white, sugar-sand beaches stretched out as far as my eyes could see. Palm trees with their leaves softly swaying with the breeze, this was definitely an island paradise. "Can I move in?"

"Let's see if you still feel that way after a week." Leif was grinning and I could see he felt the same way.

Miles checked the sturdiness of the wooden planks and gave his nod of approval. "We'll definitely need to build a bigger one, but for now this should work."

Samson unfolded a map and studied it. "If it hasn't grown over there should be a pebbled walk way to the cabin straight ahead. The agent said it was only about 400 feet back. Why don't you stay on the boat with Zoey, while the rest of us check it out?"

Leif gave a nod and the other three trekked off. I couldn't wait to get my feet into the sand so I jumped over the side, still wearing my clothes. The water was warm and inviting and I dove under with a smile. Leif didn't wait long to join me and soon we were swimming around like children.

It was already in the eighties. I couldn't imagine what it would feel like here in the summer. "Definitely could see me living out my life here." Paddling back to the shore, I wasn't sure I liked the look on the guy's faces. Samson looked pissed, while Leon and Miles just seemed perturbed.

"How bad is it?" Leif walked onto the shore and I followed behind.

"It's small." Samson was being a prude, I thought to myself.

"Well we didn't expect a mansion. Did we?" I expected some rustic cabin.

"Not a mansion, but a few beds would have been nice. As it is there's one cot and no bedroom. It does have a small kitchen and what looks like an outdoor shower outside, although I'm not sure where the water is coming from.

Samson was definitely not happy. I couldn't help it, he was so spoiled my funny bone was tickled. Once I started laughing, I just couldn't stop.

"Go ahead and laugh it up there Zoey. When you're sleeping on the floor with all of us snoring we'll see how funny it is then." Samson was trying his best not to laugh and keep his cynical expression in place. Eventually he failed and joined in.

"There's no reason to complain about it now. We should get all our supplies stored away before night falls." Leon shrugged and lifted one of the heavy boxes.

They definitely weren't lying when they said the cabin was not a mansion. It wasn't even as big as the living room in my apartment. The walls seemed to be fabricated out of ply wood and mud, but at least the floor was cement. It took four trips to get all our gear in place and I left the guys to that while I cleaned up as much as I could to make it habitable.

"When we get back I'll hire a contractor to fix something more livable for the workers that need to stay on." Leif was grinning, and the way I saw it, it could be worse. At least we weren't setting up tents on the beach.

"Um question? Where do we go to the bathroom?" I'd never been camping before, so the question didn't really arise until that moment.

"You make friends with mother nature." Miles winked at me and when I understood his meaning I groaned.

"There's a bathroom on the yacht." Sticking out my tongue childishly, there was no way I was doing my business between the palm trees.

"She wins." Leif chuckled. "I'm not really thrilled about yanking my junk out here until we know just what type of wildlife inhabits the greenery.

"We could sleep on the boat if it gets to be too much. Would anyone like to complain again about my quick purchase?" Samson was really enjoying his superiority at the moment and we all groaned.

"We've still got a few hours of daylight left, so why don't we leave that decision for later and go exploring?" Leon's idea seemed like the best one and we followed his lead.

The island was breathtaking. Lush greenery, tropical birds, even a huge waterfall that flowed into a crystal clear pool. We explored until my feet were aching in the soaking wet tennis shoes. I didn't want to be the one to complain, but honestly I couldn't take another step. "Um. Guys, I really need a break."

Of course my legs decided at that moment to cramp up and I would have hit my knees if Samson hadn't caught me. He looked horror-stricken and quickly lifted me into his arms. "Shit, Zoey. Sorry. I guess I didn't realize how far we've walked.

I felt ridiculous being cradled like a baby, but my legs were on fire. Leon and Miles both took one of my calves in each of their large hands and started massaging them. I wasn't sure if I wanted to hit or thank them because the sensation bordered on agony and relief.

"Let's get her back to the cabin. What she needs is a hot bath, but that's not happening." Samson walked forward forcing the guys to release my legs.

"I'm not that fragile, all I need is to relax for a little while and I'll be fine." Their concern was sweet but it made me feel very self-conscious.

Resting against Samson's bare chest was a little more comfortable than it should have been. Something about being held this way made me think of things I'd refused to allow myself to consider over the years. My face flushed when I understood it was actually turning me on, I tensed in his arms.

"Are you hurting worse?" The concern in Samson's voice embarrassed me even more. I shook my head no and burrowed my face against the smoothness of his skin. There was something seriously wrong with me I decided when my nipples tightened into tight buds, and my core clenched.

He was glancing down at my body and I knew the thin tank top and barely there sports bra, did little to disguise my arousal. The knowing smirk on his face told me he understood exactly what the deal was. I groaned turning myself more into his arms to hide the tell-tale signs.

Samson continued walking in long strides, but managed to lower his head to my ear and whisper. "There's nothing to be embarrassed about, all you have to do is say the word."

How in the hell did I answer that? I didn't. Tightening my arms around his neck, I could only hope that he didn't talk again until I got my body back under control. *Traitorous bitch.* How dare my breasts throw me out like that!

Dusk was falling as we finally reached the cabin. Instead of putting me down, Samson held on tighter. "Miles bring the cot over and let's see if we can get her worked out a little."

The thought of Samson working me out did very little to help with the ache between my legs and I wanted to argue. The truth was I couldn't really force myself to utter the denial because my legs were still hurting like hell.

My tank top was soaked with perspiration, and I felt grimy from the sea air mixed with it. "Could I maybe get a shower first?" It was vanity that made me long for that but I was also really uncomfortable. There's nothing worse than feeling the squishiness of wet socks on your feet.

"Leon get her shoes off." Samson was shifting my weight in his arms and I knew even at a hundred and ten pounds that trek through the jungle with him carrying me had to of exhausted him. Leon didn't ask questions, and made quick work of my shoes and socks. I couldn't help it, I sighed in content.

"It's getting dark. I'll set up one of the portable lights at the shower stall." Leif, walked off to take care of that and Samson carried me outside. He left Samson to take care of me as soon as he was assured we had enough light.

Calling the thing a shower stall was not appropriate since it was basically just the head protruding on a stand of cement. "I think I can stand. You've got to be tired of holding me." I knew I wasn't tired of being held even if it was inappropriate.

Instead of answering he slid me slowly to my feet, and I cried out in agony. Charley horse pain was no laughing matter. I grabbed onto him for support. "I don't think this is happening." I looked at the spray of water he'd started with longing.

"Don't be stupid, Zoey. I can help you clean up." He didn't know that my bra and underwear were full of sand and I wasn't sure how to say it without feeling like an idiot.

I used his arms as support and moved under the water, thinking at least part of my body could get clean. He chuckled softly at my action and I glared back. "What?"

"Are you really that self-conscious? I know my shorts are filled with sand and your clothes have to be as well. I promise you I've seen tits and ass before."

"Not mine you haven't." That came out way to whiny for my own liking and automatically made me feel defensive. "Turn your head." I knew we were both adults but I was still pretty shy about showing off my body.

Shaking his head, still chuckling he averted his eyes. I managed to let go of his arm long enough to pull my tank and sports bra off, but the moment I attempted to pull down my shorts, my legs cramped again.

"This is fucking ridiculous." He grabbed my hands, planted them on his shoulders, and quickly reached down to pull down my shorts and panties in one sweep. "Step out of them."

I was too shocked to disobey. His eyes roamed over my naked body freely and I shivered. "Get cleaned off so I can take you back in." Instead of arguing I quickly maneuvered back under the water and used my hands to wash away the grime. I didn't have time to think about standing there completely nude because the damn water was freezing.

Leif walked out with a towel and I gasped at his perusal. "God! At least a little privacy, please." The smile on his face was anything but comforting as he held out the towel, still taking in his fill of my body.

"Why the hell would I want to look away. You're beautiful." I hobbled close enough to snatch the towel from his hands and quickly wrapped it around me. In return I was awarded with a deep timbre laugh.

With their help I made it back inside the cabin. Miles patted the cot and I wasn't sure whether to be humiliated or thankful that I had all of them to help me at the moment. Refusing to think about it, I slowly lowered myself down until I was resting face up on the cot.

Leon was preparing something in the small kitchen while Miles and Leif worked out the muscles on my legs. After several long minutes the ache receded and I was just enjoying their touch. My eyes closed and I moaned softly at the magic of their fingers.

"How long has it been since you allowed someone to pleasure you, Zoey?" My eyes opened in incredulity at Samson's question.

"That's," I fumbled for the right words because it really did throw me off guard, "not something I talk about."

"Obviously. You're purring like a kitten in heat, so I'm guessing it's been a long time." Leif and Miles continued their massage and I met Samson's eyes wondering if he was mocking me. He seemed very serious and instead of making me uncomfortable it made me horny. Of course it could be that the two sexy men rubbing my legs had a part in that too.

"It's been my experience that sex is never good for the woman, so I don't indulge." I answered him honestly seeing no reason to be ashamed of how I felt about sexuality. I knew perfectly well just how open he was about the topic.

"Then the men you've been with are fucking idiots." His arms crossed over his bare chest and he studied me. That's the only way I could describe the way his eyes roamed from head to toe, seeming to take inspection.

"Or maybe men are just selfish assholes who only think about what gets them off?" There was no anger in my voice. I was so relaxed at the moment I couldn't muster up any.

"I don't consider myself selfish in that department. What about you guys?" He turned his attention to each of them and I wondered what point he was trying to make.

"Satisfying a woman is always first in my experience." Leif continued his massage and my legs were very happy at the moment.

"I feel the same. If a woman doesn't find pleasure in our fucking then I'm obviously not worth her trying again." Leon called out from the kitchen, and I had to admit he looked very domesticated plating sandwiches.

"I think a woman's body should be worshiped." Miles moved his caress down to the soles of my feet and I nearly came undone. I obviously needed the touch of a man more than I thought.

"Words are easy." This was the strangest conversation to be having while I was laying on a cot with just a towel covering me. Not that I wasn't accustomed to strange discussions with these men. We'd never focused on me during them though.

"Maybe you should let us show you then." Samson lowered to his knees at the head of the cot, and his hands moved to my temples, massaging in tiny circular motions.

For a moment their hands felt so incredible on me I was tempted to give in. Then sanity came back. "You're my bosses. I don't think us having sex would be a smart decision." Not to mention having sex with four men wasn't even possible, was it? Talk about a fantasy that needed to be added to the books.

"Not sex, Zoey. Pleasure." Samson ran his fingers through my hair as he massaged my scalp.

"What you're doing right now is more than pleasurable." If that's what he meant, he could keep going all night. I relaxed even more as the men continued their impersonal massages and I felt like a pampered queen.

"I'd love to spread those beautiful thighs and massage you with my tongue." Leif ran his hand further up my leg to mid-thigh and stopped.

My core clenched almost painfully at his words, forcing my eyes open again. "You mean, there?" My eyes glanced down and I tensed. I'd never had a man taste me that way and I wasn't sure I would ever want to. A part of me longed to know what it felt like though.

"I bleed from there." I knew it was a childish thing to say, but I had all these screwed up concerns about my body and I couldn't imagine a man really wanting to do that.

"You're not bleeding now though?" Leif winked at me and massaged higher, under the towel. I felt my heart race at the thought of how close he was to my sex and tensed.

"No, but I've never done that before." My legs tensed and not so much from wanting him to stop but excited about the possibility.

"Sweetheart, you've never really had a man worship you at all, have you?" Miles shook his head with a sad expression. "Let us show you how beautiful it can be."

Leif's hand stilled again, and I knew without doubt if I said no this would all end. The problem was I didn't really want to say no. "I'm afraid." I hated the weakness of my words. As a woman who had always stood strong, the thought of letting go that way was terrifying.

"We would never hurt you Zoey." Leon had walked out of the kitchen and was now kneeling down at my side. The seductive smile on his face made me ache to give in.

I was surrounded by four of the most handsome men and they all wanted to please me. How could I refuse that? Even if I could, why would I want to? I nodded, unable to speak the words that longed to spill forth.

"You have to say the words. I promised you nothing would ever happen unless you asked for it." Miles continued the almost impersonal massage now, and I remembered the conversation.

"I want this." I might hate myself tomorrow for being so weak, but the thought of them lifting their hands away was more than I could consider.

Leon lowered his lips to mine and kissed me gently. It was the barest touch of flesh and I sighed against the feel. With unhurried hands he separated the towel splaying it open to display my body. Without conscious thought my hands moved to cover my breasts.

"Put your hands under your head, Zoey." Samson softly demanded. "Let's us please you." After I complied he tilted my chin back slightly with his hand and kissed me. The action lifted my breasts and they were soon enveloped in two separate large hands.

Samson released my lips and rested his hands on my forearms at the top of the cot, imprisoning me gently. His head lowered and he whispered in my ear. "Watch them pleasure you." The seductive command was all I needed to lower my eyes to Leon who was cupping my right breast, then he pinched the rosy nipple between his fingers sending a shaft of pleasure down to my core.

Leif's mouth lowered to my other breast and suckled my nipple deep inside his mouth making me cry out at the bliss of duel sensations. This was insanity but I never wanted it to end.

"Spread your legs for Miles, and let him show you good he can make you feel." Samson's words in my ear felt like a caress and I slightly parted my thighs, still unsure about displaying myself so completely. "She needs a little help."

Leon and Leif released my breasts and moved to each of my thighs, parting them widely. I couldn't help it. I whimpered.

"You're beautiful, Zoey. Let us look at you." This from Miles whose long digits now stroked softly over my aching flesh making me forget everything but the feeling of desire that touch brought me. "So soft, pink, and wet." He continued to whisper positives about my body as he gently caressed the throbbing folds. My legs were spread wide with my feet touching the floor on either side of the cot.

"Keep them there and we can worship your breasts while Miles shows you how good he can make you feel." Leon moved back up and took a nipple deep into his mouth before biting down lightly. I cried out at the pleasure and felt I would combust from the two sensations at once. I attempted to pull my arms from their resting place as the feeling overloaded me but Samson refused the action.

"No Zoey. Those sweet little hands would only get in the way." He kissed me again and I was almost beside myself at the sensory overload. Leif was suckling me again, Leon never stopped, and Miles's fingers were working magic bringing me so close to the edge I knew I'd soon explode with pleasure.

Then I felt his tongue replace his fingers and I unraveled. My soft cry was captured by Samson's tongue and the sensations just kept going on and on as

Miles speared deeply in and out, forcing me to ride out the release.

I'd never known being devoured that way could bring such incredible pleasure and tears streamed down my cheeks. When his tongue laved over my clit the sensitivity there made me tense. He lifted his head and licked his lips. "Sweetheart you taste like heaven."

"She comes apart so completely." Leon released my breast then caressed my cheek. "I wonder how many times we can make her come in one night."

He stood up and Miles changed places with him. "I say we find out."

I couldn't believe they wanted to do that again, and I wasn't sure I could live through it. "I can't." Was that my voice that sounded so breathless?

"You can, and Leif and I want a chance to prove it after Leon is done." Samson was massaging my scalp again and I knew that I couldn't refuse them. Even through the languid feeling of release I'd been given, I was longing for more.

Leon's finger slid deep inside me and I gasped. It had been so long since that part of my anatomy had been invaded that I couldn't help myself. "She's so tight. Samson you have to feel her."

A part of me knew I should be embarrassed as Samson moved between my thighs, his finger taking the place of Leon's, but the pleasure? It was so incredible feeling his thick, long digit slide deep then curl. When he added a second and rode me slowly with it, I couldn't stop the moan of ecstasy that escaped my lips.

"Taste her, I want to continue fucking her with my fingers." The way he spoke was so dirty, but when Leon's tongue flicked over my clit and Samson's fingers rode me, I didn't care what they said. My hips arched off the cot and followed the rhythm of sensation. The soft cries of pleasures echoing in the room shocked me when I discovered they were my own.

My core clenched against Samson's invading digits, on the brink of finding release again. When he removed them I couldn't stop the sigh of disappointment. "I know you're close baby, but I think you'll enjoy this more." His finger rimmed my other entrance and I tensed.

"Trust me Zoey, you'll love this." With ease he slowly pressed his finger inward, the juices from my sex lubricating the way.

It felt so strange to have his finger there, but not in a bad way. "Taste her now, Leon." Samson slowly worked his finger in and out of my tight hole but the moment Leon's tongue speared my core all thoughts of what he was doing left my mind. Miles and Leif's mouths on my breasts along with being so completely pleasured by the other two was too much. My orgasm peaked and flowed over leaving me drenched in my own juices.

I barely even noticed Samson adding another finger and pressing forward except for the strange burn in the aftermath of such pleasure. "You've never taken a man this way before?"

I shook my head no, still trying to come down from the sensations of pleasure I'd been given. Now I felt the stretching of my other entrance but it wasn't exactly painful, it just let me feeling very full.

"I wonder if you can take three." Samson's words made no sense until I felt another finger join and tensed at the increased burning sensation. "No baby, don't tense up. Bare down." I tried to follow his command but the pressure was too much.

"Leif, come down here and pleasure her pussy, she's thinking too much." He quickly moved between my legs, doing as Samson asked and within seconds my hips were straining toward his tongue. Samson fingers pushed in knuckle deep while my mind was otherwise occupied, then slowly inched in further.

Leon took the place at the top of the cot by my head and gently nibbled on my earlobe. "That's it, Zoey, just relax and let them fuck you with their fingers and mouths." Miles was worshipping my breasts and again I was overwhelmed by a myriad of sensations, unable to focus on one single thing.

I could feel Samson's fingers sliding in and out of my ass, Leif's tongue plunging into my core, and the beauty of Miles suckling my breasts. Leon's gentle words in my ear was almost hypnotic as he encouraged me to just let go and feel everything. When I found paradise again my entire body was nothing but mush. When they each lifted away I felt empty and longed for their touch again.

"Let's clean up then eat." Samson winked down and held out his hand to help me stand.

I wasn't sure how I was supposed to feel now that each of them had pleasured me. I took Samson's hand and stood, glancing at my feet.

"There will be none of that Zoey. We all enjoyed feasting on you and if you'll let us, we'll do it again after we eat." Samson lifted my chin with his hand, forcing me to meet his eyes. The look of sincerity in those gray depths spoke nothing but truth. That's all it took to make me feel that what we'd done was alright.

We walked outside to the standing shower and I was shocked when all the men stripped down. They were beautiful with clothes, without them? Each was a sculpted work of perfection. Leif walked under the cool spray and pulled me with him.

I shivered as the coolness splayed across my once again sticky body, but was heated up when he began washing my breasts. All of them were sporting rather impressive hard-ons, and I could help but gape. "None of you, um, got off." I wasn't very comfortable talking about a male's anatomy.

"Would you like to watch us do that?" I was a little surprised to hear Miles ask the question, since he was usually the most reserved.

I nodded my head because I'd never watched a man do that and I was curious. Miles grinned at my response and his hand moved to his long, hard shaft. My eyes were riveted as he worked his fist in a pumping motion and it grew even larger. My hand reached out to touch him, but Samson stopped me.

"Later, Zoey. If you want us to fuck you, and I hope you do, we will. But for now just watch." Feeling almost chastened I watched. When Leif, Leon, and Samson began stroking their massive erections, I felt like I had a front row seat to the best porno ever.

Each of them had a distinct way of pleasing their body, and I couldn't look away. Leon worked his shaft slowly from base to head, Samson rolled his fist just over his wide mushroom shaped head, and Leif seemed to go at it with the same gusto he had for life. Almost yanking to the point where I was amazed it didn't cause him pain.

"I want to come on you, Zoey. Will you let me?" Miles was pumping slowly and met my eyes as he asked the question.

"Yes." Fascinated and a little shocked that he wanted to do that, I moved closer. With a few more pumps of his fist, his body sprayed my hip with his essence. It felt warm against my skin.

"We all should cover her with our pleasure." Leif grinned and waited for me to either agree or not as he continued the fast motion with his hand. I nodded. I wasn't even sure why I now wanted them to follow Miles's lead, but I did. The other three men surrounded me, continuing their hand jobs until they all found release.

I felt marked before I was ushered back under the cool spray and cleansed off by four sets of masculine hands. When I was about as clean as a girl could get, Samson took over the shower and then took me in his arms when he was clean. Being pressed against him chest to chest felt incredible, but my body was soon pulled away from his and into Leon's arms.

Leon kissed me deeply until I was dragged away by Miles. I laughed softly at how they were passing me around, but my body was soon aroused again. Leif was the last to grab and hold me against his chest. "Let's eat before I forget what a feast we have in her right now."

Food was the furthest thing from my mind as we dried off with towels. I'd just had the most incredible sexual experience of my life and it wasn't with one man, but four. None of us dressed. I kept on my towel as we sat on blankets on the floor to eat our sandwiches. The men just let it all hang out. I couldn't help that my eyes kept drifting down.

"See something you like?" Of course Leif would make a joke out of my ogling. He was wolfing down his food like a man who hadn't eaten in days.

Flushing I put my attention back on my sandwich managing to eat half before I was so full I couldn't take another bite. Sipping on the bottle of water Leon had given me, I forced myself not to stare.

"We like it when you look Zoey." Miles's humor-filled words forced me to lift my head.

"We'd like it more if we were deep inside you." Leon raised an eyebrow devouring the rest of his meal.

"Is that even possible?" I was thinking the thought. I really didn't mean to blurt it out there.

"Three of us could be inside you, and your hand would pleasure the other." Samson's matter-of-fact answer made my mouth fall open. "That's only if you want it Zoey." He was more refined in eating, seeming to study me almost like he was trying to read my mind.

"I've only had sex with one guy, and it wasn't really fun." There's was no reason not to be honest with them after everything that had happened tonight.

"Do you think we'd fuck you and not make sure you enjoy it, sweetheart?" Miles gave me an encouraging smile and I really couldn't doubt his words.

I nibbled on my lip, nervously. The thought of having sex again was terrifying on its own, but with all of them? "It was really painful the last time." I wasn't sure how to make them understand my fears.

"He hurt you?" Samson looked pissed and self-consciously I wrapped my arms around my waist, not liking him angry.

"You're scaring her." Leon pulled me into his lap and held me like a child. "None of us would ever hurt you Zoey. I think we promised you that already. If you don't want this, all you have to do is say no."

I rested my face against his chest and closed my eyes while he stroked my hair. "I know it's crazy, but I do trust all of you." I whispered the words, then kissed his chest lightly.

"It's not crazy. This isn't about just getting our rocks off baby. We want you to enjoy the things we do to that luscious little body." Leon kissed my forehead and I felt truly cherished.

"We've all had an exhausting day. I think we should let Zoey get some sleep and decide what she wants next." Samson stood, gathered all our plates and Leif disposed of the water bottles. "Tonight we can cuddle."

Hearing Samson say we could cuddle was funny and I couldn't stop the small laugh. "I think your much more of a softy then you let on."

He put the plates in the sink and shook his head. "The last person that thought that ended up with a tanned ass." He walked back over and sat down on the make-shift sleeping bag beds on the floor.

"I thought you said you wouldn't hurt me." The look in his eyes told me he wanted to pull me over his lap and not in a nice way.

"Spanking you would bring us both pleasure but that's for another discussion. Get some sleep before I prove just how much you'll love it."

I didn't want to test his theory out, because I was seriously tired. We had the cushioning of sleeping bags, but even that cushion wasn't enough to make me forget about the hard floor beneath. "This place really needs a bed." I tried to get comfortable but it really did suck.

The other guys had settled down on the floor. Miles and Leif on one side of me, Leon, and Samson the other. "Come here." Leon pulled me over on his chest and covered me with his sleeping bag. "Get some sleep before we decide to wear you out even more."

I wasn't sure that would be such a bad thing. My body was so sated after being pleased so well that I couldn't wind down. Long after they'd fallen asleep I was still wide awake. Thoughts of the pleasure I'd received made me crave it again, and subconsciously I entwined my leg with Leon's rubbing against him.

His soft growl made me realize I'd woken him and what I was doing. Of course I immediately stopped but my clit was throbbing so I pressed my legs together tightly to stop the ache.

I felt his fingers slide down, rubbing exactly where I needed them. I cried out softly before covering my mouth with my hand, not wanting to wake the others. With expertise he stroked my sex until I came undone.

"Sleep Zoey." Pulling me back over on his chest, his arms wrapped tightly around my waist. Listening to the rhythmic beating of his heart finally lulled me to sleep.

CHAPTER SEVEN

Fantasy

Waking up surrounded by all the beautiful flesh was an experience I wouldn't soon forget. My towel had come off during the night and Leif's arm was splayed over my breasts. I wasn't sure how I felt about that. The passion last night had been incredible, but was I this person?

I maneuvered my way out of fantasy land and managed to stand up. Arranging the towel so I wasn't showing off everything, I glanced around the room until I found my suitcase. Opening it I saw the string bikini resting on top that I remembered specifically unpacking before I'd left home. Rachel! Shaking my head I decided at this point showing off my body wasn't that big a deal so I slid it on.

I was at the front door when Samson's voice stopped me. "Running away?" I turned back and knew it was the wrong move when I saw his beautiful body standing in all its glory. The man was like a walking Adonis with his chiseled abs, tanned skin and even his prominent sex thick and long, giving me its own morning greeting.

"No. Just thought I'd take a walk on the beach." Yes I was staring but hell who wouldn't? The man was beautiful dressed in a business suit, with his sculptured face of the gods, undressed he was damn near irresistible.

"Let me grab my trunks and I'll join you." I didn't stop looking as that well-rounded ass walked over to his own suitcase and almost sulked in disappointment when my view was stripped away by his bathing suit. He slid on a pair of sandals and I decided that wasn't a bad idea so I rummaged through my bag until I found my own. We walked out the door leaving the rest of the men sleeping soundly.

Sunrise on the island was a sight to behold. The beauty of the waves crashing against the shore, the scent of the tropics, combined with the sounds it was easy to believe I'd stepped into another world. Having Samson walking beside me made it even more surreal.

"Tell me what you're thinking." His hand reached down and grasped mine as we continued to walk along the sugary white beach.

"I love this place. I think the Isle will be a great investment." It just felt right to be walking with him holding my hand.

"I'm glad you think so, but I was talking about last night." He stopped, forcing me to come to a standstill as well.

Glancing up into his gray eyes I knew what he was really asking. Did I want to explore what happened more? "Honestly?"

"I'd prefer that instead of you lying." His grin was easy but the look in his eyes was probing.

"I guess I'm overwhelmed? I mean until last night I wasn't even interested in sex. Taking a step that big? Well it's huge and I'm not sure I'm ready for it." He wanted the truth I was giving him nothing less. "Don't get me wrong, the pleasure was mind-blowing."

"Always tell me the truth Zoey. I'm glad you enjoyed yourself last night, and I can speak for the others when I say I'm glad we were able to give that to you." His hand lifted and he smoothed my hair away from my face. "This is about what you want."

What did I want? Definitely not four men at once, even though the feelings of passion they'd given were ones I'd never forget as long as I lived. "If I had more experience maybe I wouldn't be so afraid. But, um, maybe one lover at a time?"

"You're asking me instead of saying what you need. Zoey you're a strong women who knows her own mind. Intellectually, you may be one of the smartest women I've ever worked with. So don't ask me what you want, tell me." This was Samson from the office. The man that liked being in control and in turn made me want to argue with him about my place in our work environment.

His tactic worked because instead of feeling self-conscious I was ready to be the mouthy bitch I could be when things weren't going my way. "Fine. What I want is to fuck you right here on this beach and worry about the other shit later."

Samson tossed back his head and chuckled deeply. "Now that is sexy!"

I was amazed that my mouth filter flew off when confronted by his dominant side. "If it's so sexy why aren't you kissing me?" Obviously the filter wasn't ready to be put back on.

That gorgeous smirk that I loved found his face and he stepped back to cross his arms over his chest. "Because little Zoey, you've explained what you want, but I have my own needs. I'd love nothing more than to throw your gorgeous ass down and fuck you until you screamed in pleasure, but sand and fucking? First of all, they don't work well together that shit only reads well in books. Second if you want me to pleasure you, then it's on my terms."

Well didn't that just change things completely? I knew Samson liked being in control in the club, but what would he want from a sexual partner? "What are your terms?" Asking seemed the easiest way of finding out if I was in over my head or not. I refused to even deny the fact that I really wanted to be with him that way.

"You can start by getting on your knees and using that mouth for something more pleasurable than arguing."

"You want me to submit to you?" I remember vividly saying I'd never get on my knees for any of them the first day I walked into the office.

"Only in regards to sexuality. I love that smart ass mouth in business but when it comes to pleasure, I know you'll be a lot happier if you allow me to take control." He didn't make a move toward me, and I was somewhat shocked that he wasn't angry. Usually when I crossed him at the office he looked ready to toss my ass over his knee.

"I'm not sure I can be both those things Samson. Submissive in the bedroom, but in control out of it." The only thing stopping me from falling to my knees right now was that concern. I wanted to be with him, but I also didn't want to go back to work next week and feel I had to bow down to his wishes.

"If I didn't approve of how you conducted yourself at work, you wouldn't have a job Zoey. The last thing I want is some timid little woman saying yes to every idea brought up involving the company. You can take that out of your mind now. This thing between us will only happen outside of business hours. Well maybe during lunch."

Holy shit didn't that bring a few more fantasies to mind. Samson taking me over his desk at lunch. I think I was supposed to be focusing on what I wanted from this? "You're not making it easy to think." I went from pragmatic to horny as hell in less than a minute.

"If you want easy, you might want to talk to one of the other men. I'm sure they'll give you whatever you want on your terms." His deep chuckle did funny things to my equilibrium.

"What about them?" This was really going to sound slutty, but it needed to be put out there. "If I'm yours does that mean I can't be with any of them?"

He grinned, while shaking his head. "Now if you were mine completely, you'd ask permission to fuck them, but that's not what we're discussing here. I don't think you're ready to belong to anyone in that capacity yet. Don't add boundaries to this that we're not approaching. This is about you and me enjoying each other sexually. What you do outside of the time we're together is up to you."

"So basically you're saying that anytime you and I sleep together I'm under your control and that's it?" I really wanted to understand what he was offering. This was a new world that I was embarking on and I was clueless.

"That's it, for now. If we decide we're compatible together later on, we'll rethink things."

My mind was overwhelmed. "But isn't that dangerous. I mean having several sexual partners can't be safe." Slut. My mind was really having a hard time accepting that a person could just sleep with someone without emotions being involved.

"We're all clean and you are as well. None of us sleep with people outside of the club and they are all tested to retain membership. As long as you agree to those same terms you can do whatever you like."

That explained the medical exams I'd underwent for employment, and I knew from Rachel that the other employees did that as well. "Did you know you were going to sleep with me when I was hired?" There was no doubt in my mind now that it would happen, but it made me uncomfortable to think he was considering this back then.

"No. I had no idea. It is standard protocol for employment. When our clients ask for a fantasy, they are required to undergo the same tests. They also have a yearly exam to continue membership."

My head was spinning with so much information that I'd forgotten why this conversation started. "I guess I've gotten off topic."

"I don't mind answering your questions. Why don't we move to the boat and get more comfortable?" At my nod we walked back toward the pier and boarded.

Sitting down at the table I tried to understand what kind of relationship he wanted with me. I got that it was purely sexual but there were so many what ifs that I still wasn't sure what that meant.

"I can see your mind working overtime, Zoey." He walked over to the small cooler on deck and pulled out two bottles of flavored water. "This doesn't have to be so complicated. If you want to fuck me, then you agree to let me be in control during the act."

I couldn't believe I was sitting on a boat staring at the beautiful scenery, and contemplating sleeping with my boss. The irony was not lost. I'd lost my last job for that refusal. I took the bottle he offered, unscrewed the top, took a deep sip and made a decision. "My answer is yes." I was sitting on the long running leather couch at the front of the boat offering my submission in exchange for the pleasure I knew he could give.

He took several deep drinks of the liquid before putting his bottle down on the table. "Come with me." Holding out his hand, I took it and was led downstairs to the bedroom. "You're sure this is what you want?" He stopped in front of the bed and searched my face for an answer.

"I'm sure." My voice didn't sound sure and wobbled while looking into the intensity of his gray eyes.

"Until we leave this room all I want to hear from those beautiful lips is yes or no. Understand?" His knuckles lightly grazed over my cheek and instantly had me aching for his touch.

"Yes."

"Good girl. Now on your knees."

I knew this was what he'd want and as I did what he asked I felt strange. I'd always thought that a woman doing this would feel degraded, but I didn't. Instead I felt empowered. Maybe it was knowing that while I'd done as he asked, it was only because of the pleasure I knew his hands were capable of? I watched as he lowered his swimming trunks, putting me eye level with his beautiful cock.

"Show me how you worship a cock, Zoey."

I had no experience with this at all, but I refused to let that stop me. Reaching out my hand I gently grasped the base of his shaft, squeezing lightly. My eyes lifted to his as my tongue laved over the smooth steel.

He was already semi-erect and with each stroke of my tongue he grew thicker and longer. Going on gut instinct alone I took him inside my mouth, suckling half of his length before retreating. His width forced my mouth open wide and I attempted to take him deeper with the next downward plunge of my mouth.

"Relax your throat." His hips pushed forward gagging me, and he retreated. "We'll work on this." Pulling out slowly he watched my face as he pushed back in. By forcing my throat muscles to relax I took him a little deeper that time. "Put your hands on your thighs."

I trembled as I followed that command knowing that my hand wouldn't be there to stop him. "You have to learn to trust me Zoey. I won't do anything you can't handle." To prove his point he pushed his cock into my mouth a few inches and retreated. Repeating this movement several times until I wasn't worried he was going to choke me, I relaxed again.

I felt his hand tangle in my hair and he pushed a few inches deeper before retreating, never once abusing the trust I had given as he rode my mouth slowly. Closing my eyes, I tightened my lips and let him fuck my mouth. If you had asked me before if I thought I could find pleasure in this I would have laughed in your face. With Samson, I enjoyed knowing I was giving him pleasure.

"I'm going to give you more now, just relax and take me in."

I almost panicked when his mushroom-shaped head hit the back of my throat, but forced myself to relax and swallow instead. Instead of choking, I discovered I could easily do this.

"That's so beautiful Zoey. I love watching you suck my cock." His movements increased in speed and I focused carefully on my breathing and not tensing my throat muscles. "One day I'll come in your mouth, but I want to show you how proud I am of you right now." He pulled away and I almost whimpered in disappointment.

He stepped out of his shorts and kicked off his sandals. "Undress and lay on the bed. I want those sexy legs spread wide."

I didn't hesitate about taking off the string bikini or my sandals. Climbing onto the bed I parted my legs slightly, still not comfortable with putting myself on display.

"I want those legs spread wide. Don't make me tell you again." He wasn't asking.

"I'm sorry. It's embarrassing to know you're looking at me that way."

Samson sat on the edge of the bed and patted the spot beside him. "Do you remember what I told you to do when we were in this room?"

Fuck. I'd forgotten he only wanted me to say yes or no. "Yes." Why did I feel so guilty for opening my mouth?

"And did you answer me with yes or no?"

"No." I sure as hell wouldn't forget again.

He patted his lap. "Lay over my legs."

My mouth opened to ask him why and then I remembered he only wanted one of two words. I bit my lip indecisively not sure that I was willing to let him spank me for something so stupid.

"It's your choice. Either accept that I'm going to punish you or walk out and we forget about this." I knew that look on his face. I'd seen it in a meeting when one of the guys pushed him on a project he wasn't interested in taking on. He was serious.

The self-preserving side of me said to get up and walk my ass out of this room, never to look back. The part that wanted Samson won and my ass ended up over his lap terrified that he was about to beat the shit out of me.

I wasn't expecting his large hand to caress my ass cheeks like they were a prized possession. The tenseness of my body relaxed after he continued doing that for several long minutes. Then a resounding slap landed on my ass and I cried out softly.

That smarted like hell, but then his hand caressed again making me forget. It didn't last, his hand fell upon my ass in several quick slaps making me feel like my backside was on fire.

"Such a pretty little virgin ass. It looks better with a little color thrown in." I was ready to cry when the next five slaps fell down without mercy. He pulled me up to sit in his lap and I wasn't sure if I wanted to hit him in the face or cry. The latter won.

"You did really well."

I'd never been disciplined that way as a child and it was like a dam had broken because the waterworks wouldn't stop. I wasn't expecting his fingers to slide against my sex, or for the moisture that made those digits entering me find home easier because of it. My body actually got off on that shit. The pain in my ass receded at the pleasure his touch gave. Two fingers curled against that sweet spot in my core and I almost came.

"Not yet." I wanted to scream as those fingers slid away leaving me hanging on the edge of ecstasy. "On the bed with those legs spread wide."

I didn't hesitate this time, scrambling up to the top of the bed, resting back, and splaying my legs open. My clit was throbbing and his eyes taking me in didn't help the ache he'd left with his caress.

"Such a beautiful sight. That pretty little pussy is weeping for me. Hands under your head and don't move them."

I remembered this from last night except this time there was no one there to keep my hands in place. I complied and tried not to think about the ache between my thighs. I wanted him to touch, thought I'd scream if he didn't but when his hands did find me, it wasn't where I wanted them.

His hand stroked over my shoulder, between my breasts, across my abdomen, skipping my sex completely, it traced down my thigh then back up again. My body was clenched in anticipation and he didn't seem to be in a hurry to answer my needs.

"Such soft skin, I could spend hours just touching you."

My hips lifted up, asking him silently for the touch he was refusing. He chuckled softly. Instead of answering that movement his head lowered and his tongue trailed around my navel then made me squeal when it dipped inside. "Not the hole you want tongued?"

Closing my eyes, I groaned, refusing to answer that question. His lips trailed up and circled the areola of my breast, missing the nipple and I knew he was purposely teasing me. I whimpered and he chuckled. "So impatient."

He continued teasing me by running his tongue up my inner thigh, stopping before he reached my sex. His breath hovered over my clit briefly, and I thought I would scream as he denied me that pleasure and moved up my body again. "Do you want to fuck now Zoey?" His body moved between my thighs and I felt the head of his cock nudge against my clit.

"Yes!" I was so turned on that all I could think about was his thick cock driving home, pounding me into the mattress. The wide mushroom-head pushed slightly against my core and I gasped.

He pulled back. "I think I'd rather have you fuck me instead." Flipping onto his back he rested his hands under his head and motioned with his chin for me to climb on.

The thought of riding him was daunting but I was so ready that I was willing to do anything to ease the ache he'd left. Refusing to think about it, I straddled his waist hoping like hell I could do this right. Grasping him in my hand I lowered myself slowly tensing as his width breached me. Whimpering softly, I was convinced this would never work, he was too big.

"Fuck Zoey. You're so damn tight." The pleasure on his face made me want to continue and I pushed down taking in the head at least, then I stopped.

I didn't care if he didn't want me to talk he was too large. "Samson, I can't!" Frustrated as hell because I wanted this I attempted to take him in further.

"You're as tight as a virgin, baby." His hands moved from under his head and he lifted me by the hips, putting me on my back again.

"I've only done this once." My eyes filled with tears because I hated that I just couldn't take him. I knew he was much bigger than the guy that had taken me, but I hadn't realized how much larger.

"Stop." His fingers wiped the tears from cheek. "We can do this, I just didn't realize how inexperienced you are." Two fingers found my core and pushed in deep. I caught my breath at the fullness. He rode me slowly that way for several strokes then introduced a third, I cried out.

"Don't tense up baby. Just let me love you." Slowly those three fingers embedded deeply and I felt him widening them, stretching me almost impossibly. The sensation bordered on pleasure and pain and I closed my eyes attempting to relax.

Soon those three digits were fucking me and I was amazed that the pain was gone. I felt my body reaching toward that pinnacle of paradise and then he withdrew again.

"Now you're ready." Moving between my thighs he slid in slowly, still stretching my body but in a way now that was so delicious I moaned softly. "Beautiful, baby." He was so deep I could feel him against my womb. I didn't think it could get any better than this until he began riding me with slow deep strokes. I met each thrust of his body and felt the tides of passion rise again.

"You're so perfect I'm not going to last. Come for me Zoey." His fingers moved between our bodies he rubbed my clit and instantly I came apart. My core clenched and released as it flooded with my desire and I rode out the wave with his faster thrusts until I felt him fill me with his own.

Bathing my womb with his passion only made my orgasm continue until he collapsed on top of me, nearly stealing my breath. "Thank fuck you're on the pill."

His words slid into my passion numbed brain and confused me for a moment. Remembering that I'd disclosed that information during the physical, it gave me a sense of relief as well since the last thing on my mind had been protection.

Still joined together, he turned me over on my back to relieve me of his weight and I felt his cock soften. I didn't have the strength to move so I remained splayed over his chest. "I think I love you."

The expression on his face at my words made me realize what I'd allowed to slip out. I hadn't meant to say that, it was just so beautiful, the experience he'd given me.

"You two were fucking amazing together." I was exhausted after so much pleasure but seeing Leif standing at the door made my eyes widen.

"Glad you enjoyed it." Samson lifted me carefully off his body, leaving me exposed to Leif's eyes. That tick was in his jaw again, like it was when he was angry.

Instead of walking out like I expected most people to do when they walk in on two people making love he sat down on my side of the bed. For reasons I couldn't explain it didn't feel wrong to me having him there. I could only guess because he'd pleasured me the night before.

"The other guys were looking for you." Leif's eyes were roaming over my body and flushed.

Samson chuckled and sat up. "I'm going to wash up and grab some breakfast. Maybe you and Zoey can talk while I do that." He rolled over and kissed me gently on the lips before getting out of bed. "I really enjoyed you." With a wink he left me open mouthed staring at his gorgeous ass retreating.

How was I supposed to react? I'd just had sex with Samson and now Leif was staring at me like I was the only breakfast he had in mind. For a brief moment my feelings were hurt, but I remembered what he'd said. This was just sex. I needed to stick that in my brain and classify it the same way or I would risk getting my heart broke. I didn't really love Samson. Did I? I always thought I was the kind of person that didn't have sex unless I was in love.

"You okay?" Leif looked worried and I hated to see that expression on his beautiful face.

"I'm fine." Sitting up I pulled the blanket around me wondering if I really was. The sex had been incredible after the initial pain part, but I didn't know how to feel about it now.

"Samson can be a little insensitive." Leif had obviously read the confusion in my face but I didn't know how to reply. Biting my lip I nodded not sure why I felt like crying again.

"Damn." He pulled me into his arms and I clung to him. This was so stupid, I knew what I signed on for when I said yes, so why did I feel like shit? "We work better as package deal. I wish I'd talked to you before you slept with him on your own."

"What does that mean?" A package deal. Why should Leif apologize for Samson fucking me and basically dumping me in his lap?

"It means that he's great in bed, but emotions? Those aren't his strong point. It's not that he doesn't care, it's just? Well I guess he hasn't learned to show that part of himself to a woman."

"So you guys do this often, all sleep with one woman?" I was feeling pretty ridiculous at the moment.

"No. Believe it or not our tastes are usually pretty different. We all wanted you though Zoey.   Leon and I have had our share of three ways, and Miles and Samson usually do the same, but you're special."

"I don't feel very special at the moment."   Even though I had to admit being held in Leif's arms made the cut by Samson a little less painful.

"You should. I've never known Samson to be with a woman without her being bound to the bed before."

"I hope that wasn't supposed to make me feel better. He made it pretty clear that I was only allowed to say yes or no or follow his commands in the bedroom."   What the hell had I been thinking? Obviously with the wrong part of my anatomy because now that he was gone I was pissed for agreeing to anything.

"Still you weren't tied down. It's a start."

I knew he was trying to me make me feel better, but it wasn't working. "Thanks Leif, but I was just stupid for wanting him."

"What about me?" The hope in his voice made me smile even though I wanted to stay angry.

"I think you're beautiful and charming." I couldn't take out my anger on Leif, he'd been nothing but nice to me.

"Well yeah, I am those things, but what I meant was what about us?"

The anger I felt left completely at his egotistical charm. "Wow. Conceited much." I didn't really have an answer for him at the moment. I'd just slept with Samson, told him I loved him and needed some time to come to grips with that.

"Nah. I just know how perfect I am." He stood up with me in his arms, and lowered me to my feet. "I'm better in bed than he is too." Waggling his eyebrows he deserved the punch in the arm I gave him.

"I need a shower." Forcing a grin, I dropped the blanket and pulled my bikini back on.

"Yeah, you do." He took off running, jumped off the boat and into the ocean. I dived in after him trying not to overthink this and swallow half the sea as I made it to shore.

My mood was much better after I cleaned off and headed back to the cabin with the rest of the guys. I knew I still hadn't answered Leif, but I needed to think about what I was doing a little more before I made quick decisions.

CHAPTER EIGHT

Tempting

Miles was standing underneath the shower when I finally made it there, and instead of giving him his privacy, I joined him. Something about the island just took away my inhibitions, and it wasn't like the guy hadn't seen me spread out as he devoured my body last night. When he began washing my hair, I have to say I didn't regret the decision at all.

"I'm going to see what I can do about scrounging up some breakfast." Leif was smiling when he left Miles and me alone.

There should have been a part of me that felt bad about letting him remove my bikini, but there honestly wasn't. Of all the men, Miles was the one I considered the most trustworthy. He earned that respect even more when he simply bathed me and didn't make a sexual act of the situation.

"Did you sleep with Samson?" I hadn't expected the question but I didn't see any reason to lie about it.

Nodding my head, I stepped out from under the spray and wrapped a towel around my body. He was searching my face before turning off the water, then walking over taking my towel and drying me before doing the same for himself. "You alright with that?" He wrapped me back up, leaving his own body deliciously exposed.

"I guess?" I didn't know how to feel now. I knew they'd wanted to have some kind of orgy, which I still didn't understand the dynamics of, but he didn't seem upset.

"We were all worried when we woke up and both of you were gone. Samson's a little difficult."

These concerns that Leif and him had about me and Samson might have been better served before the act, I thought to myself. "I got what I asked for." Didn't that make me seem like slut of the week?

"Did you? Or did you get what he allowed?" Miles stepped behind me and ran his fingers through my hair, attempting to untangle the locks.

God! It felt like heaven having his fingers in my hair and there was definitely something wrong with my libido. How could I want him after just having Samson? Closing my eyes I rested my head back on his chest. "I'm not sure how to answer that?" My voice sounded almost drugged I was so enthralled with his magic hands.

"Did you tell him what pleased you?" His fingers left my hair and fell to my shoulders, turning me to face him.

Forcing my eyes to open, I met his smoldering emerald gaze. "Everything pleases me." What was he really asking me?

"Does it? If I asked you right now how to pleasure your body in a way you couldn't resist, what would you tell me?" His finger grazed over my cheek tenderly, our eyes never breaking contact.

What kind of question was that? Just listening to his voice made me feel like melting at the moment. "I don't know." My heart raced as his head lowered and those beautiful lips touched mine. This was a good start, I thought as our tongues danced together.

He broke the kiss and shook his head slowly. "Maybe we should find out then." His hand caressed over my lower back, resting on my ass before pulling me against his body. "Do you enjoy it when I hold you against me like this?"

I nodded, unconsciously rubbing our lower bodies against each other, wanting more contact. He smiled and lifted my leg until it rested against his hip, holding it there. The long length of his cock now rested against my sex and I gasped.

"I think you like this a little more." The towel had parted, and I gasped as he rotated his hips. The slide of his cock against my sensitive flesh flooded me with desire. "Miles." I bit my lip at the sensation and whimpered out his name.

"You're so beautiful, Zoey." He lowered my leg and left me aching without the connection. I didn't expect him to lower to his knees, or pull my leg over his shoulder. I definitely didn't expect his tongue to spear my core leaving me grasping his shoulders for support.

"Oh God!" Miles had a magic tongue and within seconds had me falling over the edge with just a few plunges of that wet wand.

"You smell like heaven sweetheart, and taste even more delightful." He stood and kissed me again, and I wasn't even repulsed at the taste of myself on his lips.

"That I really enjoyed." The words just slipped out and I flushed hotly.

"Don't be embarrassed. I like knowing my tongue in that beautiful pussy makes you happy."

Instead of thinking, my hand lowered to grasp his cock and I stroked it wanting to bring him pleasure too.

"Don't let us interrupt." Leon broke into the moment and stood watching us with Leif and Samson.

I wasn't sure how I felt about being caught in the act, but when I met Samson's mocking grin, I refused to release the grip I had on Miles.

"We're going to do some exploration of the island, maybe you can keep Zoey entertained until we return." Samson didn't seem upset that I was enjoying pleasure with Miles, instead it appeared to make him happy. My hand stilled on his cock, trying to come to grips with how I felt about that.

Miles gave a curt nod, and I didn't understand the look that passed between the two men. They walked away leaving us standing together awkwardly. Feeling embarrassed I dropped my hand.

"He wants you to be happy." Miles pulled me back into his arms and hugged me tightly.

"He's got a funny way of showing it." Dropping the towel I stepped back under the shower and rinsed off. "I'm sorry I really can't do this." There was no doubt in my mind if the other guys hadn't walked out I would have fucked Miles. I guess that made me a prick tease, but screwing him would have made me something far worse in my opinion.

"You never have to do anything that makes you uncomfortable Zoey. I should've asked first."

"Don't be nice to me right now." I stepped out of the shower, picked up the towel and dried off quickly before wrapping it around me. "I feel bad enough as it is."

Most men would have been angry the way I stopped things, but Miles? He just chuckled. "Sweetheart there's nothing to feel bad about. You're overwhelmed and things have moved way too fast. Let's grab some breakfast and find something else to do."

I glanced down at the raging hard-on he still had and raised an eyebrow. "Do you want me to?" I paused not sure exactly what I was asking to do. Give him a hand job or suck him off? Turning my head away I wondered if I'd turned into a whore overnight.

Miles chuckled, confusing the hell out of me again. "I think I can manage this. Why don't you go get dressed and I'll be in shortly."

Not knowing how to respond, I decided to follow his advice. Walking back in the cabin, I dressed in a pair of walking shorts and a tank top. I needed to get the hell off this island. The things it made me feel were frightening and who knew what I'd do if we didn't leave soon.

Miles had showered off again and walked in to retrieve his clothes. He looked so sexy in the white t-shirt and khaki shorts that for a moment I wished I hadn't stopped things outside.

"Sweetheart don't look at me that way unless you want to fuck." He winked and walked into the small kitchen leaving me standing there with my mouth hanging open.

He fixed up a plate of fruit and we ate in silence. After we were done, he suggested we walk along the beach. The walk didn't really clear my head, but the view was so spectacular I decided if you had to think, this was the place to do it.

"I don't think any of us wants to spend another night on the floor. Leon said something about flying out tonight and coming back after the contractors had a better building in place."

"We're leaving?" Getting back home was probably the smartest idea, but I really didn't want to leave the paradise behind. To be honest though, another night in sleeping bags wasn't my idea of great fun. I really needed to get away from this place and do some soul searching.

"I'm sure he'll talk to Samson first, but probably so. Don't worry, we'll come back when there are some comforts available."

"I'm not sure you'll need me with you the next time." After what had happened with Samson I wasn't even sure I could work with him again, much less fly out to the island without remembering what took place even if I could.

"Of course we'll need you. Zoey don't let what happened with Samson make you overthink things." It was almost like he read my mind. "Work is work, what happens outside, that's completely different."

"Maybe for him, or even you and the other guys that's true, but for me? Miles all of you had your head between my legs less than twenty-four hours ago, how am I supposed to just forget that when we're back in the office?" I felt like such an idiot.

"I'd have my head there now if you wanted it and it still wouldn't make a difference when we returned. We all rely on you. You're a great employee, but a friend as well. Seriously, you have to put what happened here in the right place sweetheart."

We'd stopped walking and were facing each other. "I'm not sure I can." How could I sit down with these guys in a board room and discuss work which was also about pleasure, without thinking of having their hands touching me?

"We'll find a way to make it work. Maybe it would be easier if you just submitted to Samson."

"I can't believe you said that." Of all the men, Miles was the last one I'd expected to say something like that. Pissed off and needing some space, I turned to walk away.

Miles grabbed my arm, stopping me. "I didn't mean it that way Zoey. Damn it! All I meant is if you belonged to Samson you wouldn't let all this shit cloud up your mind. You'd just accept that as his slave he wanted it to happen."

"Do you think I'm the type of person to belong to anyone?" Better yet, did I? So I fucked up. I'd allowed myself to submit to Samson in the bedroom. I'll be damned if it was going to look like I was bowing to anyone ever again.

"If you'd stop being so stubborn you could be in control of us all." Miles dropped my arm, more frustrated than I'd ever seen him before. "Don't you understand that we all care for you Zoey?"

That pulled the wind out of my sails instantly. "Right, because I can see you, Samson, and the other guys on your knees for me." I had to throw off on his comment because if I didn't I'd admit just how much I wanted to believe those words were true.

"We were on our knees for you last night." With those words he walked off leaving me standing alone in paradise.

My smart ass side wanted to shout out some parting remark, but how could I? They had been on their knees for me, showing me pleasure without demanding anything in return. It didn't make sense, especially with how easily Samson left after fucking me earlier today. Confused couldn't even begin to explain how I felt about what was happening.

Left alone to explore, I tried to imagine returning to the office and putting things back in perspective. Maybe if we never brought up anything that happened out here, I could manage it. It's the only way I knew how to still work at a job I loved, and stop feeling like I'd changed positions into one of their playthings. Making that decision gave me the confidence I needed to walk back to the cabin and find Miles.

He didn't bring up our conversation which helped tremendously. When the guys returned they'd decided to return back to the city and the next few hours were spent preparing for the journey.

CHAPTER NINE

Home

The trip back was exhausting and when we arrived I was glad I still had two days off before returning to Fantasy's. I'd done my best to keep things professional on the flight and by the time we'd landed, they all acted as if nothing had happened on that island. We managed small talk and kept everything on a professional level.

Keeping my emotions in check was more difficult for me I guess, and I didn't relax until I was dropped off at my apartment.

"You look beat babe. What did you think about the island?"

Rachel had ordered in and we were sitting down at the island bar eating dinner. I'd walked in the door, unpacked, then took an hour long bath before joining her. I still needed to get my head on straight and even though she was my best friend, I didn't know exactly what I'd tell her about the trip.

"It's just jet lag. The island was, well, an experience."
I needed someone to talk to and if anyone would
understand I figured it would be her. I started talking
and didn't stop until she was sitting there mouth agape,
a confused look on her face.

"You let them all? Then you slept with Samson?"

I had to laugh at her expression because never in our
many years of friendship had I been the one to shock her.
"That's about the gist of it."

"Holy shit babe. I mean I might have been afraid to
free my sexuality to that point! Holy Shit!"

"You said that already." Lifting my mouth in a
semblance of a smile, I took a sip of wine. "I just don't
know how it's going to play out in the office."

"I get that Samson was a bit of a jerk after, that's his
style, but why didn't you sleep with the other guys? I
mean shit, it's not like you made an exclusive
arrangement with him."

"I shouldn't have done any of it. Don't get me wrong,
Rach, they're all sexy in their separate ways, but me
sleeping with four men? I'm not sure I can look at my
own reflection now, if I'd taken it further I doubt I'd
have any morals left."

"That's where you need to pull your head out of your
ass. Guys fuck women like that all the time. Why
shouldn't we enjoy our sexuality?"

"What other women do doesn't concern me. I never
thought I'd have sex again, but four men? Come on
Rach, you know me better than that."

"What I know is that you've held yourself back long
enough. I get that you work for them, but having sex

with four hot billionaires? How many women can say that they've had that offer?"

"I just hope we can put that trip in the past and it doesn't screw up my job." We weren't going to see eye to eye on the reasons I'd turned it down, so I decided to stop arguing.

"I don't think they'll bring it up unless you do. I've never known any of them to be the kiss and tell types. Hell I almost get fired on a weekly basis for saying anything about what goes on at the club."

I remembered Samson putting her in place for mentioning the clients before, so I hoped she was right. "Well I guess we'll see when I make it back in."

We talked long into the night about the things that happened on the island and then vowed to never discuss it again. Rachel loved me, so I knew my secret would be safe with her. I think she was amazed that I'd finally got some action, her words, not mine.

Two days later my body had recovered from the extensive travel, and as I showed up for work, I could only hope that my mind could stay focused as well. Dean had my coffee on my desk before I'd even got comfortable and it was nice to know at least one thing was the same. She'd informed me that the meeting was rescheduled to after lunch so I had plenty of time to catch up on work.

My brain was so overwhelmed by the contracts I was working on, I had no time to think about anything else. Leif had to pull me out of the office I'd been so wrapped up with work that I'd forgotten the time. He was still the same carefree guy I'd come to admire and at least with him it didn't seem awkward being back in a business setting.

The meeting was filled with new projects and information about the building going on with Fantasy's Isle. Nothing was said about what we'd shared out there and after an hour in it felt like we'd never even taken that trip. Except for the remark about our walk where I overtaxed myself which led to the idea that there needed to be motorized vehicles in place for guests, nothing was mentioned.

We ate lunch in the boardroom during our meeting and by the time it ended I had so much information to process that I knew the rest of the week would be long. I was amazed that not one word had been uttered that was unprofessional and not one of them brought up anything that would've made me feel uncomfortable.

Things continued along that theme for the rest of the week and I was finally able to accept that I could work here without regretting the past. By the time Friday rolled around I was ready for a weekend of doing nothing but sleeping in and taking a much needed break.

Samson booked the restaurant for lunch and I was happy about not having to do another working one. I ordered the biggest steak they had on the menu and drooled when it finally reached the table. I dug in and noticed that all the guys were staring at me warily.

With a huge bite in my mouth, I quickly chewed and looked at each of them in turn. Swallowing before speaking I felt my defenses rise. "What?"

"We're not at work so can we finally talk about this?" Leif spoke first and his words made me leery.

"Let her eat first." Leon slapped him on the back and rolled his eyes.

"I think it's a little too late for that." Putting down my fork I pushed my plate back, glaring down at the food I'd just lost the appetite for.

"Dumb ass." Leif and Leon began arguing and it was so funny to see two grown men acting like adolescents, I couldn't stop the giggle that escaped.

"God, I've missed that sound." Miles looked at me longingly and I felt the own ache in my heart.

I'd missed just talking to them. I'd been so hell bent on keeping things professional that I'd distanced myself from them all. "I missed talking to you."

"All this shit is my fault. I'm so fucking sorry for being an asshole, Zoey." Samson looked like he'd just lost his best friend and I instantly wanted to hug him or slap his face and tell him to snap out of it. He was supposed to be the leader.

"There is no fault. Things just went a little too far, but it's over now. Can't we just keep the past where it belongs?" I didn't want to rehash this again even if it killed me to think about never having them that way.

"Is that what you want, sweetheart." Miles. My tenderhearted hero. I would always think about him that way. It just seemed to fit.

"What I want is to stop feeling like the biggest slut in the world for enjoying what we did." That's all I'd thought of night after night at home in bed. Of course that didn't mean my dreams weren't more erotic than they had been before the island.

"Why would you feel that way? We all loved what we did together. I know none of us thinks about you that way." Leon was sitting to my left, and his hand rested on mine on top of the table. I looked around at the other men and they nodded in agreement.

"When you walked out of that room after sleeping with me I felt like a whore, Samson. I knew the night before I'd been pleasured by the other guys, so I felt I deserved to be thought of that way." This was what bothered me the most. If he'd have shown me five minutes of tenderness after what we'd shared maybe I wouldn't have felt guilty at all.

"So it was my fault. Please know that I never meant you to take it that way. I don't do the flowery bullshit, Zoey, you know that. The way I felt after being with you made me feel things I wasn't accustomed to."

Was he saying he had feelings for me? "I'm confused. What did I make you feel?" The way we left things I figured I was just a fuck and he was ready to let Leif take over in his place. That kind of shit plays hell with a girl's confidence and I didn't have any in the bedroom as it was.

"I felt like locking you up on that boat and keeping you there until you agreed to belong to me. I wanted to slap a collar on your neck and demand that you never walked out of my life again. Since I didn't think you'd be receptive to the idea, I did the only thing I could, walked out before I screwed up any chance with you. But I've done that already, haven't I?"

I stared at him like he'd grown several heads as I let his words sink in. He'd wanted to keep me? Well wasn't that just the opposite of what I'd thought. "You could have fucking said something." I was pissed now. I felt like shit because of how he acted and if he thought I was going easy on him now? He had another thing coming.

"What would you have had me say, Zoey. I know how you feel about the domination stuff. I thought I was doing the right thing by leaving you with Leif."

The look of dejection on his face was enough to deflate my anger. "Maybe that you didn't regret sleeping with me and I didn't suck in bed?" I laughed self-consciously.

"Is that what you think? I've never had a woman feel better underneath me Zoey. If I hadn't thought you'd lose your shit I would have tied you up and fucked you until you couldn't walk."

"I wouldn't have minded watching that." Leif's comment broke the seriousness of the moment and we all laughed.

"I would have wanted to join in." Miles was sitting on my other side and his hand stroked my arm softly.

"Ditto." Leon winked at me and I was amazed at these four incredible men wanting me in that way.

"So have we lost our chance with you Zoey?" Samson's smile turned into a frown as he studied my face. The sincerity in those beautiful eyes almost made me tear up.

"I don't want to lose any of you." Keeping things on a professional level was killing me with these guys. I loved them all in different ways. I didn't understand it, but I refused to lie to myself any longer. "I just don't know where we go from here."

"Maybe we take it one step at a time. We've got a lifetime to explore this." Leon smiled warmly and my heart melted.

"I know where I'd like to start, but here in the restaurant probably wouldn't be the best place." Leif's boyish grin told me exactly what he had in mind, and the thought brought some fantasies to life.

"I'm not against the idea." Did I really just say that? Obviously I did since Samson flagged down the server for the check. Leon had our meal piled in to-go boxes and we were in his car before I had time to really catch my breath.

As we drove I was having trouble breathing knowing what I'd just agreed to. Sitting in the backseat with Miles and Leif, my heart was racing in my chest as we pulled up to a gorgeous mansion. I had no idea whose home we were at, but it didn't really matter. What would happen behind those doors was the reason I trembled when the ignition was finally turned off.

"This is your fantasy Zoey, you tell us how to please you and we'll make sure you're never disappointed again." Leif took my chin in his hand and lowered his lips to mine. I lost myself in that kiss before he broke away.

Samson and Leon held each of my hands as we walked to the front door and Miles opened it. I had no idea what would happen next, but I couldn't wait to find out. Maybe that's really what we all crave, a fantasy, custom made to order.

Devoured
Fantasy's Bar & Grill – Book 2

Michelle Hughes

Tears of Crimson Publishing

CHAPTER ONE

Comfort

Walking through the doors of a mansion with four gorgeous men that you'd just agreed to have sex with can be a little overwhelming. Who the hell am I kidding? It was terrifying. I'd made those steps without thinking through the actual act of going through with it but once that door closed behind me? The reality slapped me in the face and my body responded by seeking out comfort. Propelling myself into Samson's arms, I held on tightly.

Strong arms wrapped around my frame surrounding me with the protection I needed to feel safe again. My body trembled, heart raced, and I knew if he let me go I'd slide to the floor since my feet no longer seemed to have the ability to hold me up. Even being the strong independent woman I was, I craved that security in the face of the unknown.

"Shit baby, you're shaking." Those long fingers moved from my back to rub up and down my arms as I clung to him desperately.

I couldn't give a response. The dryness of my mouth felt like someone had stuffed cotton down my throat. Pressing my cheek against chest, I attempted to breathe, but the shallowness of my intake made it feel like my lungs were on fire.

"Talk to me Zoey." Samson's voice was laced with concern as his hand moved to my head and caressed my hair. Shaking my head, I wished I could make him understand that I couldn't force words from my lips. I was terrified.

Those beautiful arms lifted me, cradling as his long strides moved over to sit on the couch holding me in his lap. The choke hold I had on his neck was my only link to sanity. My fears were unfounded, logically I knew that. If I told any of them that I'd changed my mind they'd hold me and never make me feel bad about leading them on. These were the men I'd fallen in love with. That thought above all others helped me relax and loosen the grip I had on his neck.

"Bring her something to drink." Samson's soothing voice shot a pang of desire through my panic confusing me even more. "Shush baby." I whimpered at the sensation that moved from my breast to core, wiggling in his lap. I didn't understand my body or my reactions to the situation.

One of Samson's arms lifted and I wanted to cry at the loss of contact instead I felt the cool press of a glass against my lips and sipped deeply of the strong drink I was given. The liquid burned as it slid down my throat, but it was such a relief. My hand reached out to tilt the glass back when he attempted to take it away. After several large gulps the liquid courage seeped into my brain and helped relax the panic attack I'd almost succumbed to. I downed the rest of the glass.

"I'm sorry." Feeling like an idiot my body almost wilted in Samson's lap. Being so tightly strung and finding relief almost instantaneously with the alcohol left me in a strangely depressed frame of mind. Samson stroked my back softly, almost as if he was afraid I'd freak out again.

"Are you okay sweetheart?" Miles was kneeling in front of the couch, his hands reaching out to touch me before pulling away. The concern in those emerald eyes made me feel bad for losing it. Reaching out my hand I cupped his cheek, offering him comfort as I nodded slowly.

Leon sat down beside us on the couch looking worried and all I could do was offer him a tentative smile. "There's nothing to be sorry about. You know that right?"

I felt so foolish. My face heated and I couldn't meet his gaze. These beautiful men cared about me and I'd caused them worry for nothing. Dropping my hand from Miles's cheek I didn't know how to explain what I felt.

"Would someone tell me what the fucks going on before I go postal?" Leif's words pulled my eyes to his and I knew instantly that he didn't do stress well. Those beautiful hands were fisted by his sides and it looked like he was about to fly off the handle.

"She's fine guys. Just give her a minute to pull together." My beautiful Samson. He understood me better than anyone. "We're going to talk little Zoey, but first I think you need to compose yourself." Standing up with me still in his lap, he allowed me to slide down his body finding my own feet. "The bathrooms down the hall to the right."

With a small uplifting of his lips he motioned with eyes the direction he wanted me to go. My legs were still shaking but I knew I had to get control and he was offering me that chance while allowing me to save face at the same time. Later I'd think about how he understood me so completely. Right now I needed some me time.

Their voices, all questioning him, faded off into the distance as I shut the bathroom door behind me. Staring into my reflection I shook my head. Scoffing at that weak bitch in the mirror I told her to grow some balls. There were four gorgeous hunks in the other room that wanted to please me who I wanted to please in return. Instead of cowering away in this bathroom I should be out there telling them how honored I felt that they all wanted me.

I did want them. Just thinking about all the things they would do to me made me clench my thighs together in need. It was going from point a to point b that scared the shit out of me, leaving me panicking like some adolescent girl getting ready for her first time.

The truth was I still didn't understand how I could sleep with all of them together and it freaked me the hell out. There were only so many different ways they could fill my body and one of them? That shit was going to hurt and I wasn't big on the pain thing. Samson on his own had been so big that I was sure he'd rip me apart, add another guy going in the other direction? How was that supposed to be pleasurable?

I was panicking again. The thoughts rolled through my mind and I had to force myself to calm down. I used the restroom, splashed water on my face and had a mental argument about the pros and cons of this situation. My guys wouldn't hurt me. I knew that with every fiber of my being.

That thought process helped but when I realized that Samson wouldn't allow it in the first place, that was my defining moment. Thinking back to the conversation with Leon about me allowing Samson to dominate me, I finally understood. He hadn't been trying to make me feel like I needed someone taking control, he was offering me a way to let one person lead what would happen so I wouldn't be so overwhelmed by any of this.

When it hit me, I shook my head and gave a self-depreciating grin to my reflection. I'd worked so long to be a confident, independent woman that I never stopped to allow myself to consider it was okay sometimes to not be in charge. Obviously that didn't mean I was going to let anyone tell me how to live my life, but in this case it made perfect sense.

Just that quickly the fear that had me ready to bolt for the front door eased away and I knew what I needed.

"Huh?" I wanted to allow Samson to control this. Didn't that just put a cherry right on top of the cake? The soft laugh that escaped would have made me look crazy if anyone else had been in this room. Zoey Summers, the feminist, was ready to walk back into a room and fall to her knees in submission. I couldn't stop myself from laughing.

When I finally had some self-control again, I knew what I needed to do. Taking a deep breath, I gave myself one last convincing look in the mirror before walking back out to join my guys. The expressions on their faces told me everything. Only Samson smiled as I made my way back to them, the others looked ready to apologize or in Leif's case, ready to bolt in case I freaked out again.

Meeting Samson's beautiful gray gaze, I stopped only scant inches away from where he was now standing. His look was intense and I gave my own back. I knew he'd understand this just as he understood earlier. I broke eye contact first then lowered to my knees in front of him.

This I didn't know, how to be his submissive. I didn't know how to be subservient to anyone, but if I wasn't convinced he knew, I'd never had made the move. That large hand caressing the top of my head told me more than any words could ever explain.

What I hadn't expected was Samson finding his own knees, and lifting my chin with his hand to make me look at him directly. "I'll never let you regret this, Zoey."

I knew he wouldn't. All I could do was nod, the emotional overload of giving myself to him completely took everything I had. His lips moved to my forehead, kissing me gently, then his hand grasped mine and pulled me up to stand with him. "Now we're all going to talk."

The last thing I wanted to do was talk now that I'd made my decision. Biting back those words took tremendous effort and for the first time in what seemed like forever, I kept my mouth shut.

"Someone needs to talk. I'm so fucking confused at the moment I could drink my way through the bar." I felt almost sorry for Leif at the confusion he felt. He didn't know it but he wanted to be led too. It was so much easier to understand that now that I'd accepted there was a part of myself that needed direction.

"No one else drinks or everything else tonight stops. We all need to have a clear mind so we don't confuse things." Samson was in what I liked to call his business mode as he addressed Leif. For the first time it didn't make me want to smack his face for exerting that control.

"I agree with Samson. I'm not sure what happened Zoey, but if you've changed your mind all you have to do is say the word." Miles was just as confused as Leif but in a different way. He didn't panic, even a blind person could tell he was only concerned with how I was feeling.

"I don't think she's changed her mind." Leon's wink my way made me feel a little less embarrassed as he talked to Miles. "Zoey just needed someone to take control of the situation, and I think she made the right choice."

The strong male I saw in him as he led the conversation enlightened me that he was just as dominant as Samson, just with a different style. "You're not upset?" Instinctively I knew that one of them would have had to be in control, and wasn't sure how Leon felt about it not being him.

"Of course I'm not." His hand reached out and he tugged on a lock of my hair playfully before releasing it. "I think for you Samson is just the type of master you need."

I didn't take that the wrong way, which I easily could have, because I understood what he meant. Leon was a dominant male but not as strict as Samson. Intuitively I understood that, even with no experience in the world they played in.

"So what? You own Zoey now?" Leif looked at Samson and I could see the idea pissed him off.

"No one can own Zoey." Samson chuckled warmly, and I flushed at his meaning. "What she needs is someone to take over in the bedroom so she can stop worrying that what she wants is wrong or that she doesn't know how to do the things we ask."

"These games work for our employees, but this is Zoey we're talking about. I don't like the idea of anyone telling her what to do."

My tender hearted hero, Miles. I walked over and hugged him tightly. "Do you think I'd ever let anyone make me do something I really didn't want to?" Pulling back I looked into his eyes and gave him my most confident smile.

"No. I guess not." He smiled back and finally there was a dawning of understanding in his emerald orbs. "If this is what you need, I understand."

"I don't understand but if it stops you from freaking the fuck out again, then I'll learn to live with it." Leif's anger deflated and I saw again how he really just wanted anyone else to take charge. He was all about enjoying life not trying to understand it.

"Great. Now that we've got all that out of the way, let's talk." Samson sat down on the couch and patted his lap for me to join him. I didn't think twice about crawling into that safe haven. I felt much calmer with his hands around my waist.

Resting my cheek against the crisp linen of his shirt, I relaxed and allowed him to start the conversation. "Zoey's only had sex twice, so throwing her into a room with four men was a bit much. Since she's sitting here and not running out the door, apparently she wants to continue but there need to be boundaries."

"Damn girl." Leif grinned, shaking that sun-bleached head full of hair. "Sounds like you need to make up for lost time."

Leon rolled his eyes at Leif's enthusiastic words. "What it means is it probably scared her shitless to think of all of us inside her that way. Am I right?"

"That's an understatement." I mumbled the words under my breath still not sure sleeping with them all would be enjoyable.

"What scares you the most about it sweetheart?" Miles was sitting beside me and his hand patted my knee gently, like I was a child that needed to be comforted.

I bit my lip for a moment, not sure how to word what I wanted to say. A first for me. "I've never done, um, the backdoor thing. But it's not just that." I paused again trying to get the courage up to talk about sexuality in a way I never had before.

"Anal.   We'll work on definitions later." Samson corrected quietly. "What else?"

"Don't take this the wrong way, but when we were together you filled me completely, so the thought of having you all, well I'm terrified it will hurt." Honesty. That's the only way I could move forward with this. They'd seen my body, had their lips on me, how could I not give them the truth.

"I'd never allow that to happen." Samson's arms tightened around me and I felt secure in his embrace.

"We'd rather cut off our own cocks, before hurting you Zoey. You have to know that." Leif looked horrified at the idea that he could cause me pain and I grinned.

"I know you wouldn't on purpose. It's just? The idea of being so full of you guys, that's a huge step for me and I don't have a lot of background to go on."

"It doesn't have to be all about penetration." Leon winked and I was happy he didn't think less of me for being afraid. "We could take turns, you could do oral, or hell even use your hand."

"I never thought about how much work that would be for you." Miles's tone was regretful. "I could take myself out of the equation."

"No!" I shouted the word before realizing what I'd done. "I don't want that." I continued in a softer voice. "I want to experience this with all of you, I just don't know if my body has the capability of giving that much pleasure."

"Our pleasure isn't what's really in question at the moment. We're grown men, and what we're asking of you is more than I've ever asked of woman before. You come first Zoey." Samson's words made me fall in love even more.

"He's right. I've used my hand before." Leon chuckled softly. "What we don't want is to hurt you in any way. But for that to happen, you have to tell us exactly how you feel and not be afraid to hurt our feelings." His tone became serious at the end and I saw the stronger dominant in him that he'd apparently kept hidden from me before.

I nodded quickly, not ready to see just how domineering he could be when pushed. That earned me another chuckle and his facial features relaxed out of the stern set they'd taken. Instead of turning me off, I squirmed in Samson's lap.

He groaned and I felt the answering hardness grow under my ass from my fine vantage point in his lap. "Stop doing that unless you want me to fuck you right here."

I stilled but not before I figured out that I was just as in control of him as I was allowing him to be of me. The thought gave me a huge boost of self-confidence. "Would that be a bad thing?" I definitely didn't think so and wiggled my hips against his erection again. In that moment I was done talking, my hormones were starting to take over. The thought of Samson taking me in front of the other men filling my head with a pretty vivid fantasy.

"Leon, take her." I was lifted off his lap and onto Leon's before I could blink. I thought he was pissed until I noticed him adjusting his pants and understood completely. "No it wouldn't be a bad thing, Zoey but we need to make some rules before things go there."

Leon's arms were like a steel cage around me and I sighed. "Fine. What rules?" The fact that my voice sounded petulant wasn't lost on me. I'd regret that later I'm sure.

"Brat. You have no idea how much I want to take you over my knee for that but I'll give you a reprieve. This time." When he glared at me, I lowered my eyes thinking having my ass tanned wasn't really what I wanted at the moment. Although what happened after I was spanked last time wasn't something I regretted.

I batted my eyelashes as I met his eyes again and he couldn't hide the smirk that turned into a full blown smile. "Topping from the bottom already." He shook his head and Leon laughed. I had no idea what they were talking about. "Rules my little smart ass like listening when I tell you to do something and telling me when we're crossing into territory that makes you uncomfortable. We tried the yes and no thing on the island, but that obviously didn't work, so just open your mouth and say something if you're overwhelmed. Got it?"

"Got it boss." I was goading him on purpose knowing it was the fastest way to get him to stop talking and into the action.

"May I?" Leon looked at Samson and I didn't like the conspirator look he gave back.

"By all means." I didn't have time to question since I was turned face down over Leon's lap and his hand delivered several hard slaps to my covered ass. I waited for the soothing caress like Samson had given or even the graze of his fingers over my sex, but they never came.

"Ass." I grumbled under my breath as I struggled to sit up and he kept me pinned over his legs. Thankfully I was still wearing pants or my ass would've been throbbing.

Several more resounding swats landed there and I decided my addition of clothing didn't matter. I kept my mouth shut. "I don't give sweet spankings baby girl." Finally he sat me back upright in his lap and my arms crossed over my chest, pissed at him. I did learn a valuable lesson though, I didn't want to test Leon again.

"Still want me?" His teasing voice spoke softly into my ear before he gently bit down on the lobe.

I probably would have said no, just to be a bitch if the shiver didn't betray me from the innocent contact. "Yes." I whispered back not sure if I liked myself for being so easy.

"Let's take this upstairs." Samson held his hand out for me, and I slid off Leon's lap to take it. Walking up those stairs made it all too real and I was clinging to him as he opened up a door at the end of the long hall we'd just stepped into.

CHAPTER TWO

Loved

With all four men inside, what was a huge room seemed
to barely give enough space. I clenched Samson's hand
and he returned that squeeze gently, helping me relax.
Taking several deep breaths I glanced at each of them
and the looks of desire on those beautiful faces gave me
more confidence than I'd felt even cradled in Samson's
lap.

Leading me over to the bed, he patted it and I sat
down there. Standing before me he unbuttoned his
oxford, then slowly eased it off his large shoulders. My
eyes roamed over the expanse of his broad chest, pleased
at the vision he'd revealed. With a look to the other men
they began undressing as well. Talk about a strip tease!
My men were gorgeous as they bared their flesh for me.
My eyes couldn't decide which delicious morsel to take
in because they were so beautiful in unique ways.

When they were all gloriously naked, my eyes trailed over their anatomies taking in the differences of their cocks. All were impressive, but again in different ways. Samson's girth wasn't as large as Leon's but he made up for it in length. He'd stretched me so well I had no idea how my body would accept Leon's.

Leif had a beautiful body and that didn't stop with his cock. Smooth shaven, thick and long but not nearly as overwhelming as either of the other two men. Miles on the other hand forced a gasp from my lips. He was longer and wider than all the men and I cringed at the thought of being taken by him. None of them were as small as Brad had been and at the time I'd thought he was well endowed.

"When we make love Zoey, you have my word I'll take things slow." Miles must have noticed how my eyes were now focused on his sex. He hadn't seemed that large on the island, even when I was grasping him in my hand.

"You seem bigger." I voiced my astonishment, still eyeing his shaft with trepidation.

"I wasn't fully hard sweetheart. Knowing that I'm going to be inside that tight little pussy makes me excited."

"Maybe I like you more a little less excited." I mumbled the words but with the chuckles filling the room I didn't mask my voice good enough.

He walked over and sat beside me on the edge of the bed. "You have my word that I'll never cause you pain." His sultry emerald eyes searched mine and I knew he'd never break his word. I nodded.

"You're a little overdressed." Samson smiled and held out his hand. I left the bed and stood in front of it joining him. "Make yourself comfortable men." He spoke to them before lowering his mouth to my ear. "Show them how beautiful you are, Zoey."

He joined Miles on the bed in my spot, and the other two men walked to either side, sitting down. I knew he wanted me strip for them but my fingers faulted when they reached the first button on my blouse. Biting my lip hard I looked into Samson's eyes.

His small nod of encouragement gave me the confidence to begin undoing the small line of buttons. I had no idea how to do a sensual strip tease, and wasn't about to try. Just taking my clothes off while they watched made me nervous enough. I managed to remove my shirt and skirt, standing there in my underclothes, heels and thigh-high stockings before I hesitated again.

The way they were looking at me was almost unnerving. Fidgeting from one foot to the other, I didn't think I could go on. "Samson please?" My voice was pleading and for what I wasn't sure. For him to finish this for me, or just call a halt to the entire scenario.

"Undress Zoey." His voice was stern and instead of wanting to fight, I truly wanted to obey, still I hesitated. "Now!" I jumped slightly at his command but my fingers moved behind me to the clasp of my bra. Freeing my breasts from the restrictive garment, I allowed it to slide to the floor. I forced myself to meet his gaze again as my fingers hooked into the elastic of my panties. There was no sympathy in that gray gaze only a steely demand. I slid them off and stepped out.

He stood then and joined me. I was shaking and feeling a little stupid for being so worried. His arms wrapped around me and his mouth lowered to my ear. "I'm proud of you Zoey. You're so fucking beautiful baby."

My heels slid off when he picked me up and carried me over to the bed. Leon stood, giving him room and I was laid down in the center wearing only my thigh-highs. It was a king-size but with all the men together there wasn't much room left to move. Miles was at the top right of the bed sitting, Leif at his bottom. Samson and Leon filled up the left side in the same order.

None of them were touching me, instead their eyes were taking me in making me feel more than a little self-conscious. "Guys?"

"You're just so lovely that we want a few minutes to admire." Miles stroked a wayward strand of my thick hair away from my face.

"Whatever shall we do with this beautiful body?" Samson smirked taking in every inch of my frame with a hot glance.

"I'm not sure Samson, what do you think?" Leon edging him on was probably not in my best interests, I thought nibbling on my lip nervously.

"I could think of a few things." Leif laughed, his hand reaching out to caress from thigh to ankle.

"Maybe we should ask Zoey what she wants us to do to her." Miles. Always so concerned with my needs. I smiled up at him. Truthfully I didn't know what I wanted them to do.

"I think I have a few ideas." The smirk on Samson's handsome face turned playful and I probably should have been concerned. Instead I was curious as he slid off the bed, walked over to a closet, and pulled out a large leather bag that looked rather imposing. "I want you to relax and trust me Zoey. Can you do that?"

Could I? I was naked in bed with four hot men so I guess I did. "I trust you Samson." That didn't stop me from looking at him warily when he opened the large leather bag.

"Leon she's looking around a little too much for my liking. I'd rather make her feel." Samson lifted a black silk sash out of his bag and put it in his hands. "Help me out?"

"Gladly." Leon helped me sit up and I could only stare at him in confusion until the black sash ended up around my eyes. My hands moved over it as it blocked my vision and I wasn't sure I liked the idea of not seeing. "Trust. Zoey." Those simple words made my hands fall back to the bed. His hands lowered me to a prone position.

My breathing increased as the world turned dark around me, I couldn't see anything this way. My hands clenched and released the duvet nervously under my grip.

"Hands under your head Zoey. I want to tie you down but if you keep those hands where I ask I'll allow that freedom this time." My hands slid under my head quickly because being blindfolded and tied up scared the living shit out of me. Samson chuckled.

"This little bag has lots of toys. What do you think she'd enjoy most Miles?" I felt the bed shift and assumed

Miles had stood up to look at his offerings. All I could think was I'd never even owned a vibrator so what kind of toys were they thinking of using on me.

"Most women love this one. We could start with that?" I wanted to ask what 'that' was as Miles spoke, but instead I kept silent trying not to worry overly about what they planned to do to me.

"That one does seem to be a favorite. See if it pleases her." I heard a soft humming sound and Samson's chuckle. "Just don't let her come yet."

I felt my thighs being opened and tensed at the coolness of the object that vibrated against my clit. Holy mother of pearl what was that thing? My hips arched up as it gave me the most incredible sensation of pleasure. "Oh!" I never wanted him to stop the circular movements with the toy and was crying out within seconds.

"I'd say she likes the bullet a lot." Miles laughed softly pulling it away.

My clit was still throbbing and I shut my legs together tightly to stop the ache the little toy had left in his wake. I didn't want it to go away, I wanted more.

"Keep those legs spread Zoey." Samson's demanding voice made me groan before I did as he asked. There was no relief this way. "She needs a little less stimulation I think. Leif, try this."

I felt a soft caress of something trail over my clit and the pressure was so light it stroked almost like a feather being dragged across my flesh. Lifting my hips, the sensation grew even lighter and I whimpered. "I'm not sure she enjoys being teased with this one." Leif chuckled warmly and continued the feather-light caress making me ache for more.

"Those beautiful tits look lonely, maybe we should focus some attention there." Leon suggested and I could hear the humor in his voice.

"I believe we'll start with something easy first. Try these."

"I haven't played around with these in a while." Leon's words were followed by a strange sensation on one of my nipples that felt like suction.

"There's a set of them to increase the pull." Samson replied and I tried to pay attention to his words instead of the tugging on now both of my nipples from whatever he'd placed on them.

"Look how hard those nipples are now. I think our Zoey enjoys this."

I wasn't sure if enjoyed was the right word as the suction increased. Then a soft popping sound escaped and I cried out softly at the stimulation being removed so quickly.

"You could use them for both pleasure and punishment." Leon seemed thrilled with his deduction.

"I think she can handle a light clamp." Leon squeezed one of my nipples with his thumb and forefinger and I gasped, arching upward. I heard the rattle of what sounded like chains before my mind was focused on the new sensation of pressure on my breasts.

"Leon!" I cried out softly as I felt my nipples being tugged by some action.

"Too much?" The sensation instantly stopped as he waited for me to answer.

"I don't know. It just startled me." With a chuckle he tugged slightly again, not startling me again. Instead it felt both pleasurable with a hint of pain.

"She likes the burn." Samson seemed pleased by that. "I wonder if she'd like to feel a different kind." I didn't have time to think about his words as a cool drop landed directly on my clit. Almost instantly my body was on fire.

"Oh God!" This I didn't like but when I felt a warm tongue licking away whatever he'd placed on me I decided he could do it again if he followed up that way.

"We should really stretch her." Leon's words muffled through the blaze of ecstasy I felt as a tongue suckled my clit almost brutally. The sensation effectively made me burn in a different way.

"I'll add some lube to this one and we'll see how big she can go." That pulled my mind out from between my legs. What exactly was he lubing up and how big? That didn't sound fun at all. The mouth raised from my sex, and I felt a pair of hands spreading my thighs impossibly wide. A cool liquid was spread over my anus and I tensed instantly.

"Zoey baby, I want you to relax for me. This little toy is a butt plug, but it also has the ability to expand. I want to stretch you, but I also need you tell me when you can't handle anymore. Understand?"

What the hell was Samson talking about? I didn't even know they made things like that. "Will it hurt?" I wasn't a pain junky. As a matter of fact I didn't relish the idea of pain at all.

"No sweetheart. It might feel a little uncomfortable at first, but it won't hurt. Trust me. Okay?" Samson's lips lowered to mine and he gave me a gentle kiss.

"Okay." I wasn't sure it really was but I trusted him explicitly. His finger slid slowly in my back door, and I felt the squishiness of the lube easing his way. I must have made a face because he chuckled deeply. He eased another finger in and even more of the lubrication and I tried not to tense up. I understood why he wanted to do this but I couldn't allow myself to think of something larger than his fingers sliding in there yet.

After a few minutes I felt his fingers slide free and a colder object slowly working its way inside me. It wasn't that large and outside of knowing it was a toy and kind of freaking on that, I could handle it.

"I'm going to inflate it now. You tell me when I need to stop." It began to expand and I gasped not used to the sensation of anything filling me that way. Keeping my body as relaxed as possible I tried to accept the increased sensation until it was growing uncomfortable.

"Stop." Biting down on my lip I wasn't sure I enjoyed this at all. It felt like I had to go to the bathroom and my first instinct was to push it out.

"Don't push it out baby, just relax and let your body grow acclimated." I heard his words and then felt another set of fingers lightly stroking my sex. Giving me something else to focus on helped because after a few minutes of feeling the pleasure I stopped fighting against the other foreign object.

I liked the sensation of being touched and it seemed heightened by the presence of the other toy. "Will it feel that way when two of you are inside me?" I cried out softly as my body responded to those gently fingers massaging my folds.

"I've heard other women say it's even more amazing." Samson said and I could hear the smile in his voice. "Think you can handle more now?"

The pressure there had eased and I nodded. I held my breath as he stretched my body tighter with the toy but it wasn't really painful, just uncomfortable. The toy widened several times before I asked him to stop again.

"You did so good baby, I think you could take Leif inside you. Are you ready to try?"

Leif was the smallest of the men and that wasn't small. If they were going to love me in the way I wanted, I needed to try this. With more bravado than I truly had I answered. "I want to try." I felt the toy deflate and then slowly ease out. It was such a relief having it removed I couldn't believe I was going to allow something bigger to take its place.

"On your hands and knees sweetheart." Samson removed the blindfold then helped me find the position he wanted. "Now lower your face down on the bed."

I felt completely exposed with my ass in the air and even more so when Samson widened my cheeks applying more lube. My body was trembling when I felt Leif move behind me and I clenched the duvet again in my hands not sure what this would feel like.

Leif leaned his body over my back and whispered softly. "I'm going to go slow and easy baby, you let me know if I need to stop." He lifted up and I felt his hard cock nudge at my entrance.

Without thought I tensed, worried he'd be too much. "Relax for me Zoey, the more you do that the easier I can fill you up." Forcing my body to relax his mushroom shaped head pressed in. I took an intake of breath remembering that I couldn't tense but it took everything I had not to.

"So damn tight Zoey. God you feel like heaven on my cock." He pushed slightly and the ring of muscles screamed in protest at the burning pain. I groaned. "You're doing so well." Another inch slid inside and I wasn't sure I could take much more, still I didn't tighten up around him.

Several more inches found me as he pushed forward again and I was amazed that the burning hadn't increased. Relaxing even more at this, I felt him finally push forward until his balls rested against my ass. I'd done it, I'd taken all of him inside me!

"Look how beautiful she looks with Leif's cock so deep in her." Leon's words seemed almost amazed and I felt proud that my body had the capability of taking him that way.

"I'm going to ride you now." Leif carefully inched out to the hilt, and with a little maneuvering found home again. He rode me slowly until I was pushing back against his gentle thrusts and I was shocked at the pleasure that filled me in this act.

"I think I like this." I moaned softly at the gentle pulling and pushing action, feeling my sex dripping with pleasure as he continued.

"I want to feel you both, can I fuck her Samson." His words confused me. I knew he wanted to be inside me but what was the deal with the 'both' words. I didn't care I was amazed to be enjoying the anal and pushed back against Leif telling him with my body I was ready for more.

"Turn her on her side Leif." He responded to Samson's words by pressing as deep inside me as possible, grasping my hips and doing as he asked. This was a different sensation, having him from the side. It still felt incredible.

Leon laid down in front of me, lifting my leg over his hip. "I can't wait to feel you." Taking his cock in hand he stroked it over my folds first making me ache to feel him too. Slowly he inched inside and I tensed at the width of him stretching me. The man was huge and with Leif already so deep it seemed impossible for him to join in.

I lifted my eyes to Samson, not sure if this would work. "Just relax and let him fuck you sweetheart, you'll love it." His answering smile, full of confidence helped me relax. Leon fed me his length inch by inch and it took everything I had not to pull away he filled me so completely.

"How in the hell are you this tight." I had no idea and his lips crashing down on mine gave me no time to answer. I was overfull as his shaft finally embedded as deeply as it could possibly go. "Hang on tight, this shits about to get intense."

He slid out to the tip as Leif surged forward, then as Leif retreated he filled me with one powerful thrust, nearly taking the air from my lungs with the force. I cried out loudly, not sure if it was from pain or just the shock of his motion.

"Easy Leon. That sweet little pussy hasn't been rode hard before." Samson was stroking his cock, pleasuring his body but still in control. I think I needed someone to be as they commanded my body.

The next strokes were almost synchronized as Leif and Leon rode my body with an easier rhythm, allowing me to breathe but also sink under the sensation of having two beautiful men loving me so tenderly.

Closing my eyes I surrendered to their mastery riding the peak of my own desire until it shattered me completely. My nails dug into Leon's shoulders as the pleasure washed over me, refusing to end as their slow, steady pumps continued.

"Fuck Zoey, you're gripping me so tight!"

His word enflamed me almost as much as the steady thrusting from both ends and my body clenched as my release overflowed. Crying out helplessly I surrendered to the pleasure, and felt Leif fill me with his desire. That sensation only drew out my orgasm and even after he slowly slid free of my body, Leon's thrusts increased in tempo.

He pushed me over on my back now that he was riding me on his own. "Wrap those legs around my waist baby, it's time someone rode you hard."

I didn't question his command, instead I complied and then gasped as his hands gripped my ass cheeks and pounded into me, leaving me breathless.

"You. Feel. Fucking. Amazing!" If he wanted an answer he wasn't getting one I could barely take in a breath as he unleashed his power, pushing my body further up the bed with each forceful stroke.

I whimpered as his hips ground into mine, pinning me down as he came undone. I'd never felt more devoured in my life and my body loved it. When he finally slid free I gasped softly at the stinging pain of being so well used.

"She might need a little recovery time." Leon chuckled softly looking somewhat abashed.

Leif was resting on his back, trying to catch his breath and I grinned. "I'm not the only one who needs a break." I flushed at my words, pleased that I'd given Leif pleasure but still self-conscious.

My eyes took in Miles and Samson and I felt guilty that they were both still aroused and unfulfilled. Without thought my hand reached out to Samson's cock, stroking him. "Can I taste you Miles?" I didn't like the idea of them not finding fulfillment.

"Any day of the week sweetheart." Miles rested back on the bed and I maneuvered my body down until I could take him in my mouth. His cock was so impressive that I knew I couldn't take him all in, but I was damn willing to give it my best shot. Releasing Samson's cock, I grasped the base of Miles's and slowly suckled the large head.

He was huge, and stretched my mouth so wide I felt the strain in my jaw as I widened enough to slide a few gorgeous inches in. Going on instinct, I used my hand and mouth to pleasure him and felt my core tense again at the sounds of guttural desire falling from his lips.

"I'm going to fuck you while you taste him Zoey." Samson's hands moved to my hips and he lifted me to rest between Miles's legs. I lost my rhythm for a moment at the change of positions but quickly found it again.

Once again my ass was lifted in the air as my mouth and hand worked over Miles's impressive cock. I loved knowing he enjoyed my touch, those soft grunts fueling me on to take him even deeper in my mouth. I focused solely on that until I felt Samson nudging his cock against my clit and instantly I wanted to be filled again.

Much slower than Leon, Samson rode my body, inadvertently forcing me down on Miles cock with each thrust. I loved how it felt as he rode me and I shared that pleasure by using my mouth on Miles as the crest of desire rose again to full peak.

"Fuck I want her again." Leif's words of need filled the room and I ached to give him what he needed.

"I want you." Leon's words shocked me and I lost my rhythm with Miles in the process. He was speaking to Leif and I hated to admit it but the thought of the two of them fucking turned me on. I groaned as Samson's thrusts increased forcing my attention back to the two men rocking my world.

"I've never been with a man." Leif's words sounded almost as worried as I'd been earlier and my heart ached for him. Then I couldn't focus on anything but my own need as my body tensed on the pinnacle of ecstasy once again.

My grip on Miles's cock tightened and I felt the first drops of his essence on my tongue. Instead of repelling me I suckled him deeper in my mouth as he filled me. My body found fulfillment at the same time and the overload of sensations made me gulp deeply, the taste of Miles almost as incredible as finding my release.

Samson's deep growl fueled my orgasm on and I felt him fill my body with his pulsing seed. This was nirvana, being loved so completely and giving pleasure at the same time. Why had this terrified me? I wanted to do this again and again and couldn't imagine being this satisfied with only one lover.

My cheek rested on Miles's abdomen and I closed my eyes for a moment only to open them again at Leif's sound of pleasure. They widened as I watched Leon take him into his mouth. I'd never had gay friends so seeing this was a new experience for me. It was almost breathtaking watching how expertly Leon suckled him.

"About time." I heard Samson chuckle softly and he pulled me from Mile's, cradling me in his lap at the end of the bed.

I was like a ragdoll in his arms my body was so exhausted but the show before me was something I couldn't pull my eyes away from. "You knew he wanted him?"

"For years." Samson stroked my hair as we watched Leon love him. "Leon's always been bisexual but he's never admitted to Leif that it was something he craved with him."

Leif's hands were fisted in the sheets, his neck arched back in ecstasy as Leon took his cock in to the base. I could only watch in wonder at how he did that with such beautiful ease.

"Have you ever wanted to do that?" I whispered softly not wanting to disturb the gentle way in which Leon was initiating Leif into male love.

"No. I hope that doesn't disappoint you baby, but I'm only into females." Samson's soft chuckle made me blush and I guess it was apparent how much watching them was turning me on, because my hands were clenching around his neck at the sight.

"Of course not, but you have to admit it's beautiful to watch."

Miles lifted my feet into his lap and grinned, seeming to enjoy the show as well. "They do look incredible together, and I know Leif has always wondered what it would be like to experience this with another man." Miles's hands were massaging my feet and I sighed in contentment.

I'd just made love to three of my four men and my body was as relaxed as it could be. Now I also was watching Leif discover a new part of his sexuality and it just felt fitting that it had happened this way.

"How sore are you baby?" Samson's hand trailed across my abdomen, and his fingers found my core. I tensed at the slight burn there and he slowly removed them. "That answers the question." Instead of entering me again, he massaged my clit and I groaned in pleasure. "Watch baby."

Leon released Leif's cock and I saw him reach for the lube. "I'll do my best to make this easy on you." Those sweet words coming from Leon made me smile even as Samson's fingers were making me ache to be filled again myself.

Leif looked almost afraid as Leon positioned himself over him and I was shocked he wasn't on his hands and knees. I assumed that's the way men would fuck, but apparently it wasn't the only way. In sympathy I understood Leif's groan as Leon entered his body, knowing how strange it felt the first time someone took you that way.

He was so big I knew that it had to stretch Leif in a way that was uncomfortable and was glad for a moment it was his ass, and not mine, being broke in by him.

"Fuck me." Leif demanded and I'm not sure who was more shocked. Maybe he enjoyed pain because when Leon slid in to his balls, Leif cried out in ecstasy instead of pain.

"That gorgeous ass is going to be sore as shit if I fuck you like I want to." Leon slowly slid out to the tip and found home with a gentle thrust.

"I don't give a damn Leon, fuck me!" I'd never seen Leif so vocal about anything and could only clench when Leon did as he asked, riding him like a man possessed.

I turned my face into Samson's chest, afraid he'd be hurt but within moments Leif's cries of pleasure filled the room and it was obvious to all of us how much he enjoyed what he did.

"He's not hurting him." Samson's fingers continued caressing my folds and I felt my body once again on the edge. "Watch him take Leif and feel baby."

I couldn't refuse that soft command and my eyes opened to see the pleasure written on both men's faces as I unraveled again. It had to be a crime to feel so much pleasure but it was one law I was willing to break over and over again.

Even after I was sated watching Leon pound into Leif's untrained body left me wanting to explore even more passion at the hands of my men. I was too exhausted to do anything more than watch and what a beautiful scenario it was when they came undone in each other's arms.

CHAPTER THREE

Aftermath

We fell asleep in a tangle of limbs and I have to say it was the best night of sleep I'd ever gotten. My body was so exhausted that it probably had no other choice but to rest. The light of dawn was peeking through the window when I finally awakened, and I carefully slid from the bed, trying to let them all sleep. Leon and Leif had enjoyed each other several times during the night and seemed pleased that I enjoyed watching them together.

Walking into the bathroom, I quickly used the facilities before adjusting the water in the shower. I fell in love with the thing because it had eight different shower heads and the feel of that heat beating down on my body from different directions was incredible! For long minutes I stood under the stream just soaking up the soothing pleasure.

"Can I join you?" Miles's soft voice pulled my eyes open and I nodded. He stepped in and grinned as the water hit his firm body.

"How are you feeling sweetheart?" He talked as he picked up a bottle of body wash and soaped himself down.

My heart raced at the view, and I knew that they'd woken up my sexuality in ways I'd never imagined after last night. "Wonderful." I bit my lip as he washed his cock and my hands clenched at my sides to stop from reaching out to take over the job. My eyes riveted to his beautiful sex.

"I don't mind you touching me Zoey." That sweet grin of his didn't make me feel embarrassed, instead it left me longing. Stepping forward I gripped him in my hand, biting my lip again when I realized my fingers wouldn't even close around his wide girth. "I love feeling your hand holding me." Closing his eyes the pleasure on his face was all I needed to forget how large he was. I began stroking him.

His cock grew longer with each stroke and my eyes widened as my hand stilled. Only then did he open his eyes again. Pulling back he smiled and shook his head. Lathering his hands he began washing my shoulders, arms, back, across my now trembling abdomen, even down my legs missing all the parts that suddenly longed for his touch.

Finally his hands cupped my breasts, then he lathered them and massaged bringing my body to life instantly. Gripping his shoulders, I almost lost my balance when his hand slipped between my thighs, thoroughly washing away the evidence of the love I'd experienced last night. I wanted him to continue touching those folds, and almost whimpered when he turned me around washing away the stickiness from my backside. Those long digits smoothed over my anus, reminding me of taking Leif there.

Pulling me under the water he rinsed me off with such gentleness that I felt adored and more than a little turned on. He lathered my hair and I wanted to scream that that wasn't where I wanted his hands, but it felt incredible as he massaged my scalp. I couldn't voice the words. He rinsed my hair as well, making me feel completely pampered.

"I want you Zoey, but if you're too sore, I need you to tell me." His hands moved down to my hips, pressing me against him. The large erection resting against my stomach told me just how much he wanted me.

It didn't matter that I was still a little tender this morning, I wanted to feel him inside me. He was the only one of the men that I hadn't loved that way yet. "Take me Miles."

"Oh sweetheart, I'd rather give instead of take." Lowering to his knees in the shower stall, he lifted one of my legs over his massive shoulder and his tongue gently ravished me. I clung to him as he worked my body with a mastery that left me panting for more.

"Miles, please. Inside me." I didn't want to come this way. I loved how his tongue worshipped me, but I needed to feel him driving into my aching flesh.

He stood, his face glistening with my pleasure and the smile he gave me was so heartwarming I sighed. I loved this man, he was so giving that it almost made my heart ache with the knowledge. Miles lifted me in his arms and winked.

"Wrap those beautiful legs around me Zoey. Let me love you." I complied, how could I not when even knowing how aroused he was he still took the time to make sure I was ready for him.

My arms wrapped around his neck and my legs around his waist. Surrounded by Miles. I wondered if there was any place better to be at the moment. I felt his cock nudge against my clit and nearly came at the feeling he'd turned me on so much with his mouth.

Slowly he entered my body, stretching me deliciously with each glorious inch. The sweet burn already in place from being loved so well last night heightened the sensation of his thickness widening my body to new levels. I clung to him as he worked his way in until I felt his hips resting against mine.

Glancing down I was amazed that my body was able to take him so deep inside. "I love you." I didn't mean to say the words but they slipped out so effortlessly in the heat of passion.

"Sweet Zoey. I think I loved you the moment we first met." He winked down and began inching his way out only to find his way home again. Somehow I knew he'd be just as tender a lover as he was as a man and it made my heart soar as well as my body. Each delicious thrust felt like he was paying homage and I met those movements with my own the best I could in an unfamiliar position.

Those large hands rested on my hips guiding him in and out of my body and our eyes never once broke contact. It was such a beautiful experience that I felt tears sliding down my cheeks as he continued to love me. He filled me completely, leaving no room for anything but the sensation and I was consumed.

When my release found me, I still wanted more because I somehow knew that my body would never be loved this completely again. I knew that loving the others meant just as much but with Miles it was more than just physical. It felt like our souls connected and when he filled me with his seed, I cried out softly because it just felt complete.

He held me in his arms even after his body had softened inside mine. I couldn't let go. The emotions were almost overwhelming and I found myself sobbing as I clung to him.

"Sweetheart you're breaking my heart here. Have I hurt you?" His hands caressed my hair tenderly. We were still joined together but when he tried to break the connection, I clung to him tightly. Not wanting to let go.

"Please just hold me Miles. I'm fine, I just don't want this to end." I didn't understand my emotional response to our lovemaking but it didn't matter. A part of me worried that when I left this bathroom with him, and eventually returned home, that somehow I'd never experience all the pleasure they'd given me again.

"I'll hold you forever sweetheart, just tell me why you're upset." The concern in his voice gave me strength because I believed he truly would never let me go if I asked it of him.

"I'm so afraid this will all end, and I'm not sure I can imagine a life without you in it." My tears wouldn't stop so I held on to him tightly, hating myself for the sudden weakness.

"Is this a private party of can anyone join?" Leif's boyish charm made me smile and when he stepped inside the shower stall with us, I felt my mood lighten somewhat.

"What the hell did you do to her Miles?" My legs finally unwrapped from Miles's waist and my feet found the floor. His cock slid free and for a moment I wanted to wrap around him again so I didn't feel so lost.

"I would never hurt her." Miles was pissed. I could hear it in his voice and see it in his face that the thought of ever causing me pain was foreign to him.

I was drawn into Leif's arms and I hugged him tightly, speaking through my tears. "He didn't do anything, I'm just overly emotional right now." Wuss, my mind screamed.

"That I can understand. Hell I had sex with Leon." He chuckled but it was self-derisive. I could tell from the look on his face that he was trying to come to grips with his new sexuality.

"It was beautiful watching the two of you." At his fears being put out there, my own shrank to the back of my thoughts.

"You don't think less of me?" I wanted to laugh because we were standing in the shower having a serious conversation but I knew it would hurt his feelings.

"Why would I?" I had never seen two men make love but I wasn't homophobic. If anything it had been more of a turn on than I thought possible.

"I don't know. I think your opinion matters more to me than anyone else's." His words made me tear up again, and I hugged him against me tightly.

"There's nothing you could ever do that would make me love you less." The truth of that was felt deep in my heart and I was in the mood for confessing my true feelings today, I guessed.

"I hope you have enough of that love to go around little Zoey." Leon had joined us in the shower and the space was getting more crowded by the second.

"How could I not love you Leon." Grinning I left Leif's arms and hugged him.

"She still loves me the most." Samson smirked as he joined us and I was glad that whomever built this house had a huge shower. I was pulled out of Leon's arms by Samson and hugged so tightly I almost lost my breath.

"Air." I laughed until he released me somewhat. "Whose house is this anyway?" It was a stupid question but I didn't want to get into the 'who I loved more' debate. Truthfully I wasn't sure I could love any of them more than the other, it was just a different kind of love.

"It belongs to me, as much as you do." Possessive Samson wasn't something I was prepared for and my eyes widened, looking up at him. "Don't look at me that way sweetheart, I told you once that if you were mine things would be different."

I remembered vaguely him saying something to that effect when we were on the island. "I think I remember you saying I wasn't ready for that." I'd submitted to him yesterday. Fallen on my knees in front of him, but I still wasn't sure what that really meant to him."

"Clean us Zoey, then I want you and me to talk, privately." There was no room in his voice for a denial even if I'd planned on giving one. I didn't. I needed to know what he expected and see if I felt comfortable with truly belonging to him in the sense he asked.

Miles gave me a sympathetic look that made my soul ache. "I'm finished here." He turned me from Samson and kissed me tenderly. "Just remember Zoey, you never have to do anything you don't want." His fingers grazed my cheek and I noticed the heated look he gave Samson before stepping out.

"Is he upset with me?" I had no idea what was wrong with me, but my emotions were in an uproar at the moment. Like at any moment I was going to burst into tears again.

"He's not upset with you sweetheart, it's me." Leon began washing Leif and I could see the tenderness in his touch. There was something blooming with these two men that made my heart ache it was so beautiful. "I think you can just focus on washing me." Samson chuckled softly.

I didn't think about his words, instead I grabbed the body wash and lovingly cleansed away the passion from the night before. I loved touching him, feeling the strength of his powerful muscles beneath my hand as the suds smoothed over his flesh. When my hands moved down his six-pack and circled his cock, he stopped me.

"I think I'll take care of this for now." Shaking his head as his length hardened I grinned. "Those sweet little hands will make me want to fuck you again and you need a little recovery time."

I watched as he finished bathing and my eyes couldn't help darting over to Leif and Leon. Even a blind person could see where their bathing was going and I had to admit I wouldn't mind watching again. I was somewhat disappointed when Samson pulled me out of the shower and began drying me off.

"They need alone time too." The way he dried me was almost clinical and again I was disappointed. "Don't look at me that way Zoey. I'm trying my damndest to remember how hard you were used last night honey. Miles should have given you time to recover!"

Knowing that he was concerned about my well-being brought tears to my eyes. Shit! What the hell was wrong with me today? I turned away so he wouldn't see that I was an emotional wreck. After a few minutes he reached down to grasp my hand, the towel wrapped around his waist neatly.

"Let me grab you a shirt so I can stop thinking about how I want to feel you beneath me again." He led me into the bedroom and over to his closet. Pulling out a button down, he guided my arms through the sleeves and had me buttoned up before I could catch my breath.

The shirt fell almost to my knees and he rolled up the sleeves so they wouldn't fall over my hands. Leaving me standing there he walked over to a chest-of-drawers, pulled out underwear and shorts, sliding them on quickly. "The sooner I get you out of this bedroom the better!"

He grabbed my hand again and we walked downstairs. The tick in his strong jaw made me worry he was angry and it did things to my heart that seemed to be commonplace for this day. I was worried he was disappointed in my actions and ready to bolt out the door to go home and lick my wounds.

"Why are you mad at me?" I knew the words were whiny but I had no control over my emotions at the moment.

"I'm not mad!" At his increased volume tears slid down my cheeks and I attempted to walk away. He wasn't allowing that action obviously since he pulled me into his arms almost squeezing the breath out of me. "Damn it Zoey, I have no control with you. Don't you get that? I want to toss you over the edge of the couch and fuck you until you can't walk!"

I looked up at him in complete shock. Samson was a control freak, so him having none with me spoke volumes. That dried up my tears instantly. "Then say that first. I just slept with you and three other guys so I'm not dealing well with my emotions at the moment. The last thing I need to think is you think badly of me because of it!"

I was shouting at him and it made me feel a hell of a lot better just getting the words out there. I wasn't prepared when he tossed back his head and chuckled loudly. If anything I expected him to toss me over his lap and beat my ass for being so vocal about my feelings. "You're confusing the shit out me Samson." Pulling out of his arms I stomped over to the couch and sat down. My arms crossed over my chest and I refused to look at him.

His laughter ceased as he joined me. "I know I am baby, and that's why we need to talk. We need to set some boundaries for both of our sakes. The last damn thing I want is to make you confused."

I glared at him not sure what he was talking about. Uncrossing my arms I lifted my palms to the sky asking without words for him to explain.

"First of all I don't think badly about you for enjoying our company. It was so fucking hot watching you with the other men, so you can get that out of your pretty little head. I loved that you trusted me enough to lead you through that and I plan on doing it again some night when you and I have worked through what we hope to gain from this."

"Are we supposed to gain anything?" My temper released the moment he took over the conversation and that was something I'd have to think about later. "I thought that was where things were supposed to end?"

"If that's what you want, then yes. But it doesn't have to. I'd love nothing more than to collar you and make you my submissive Zoey. I think somewhere in your heart you made that decision last night as well." The tentative smile he gave me showed a side to Samson I rarely saw. The one that didn't have all the answers.

I hadn't thought that far ahead. Yesterday, all I'd known is that I needed Samson to be in control. He'd taken control of the situation but what he was talking about now was so much more. "I'm not a very submissive person."

"Tell me about it." He chuckled warmly and that beautiful smirk I loved found his face again. "But I think you could be at least sexually. I know you need and should have control outside of the bedroom but inside it? Sweetheart I could teach you things about yourself that would change all your thoughts about sexuality."

There was no way I could deny his claim on that front. After last night the point had been proven. "I like you being in control there." I wasn't going to lie about my feelings. Had he not taken control I'd never have relaxed enough to allow the things that had happened.

"I think it's pretty obvious that I enjoyed that too, but there's so much more that I could teach you. All you have to do is agree to be mine, Zoey." His hand reached up to cup my chin, forcing our eyes to meet. "Do you want that?"

Did I want to belong to him? My body did, but that was about pleasure. I knew instinctively that for him it would be much more than just the sex he wanted to control. "If this were just about sexual pleasure, I wouldn't hesitate. But it's not, is it?"

"We've discussed before how much I value your opinion with the business, so that wouldn't change, but yes other things would be different." His eyes were searching mine, and I knew he wanted me to accept his offer.

"What things, Samson. I loved what we did but before you ask me something like that and I agree, I have to know what you mean." Sexuality was taken out of the equation for the moment because as much as I loved being with him, I needed it written out.

"There's a different kind of contract we could work up for the two of us. I think it would be mutually beneficial and I would love to train you."

Thinking about a contract for sexuality between us was a little daunting. It was one thing to write up one for fantasies but I knew he meant something entirely different. "Show me what you're talking about." I wasn't going to accept something like this blindly, and I was in over my head at the moment.

"Follow me up to my office and I'll show you a standard contract. We can alter it to suit both of our needs but I think you'll find it enlightening." With a smile, he stood up and held out his hand for me.

I was curious now, and stood accepting as I followed him back upstairs. This was turning into the strangest day and I knew if nothing else I'd understand what he was looking for in a relationship. Relationship was the only word I could use to define two people signing an agreement involving sexuality.

CHAPTER FOUR

Bond

Sitting in front of Samson's home office desk, I felt like we'd just stepped back into the boardroom. His expression was professional and I took the document he offered trying to keep my own emotions in check. I read through the contract and my eyes widened at the outline of the terms.

"You know none of this would be admissible in a court, right?" My heart raced at some of the terminology included that I wasn't even sure what definition they had.

"Of course I realize that, but it's not meant to be enforced except between you and me." His soft chuckle, along with how he rested back in his chair showed that he was completely at ease in this scenario.

I knew my mouth was hanging open when I got to the part about what was expected of his submissive and how he would punish if those expectations weren't met. "You would actually punish me with a cane?" Hell to the no he wasn't doing that!

"Like I said earlier, this is a base contract and things can be altered to fit our needs." The humor left his face at my reaction. "To train you correctly I need to be able to implement disciplinary actions. You have to trust that I would never do anything that I felt you couldn't handle."

"Trust is one thing Samson, some of this shit seems pretty painful. I'm not into that at all." Outside of the spankings I'd never been disciplined in my life.

"The idea is that you'd never give me a reason to punish. Some of those things you might actually learn to enjoy."

"I don't know how anyone could enjoy being whipped and enjoy it." The thought of something like that being used on my flesh terrified me.

"It's not something you start out with Zoey. You build up tolerance to certain things and as you do you find that your body needs a higher level of stimulation." He smiled at me and I wasn't sure I liked him very much at the moment. The thought of him chaining me up to some equipment that I still didn't know what looked like wasn't my idea of a good time.

"Women seriously let you do this shit to them?" I was blown away as I continued to read and not thinking very highly of him at the moment. I sneered unintentionally.

"Yes they do and usually walk away with a smile on their face after. Sweetheart you're reading into this the wrong way. Most of what's in that contract is there for your pleasure and mine. The punishment aspect is just the result of not trusting me enough to do the right thing for you."

"Yeah well pleasure is one thing, even though I don't understand half the shit you've got listed there for that." This was a world of deviant crap I was clueless about.

"Then maybe you should learn. We don't have to work out a contract today. Take some time to research what's listed here and come back with a better idea of what I'm asking you to work with me on." If he'd been condescending in his remarks I'd have refused him outright. I could hear the sincerity in his words and that he was asking me to try for him.

"I want to talk to Rachel about this." I knew she got off on the games played and if anyone could help me understand, it would be her.

"I don't mind you doing that, but remember Rachel doesn't play with me that way. If something she says confuses you or makes you uncomfortable in the definition, I want you to ask me about it. Can you do that for me?"

Samson was being gracious? How the hell could I refuse that? "I think that's fair."

"I won't touch you again until we have sorted this out. Neither will the other men. I'm not telling you this to make you angry, Zoey, I just think it's fair to both of us if you give what I'm asking for your full attention."

He'd introduced me to pleasure and was now taking it away. I wasn't sure how I felt about that. "Why would the other men agree to that?" Miles hadn't been exactly happy knowing Samson and I were going to have this talk.   And Leif?   He didn't seem like the type that listened to anyone telling him what to do.

"They'll agree because we've always wanted to find our perfect partners to share in a relationship this way. We've talked about it for years."

"Then why was Miles so upset?" It bothered me greatly that he'd left without saying goodbye.   "And what do you mean perfect partners?" This conversation was confusing me again.

"Miles was upset because I think he wanted you to belong to him. I'm not taking you away from him Zoey, but make no mistake if you agree to this, you will be mine. By partners I mean we've wanted to find four separate people that would belong to us individually but that we'd share also."

"So Miles, Leif, and Leon would all find other women too?" I couldn't think about that and deal with what Samson was offering me. It was just too much.

"Miles definitely would. I'm not sure that Leon and Leif won't consider a relationship together after last night. I know that's what Leon has always wanted."

"But we'd all still be together?   How would that work?" My sense of reality was bordering on confusion now. I could actually see Leif and Leon together, they were such a perfect match.

"It would mean that while we enjoyed our own personal relationship with our partners, we'd also come together in ways like we did last night." He stood up, walked in front of my chair and knelt. "I'd love nothing more than for you to be my side permanently."

Holy shit! I definitely was prepared for him to take things to this level. It thrilled me that he wanted me to be with him that much, but at the same time it terrified me. "Are you asking me to marry you?"

"I'm asking you to commit to me completely sweetheart. I know what I want, and that's you, if you need marriage to accept my terms then I'll offer it, but I'd accept you without that type of ceremony."

"Let me deal with the contract first?" I couldn't even begin to make a commitment as big as marriage without understanding what he wanted in a relationship yet.

"I'd prefer we do things that way too, for now. But know something Zoey, if you agree to be mine, you'll be just as committed to me as if we'd walked in front of a preacher and said I do." His gray eyes filled with deep emotion and the glint of hardness there made me shiver.

I swallowed deeply and nodded my head. Something inside of me was changing and I couldn't understand it fully. Perhaps a part of me really wanted to belong to him because all I could do was wrap my arms around his neck and hold on tightly.

We remained that way for long minutes, he had to break contact first. "Take the contract home with you. Research it completely, talk with Rachel, and let me know if you have any questions. I want you to recover from last night so you need to leave now."

He stood up and I could see the very noticeable tent in his shorts. I understood immediately that he wasn't going to remain in control long. That thought did things to my libido that made me want to just agree to anything to be with him one more time. Instead I nodded, walked upstairs, dressed and let his driver take me home.

Rachel was still sleeping when I made it back to the apartment and I was happy about that. I needed some time to wrap my head around the things that happened last night, today, and with the contract Samson had given me.

There was not an ounce of guilt about the pleasure I'd experienced with the men. I knew the old me would have balked at having done the deed with all of them, but that frigid bitch had disappeared. I was twenty-two years old and had only slept with one guy before them. The way I saw it I'd taken Leif's advice and made up for lost time.

That really wasn't it though. With the guys, I knew that they all cared about me and it was hard to feel guilty when you were surrounded by so much love. I was a grown woman and not living my life to please anyone else, so what I did in my life? Well that was my business. Of course I wouldn't be writing home to my mom telling her I'd just had the best sex of my life with four men. My parents were happy in their retirement and didn't step into my affairs, so they didn't need to know what I was doing either.

By the time Rachel finally woke up I was in a much better frame of mind than I'd been after Miles and I had showered together. I guess it was just really emotional coming out of my sexually repressed shell after all those years.

We talked for hours after the whole submissive master relationship and after she got over the shock that

I'd slept with the guys, she helped me put things in perspective. Rachel didn't do committed relationships, but she was a wealth of information about the situations listed in the contract. Outside of a few implements of punishment I wasn't really freaked out anymore by that either.

Roses flooded my apartment by late afternoon from each one of them, and my heart was just overwhelmed at the sincerity in the cards. I also got a phone call from each of them, making sure I was okay and thanking me. I was a little shocked at them doing that when I felt I should be thanking them.

Monday morning at work would be the real test. If I could make it through the day without thinking about what we'd done, I'd consider everything a positive. I voiced my concerns to Rachel and she told me I was worrying for nothing.

CHAPTER FIVE

Work Affair

I had an hour before the nine o'clock board meeting and several new contracts to go over. That kept my mind busy enough that I couldn't worry about how our night would play out in the office. The strangest fantasy request to date crossed my desk and I wasn't sure how to deal with it. I decided to take it in to the meeting and give a topic in case things were not as professional as I wanted them to be here.

After the first twenty minutes of the meeting I knew I'd worried for nothing. Samson was ornery as a bear about the delays on the Island construction and was ready to cut off heads and shit down throats. I had to remember this was the same man I'd slept with less than 48 hours ago.

Leif and Miles were arguing now because the costs for building were higher than anticipated and Miles was quick to let him know it was his damn idea and he needed to sort it out. I tried my best not to laugh at their testosterone filled antics and rolled my eyes with Leon as it escalated.

"I've got a little problem with a file that just crossed my desk." Trying to disrupt the temper tantrums I decided now was the time to bring it up. Instantly I had all their attention.

"What's going on?" Leon looked pleased that the shouting match had stopped. I handed over the file and walked around to his side of the table to look over his shoulder.

"Well apparently there's a member of the club that wants to buy a fantasy for her younger sister. While I know we've done that before, this one is a little unique. The woman in question is a virgin and wants to set up a fantasy where she's taken against her will."

"Virgin? Do they even make those over the age of eighteen?" Leif was curious and moved to sit next to Leon, reading over the file.

"That has trouble written all over it. The last thing we need is a lawsuit where some young girl claims she was raped at Fantasy's." Samson grabbed the file from Leon and began thumbing through it.

"She's twenty-one, just turned. Very pretty woman. Amazed that she wants to pay someone for that though." I could see dozens of guys begging her for the chance to be number one, so it made no sense.

"Nothing wrong with setting up your perfect introduction into sexuality." Miles seemed lost in thought for a moment. "I'm not sure using one of our actors would be responsible though. A women needs a little more sensitivity as an innocent."

"You've always wanted to be a woman's first." Leon chuckled softly. "For what reason I have no idea. Those types usually think they've fallen in love when it's just the experience they're in love with."

"I wish I had you guys for my first." They hadn't mentioned anything about our encounter and leave it to me to be the first to bring it up. I flushed.

"We can talk about that after hours." Samson's words made me blush deeper. He was right though. If we were going to keep things professional here, I didn't need to bring up what went on outside the building. "Miles if you want to take on this fantasy personally I'll agree, but as far as putting it out there for an actor? I don't think it's a good idea either."

I knew he'd rolled over his words to me by moving on to another topic, and was thankful. "So you guys have been a part of the fantasies before?" I wasn't sure how I felt about them being with other women, but did I have the right to feel that way?

"When we first started Fantasy's we were the crew. But no, not since year one. This fantasy will require a little more finesse though and I wouldn't want to risk one of the staff screwing this woman over emotionally. There are things to look for and ways of wording a fantasy that keeps it professional and still what the client is looking for."

I was amazed at Samson's grasp of the situation. It shouldn't have surprised me though, he had a firm handle on the business here. "What do you want to do

Miles?" I needed to contact the member and let her know either way.

"Our theme here has always been about delivering the fantasy for the client, so yes I accept. I'll have a few things to add to your interview to make sure things go smoothly and a mental evaluation will need to be set up with one of our counselors on top of the physical. We need to make sure this woman is ready to deal with the consequences of her fantasy."

"I agree with Miles. The last thing you want is some woman thinking its love when it's just pleasure." Leon shook his head and I could see he wasn't convinced taking on this contract was a good idea.

"We're not here to tell them what fantasies are acceptable." Samson threw that out on the table. I had to agree with him because there were fantasies that crossed my desk every day that I found disgusting. "So other business. Leif you're going to call the contractor today, tell him he has ten days to get the blueprint in our hands or he's fired. Anything else?"

The meeting went on for another hour as other concerns were brought up. I was ready to get back to my office by the time things finally ended. Just like that the day continued, and the rest of the week didn't let up. We were swamped with new membership interests, fantasies waiting to be arranged, and the new construction going on with the island. I already had a client list three pages long for vacation themed destinations.

By Friday my ass was dragging, and I still hadn't given Samson an answer. I knew my decision but work had really been exhausting and there hadn't been time to set aside personal time. I was so looking forward to our lunch and calling it quits after. A unanimous decision had been reached that Friday's were half days because the guys still had the bar to run at night.

I'd interviewed the woman on Tuesday that wanted the scene set up and was amazed at how much I liked her. She was definitely an introvert but it was almost charming how sweet and innocent she was. A part of me wanted to take her under my wing because I saw things in her that reminded me a lot of myself before I'd met the guys.

When we finally arrived at our normal restaurant, I informed them of how that first client meeting went. "I think you'll really enjoy teaching Amber, Miles." We'd ordered our salads and were sitting back enjoying drinks. "She's just the sweetest thing. Reminds me of a little pixie doll, just adorable."

"Do you think she's emotionally stable?" Miles sat forward in his chair.

"From the hour we talked I think she is. Very shy. You just want to hug her and tell her it's okay to explain what she wants. I think we could be friends." I really had gotten a great feeling from Amber.

"Interesting." Samson had this strange look on his face that I couldn't decipher. "What about looks wise. Do you find her attractive?"

His question surprised me. "Well yes. I'm not into women, but if you asked me as one would I find her attractive, definitely."

"Have you ever been with a woman before?" Leon arched his brow and gave me a sultry look. When I shook my head no he chuckled. "Then how could you know you're not into them." He winked and took a sip of his brandy. Wrapping his arm around the back of Leif's chair I understood his point immediately.

"Fine. Let's concentrate on the client for a minute though, since that wasn't on her 'I want to do' list." Grinning I rolled my eyes at him.

"What was on her list?" Miles was suddenly very interested and that made my grin widen.

"Well that's the thing. She hasn't had any experience outside of a few kisses, so she doesn't know. I'm not even sure how to broach the subject because she was blushing when I mentioned the words anal penetration."

All the men got a good laugh out of that comment and it took a few minutes before we turned back to the conversation. "I just wanted to find out which virginity she was interested in losing?" With a shrug I silenced my thoughts as the waiter delivered our salads.

"Maybe you should set up a meeting with all three of us. The last thing I want is this young woman walking into this blind." Miles finished a bite of his salad.

"Or you could scare the shit out of her and have her meet with all of us." Leif grinned my way as he said that reminding me of our first meeting.

"Yeah. Uh, no. I think Miles sitting down with us would be a good idea though. This scenario is a little different than what we usually arrange so I'd feel more comfortable knowing she's getting exactly what she wanted."

"You weren't that freaked out the first time we met, were you?" Leon found it amusing probably because I had no problem telling him exactly what I felt now in the business world.

"Are you kidding me? I almost wet myself walking into that boardroom. You guys aren't exactly the most comforting souls. I mean hell you all look like fashion models!" I couldn't stop grinning at their looks of pride.

"Yeah we are pretty sexy." Leif and his ego! I was so glad we could sit down together and still be friends after what we'd shared. Honestly I'd done little but think about that all week long. I wanted to experience it again, but Samson and I still had things to work out. True to his word, not one of them had made a move on me since.

"You look the sexiest underneath me though baby." Leon licked his lips and I giggled at the flush on Leif's cheeks. If anyone could shut him up it was Leon.

Our meal came and we finished it off while enjoying casual conversation. I promised Miles I'd set up the interview for next week and he seemed very pleased at the idea. Secretly I hoped that he'd see more in Amber than just a client. As jealous as it made me to think of him with another woman, she was just his type.

Samson paid the bill and we were about to go our separate ways at the door when I stopped him. "I'd really like to talk to you alone if you have time." Suddenly I was nervous and found myself looking at my feet.

"I don't like it when you look down Zoey. I'm ready to talk if you're sure you're ready?" I met his eyes quickly somewhat amazed he didn't like my submissive stance, it seemed to be what he wanted after reading the contract.

"I'm more than ready." As nervous as I was, it was time to give him a decision. I'd barely slept and until today I'd had little appetite as well.

The other men walked to the car, leaving me alone with Samson outside the restaurant. "We'll drop them off them go back to my place then." His hand fell to my lower back and I allowed him to lead me to join the others.

Making small talk with the other guys on the drive back helped my nerves but once we were alone again they came back full force. I was trembling by the time we arrived back at his house.

CHAPTER SIX
Contract

He offered me his hand when we'd parked in front of his mansion and I took it with a little hesitation. This was the biggest decision of my life and I hoped that I was making the right choice. I knew Samson cared for me, possibly even loved me, and I had no doubt about my feelings for him. What I did doubt was this step I was about to take.

We walked through the front doors, not talking. He led me straight to his office and sat down behind the desk. "How are you Zoey?" Those words weren't what I expected. I'd assumed he'd want to get straight down to business, not that I was disappointed.

"Missing being in your arms." I wouldn't lie to him. When he held me I felt like anything he asked of me was possible, it was only away from him that I doubted my ability to be what he needed.

"Then why don't you come over here and show me how much?" Playful Samson was breathtaking and I didn't hesitate. Walking around the desk, I sat down in his lap and wrapped my arms around his neck.

His strong arms wrapped around my waist and I sighed in relief. We'd been together all week at work but not once had he touched me or shown any indication that he'd missed my touch. Judging from the growing erection under my ass, he had.

His hand tangled in my hair and he brought my lips to his, kissing me possessively. His tongue consumed mine and I was out of breath only seconds after it began. Frantically I wiggled my bottom in his lap, the desire washing over me in waves. I was amazed at how quickly my need for him rose. I was lifted off his lap abruptly and whimpered at the loss of contact.

"Contract. Now. Before I fuck you in this chair!" His hands were gripping my hips and his head fell against my abdomen. He was just as hungry for me? That did things to my ego that I can't even begin to explain.

"I wouldn't mind." My fingers threaded through his thick hair, holding him against me. Mind? Hell I was ready to unbutton his pants, grasp him in my hand, and ride his body until this insane desire was sated.

He stood, making me lose my grip on his head, taking several steps back. "I told you I wouldn't touch you again until we had this sorted out. Running a hand through his hair impatiently it slid to his neck and he stared at me with an intensity that left me breathless.

"I'll sign your contract." Crossing my arms over my chest I glared at him, not sure if I liked being this out of control or his ability to just step away when all I wanted was to be back in his arms.

He chuckled softly. "And be pissed off because I'm not giving you what you want now?" Smirking he shook his head. "I don't think you understand how little control I have with you. I need that tempting little body of yours bound and still so I can give you what you need."

The thought should have terrified me but instead it made me ache to imagine what things he could dream up when I had no way of stopping him. My core dripped from just hearing him say the words. "Stop telling me and show me then!"

"Demanding little thing aren't you?" Shaking his head again he grinned. "I can't wait to teach you patience." He motioned with his hand for me to find my chair and like an obedient, but somewhat pissed off, puppy I found my seat again.

How he went from turned on to control freak in five seconds flat I'll never understand, but when he sat down in that chair he was all business. Outside of the tick in his jaw I'd never guess he still wanted me. Pulling out the contract he slid it over to me. "We're going through these points one by one. I want no doubts about where we're going with this."

I hated the fact that I had to cross my legs to stop the ache that now reminded me how much I wanted him. Needing to be in control I schooled my expression into the same unemotional response he was giving me. "Fine, let's get this over with."

"We'll start with the easy things. What I expect of you when you're in this house." He knew the contract by memory I discovered as he went over every line of how I was to dress, act, and respond to any command he gave. I'd read over these points at home and only had a few concerns.

Undressing the minute I walked through the door, I guessed that was fine, because judging from his earlier reaction I knew where it would lead. "Nude at all times, fine, but what if you have company over?" I wasn't here to give a peep show unless it was for him and I wanted that point made clear up front.

"I don't entertain here unless it's with Miles, Leif and Leon, so unless something out of the ordinary is happening, you'll follow that rule."

"Do you have a staff?" I could agree with the other men being here, but this house was huge so I assumed someone had to be doing the daily chores.

"I have a maid that comes in in the morning, and if you're here when she is, clothing is fine. Outside of her and the driver who lives in the servant quarters that's it. I don't like having people in my home when I'm not here. The driver will only enter when I call for him, so he's not a concern."

"Control freak much?" I had to grin at the thought of him not having a live in staff because of his need to protect his territory.

"Enjoy that smart ass mouth while you can." He smirked. "But yes I am. I don't like the idea of servants running their mouths about what I do here."

That was understandable. The press had a field day with him as it was and he didn't need the added fuel of people in his home giving away his interests. "Wait a minute, are you saying I can't talk to you like this after the contracts signed?" I wasn't sure how I felt about not telling him what I felt.

"Read the last section on expected behavior." He waited until I found that paragraph and smiled a little too cockily for my comfort.

"The submissive agrees to be respectful at all times, and understands the disciplinary consequences if she fails to adhere?" I quoted the sentence to him, my eyes widening. "So you expect me to smile and just deal with it if you're an ass?"

"I expect you to be respectful when you're in this house and not use that smart ass mouth any way you choose."

"Something tells me my ass is going to be on fire." I made a joke out of it, because the thought of changing how we related to each other made me really nervous.

"Probably so, but you'll learn." He winked at me like this wasn't a huge deal and I nibbled on my lips fretfully. "Stop overthinking, we'll work through these things."

"Maybe we should skip ahead to the discipline stuff. I'm still not comfortable at all agreeing to the caning or whipping. I'd like to be able to walk the next day at work."

"Zoey do you think I'd ever hurt you in a way that would debilitate?" He looked shocked that I would even let that thought cross my mind.

"I didn't think you would, but I have no idea what will happen once I accept your rules." That was what really frightened me. Could he have a complete personality change once I said yes and not be the same man I'd fallen in love with?

"You really have no idea what you're agreeing to, do you?" Looking wounded, he stood and walked around the desk to kneel down on one knee in front of me. "Screw the damn contract Zoey. Just agree to let me teach you and we'll go from there." His arms wrapped around my waist and his face rested on my chest.

I felt bad that he was willing to give up what he wanted because of my ignorance. I smoothed his hair with my hand and made a conscious decision. "I'm already yours Samson, if you need me to follow these rules, I'll try, but no I don't know what you're really asking of me."

He lifted his head and met my eyes. "You'd willingly sign on to doing whatever I asked of you, just to please me?" At my nod he looked abashed. "Fuck baby that's not getting what you need out of this. We're going to do this differently. Just agree to be mine and let me lead the way and we can say to hell with all the other bullshit for now."

"Like I said before, I'm already yours Samson." The truth was I'd sign anything he asked because the thought of losing him ripped my heart from my chest.

"Then we'll make this work." He stood up again and held out his hand. I took it having no idea where we went from here but knowing he had a plan.

CHAPTER SEVEN
Tutor

We walked down a long hall and stopped in front of a set of wooden doors. He opened one of them, leading me down a long flight of stairs. My eyes widened as he flipped a switch when we reached the bottom and a room full of what looked like torture devices filled my vision.

"This is my playroom. I don't want you to be afraid of the things you see here, because I promise I'm going to introduce you slowly. Can you do that for me?"

Fuck no. I thought to myself as I looked around the room, then I lifted my gaze to his face. He looked so worried that I was going to bolt that I couldn't give him that answer. I nodded, wanting to make him happy but holy shit! What had I just walked into?

He maneuvered me around the room giving names to the devices and believe me when I say my comfort level didn't improve much. One of the chairs he stopped in front of looked like a cross between a table at the gynecologist, mixed with something seen at the dentist office and it scared the hell out of me. There were so many gadgets attached that I was sure it had to be used to torture the shit out of someone.

"It's not as scary as it looks." He chuckled, wrapping his arms around my waist. "The stirrups help keep your legs spread wide so I can have my wicked way with you. The other things are just a variation of different tools I can play around with."

"Um, it doesn't exactly look like fun." I lifted the rubber phallus attached to a board and thought I wouldn't want to have that thing impaled inside me, it was bigger than he was!" The thing had four damn belts attached that I understood immediately would be used to hold a person in place. Not to mention arm rests with some type of wrist restraints of leather.

"We'll work up to this one." He chuckled and I wanted to tell him when hell froze over. Instead I allowed him to lead me to another strange looking device.

It looked like a chair swing for adults and I couldn't imagine why he'd want to push me through the air in this room. Granted of all the things I saw here this looked the less lethal.

"You like my swing? I can strap you in there and we can try out dozens of new positions." He showed me how flexible the leather chair swing was and pointed out the restraints. Everything in this room had some way of tying me down and it gave a new meaning to my mind about being bound.

"So it's not as innocent as it looks." I spoke the words out loud when I was really just commenting to myself. So much for my thoughts about it not being lethal.

"All of these things can be innocent or as naughty as we want to make them." Turning me in his arms he lowered his head and kissed me deeply. None of these strange things mattered when he kissed me. I surrendered to the mastery of his mouth and felt my body surrendered instantly.

"Undress for me Zoey." Pulling back, his eyes met mine and I shivered. He wanted to start my introduction here and I was torn between wanting him and afraid of what evil thing he planned on testing out first.

Taking a deep breath, I knew he wanted this and somehow I'd find a way to accept that to please him. I had to trust. My fingers trembled as I lifted my shirt over my head. He never spoke a word as I slid out of my skirt, then followed with my panties and bra.

"Leave your heels on baby, I love how sexy you look in nothing but them." Thigh highs and heels turned him on, I made a mental note to wear those every time I visited him here.

He pulled me into his arms and I wished he was as undressed as I was. "Take off my shirt." He gave me that gorgeous half smirk of his, reading my mind and my fingers quickly moved to the buttons on his oxford. I loved the smoothness of his chest and my lips landed on one of his nipples the moment I dropped his shirt to the ground, unable to stop myself.

With a soft growl he took a step back. "That's why I want that gorgeous body at my mercy. Shit baby, all I can think about doing when you touch me is sliding into that hot tight pussy and fucking you like a madman!" Lifting me up into his arms, he tossed me over his shoulder and stalked away to some weird looking leather covered bench.

He sat me on my feet quickly and glared. "Lay face down over it." When I hesitated I could see the tick in his jaw pulse. "Now Zoey, don't make me ask you again." He didn't raise his voice but the demand made it apparent he wasn't asking again.

I quickly maneuvered my body over the long length of the bench, resting face down. I was shaking so bad that I couldn't stop.

"I'm not going to hurt you baby. Reach your hands down and you'll feel two handlebars." His tone softened by volumes and I tried to relax. This was Samson, and I knew my fears were unfounded. I felt for the bars and he was right they did feel like handlebars on a bike. "Don't let go of them."

My hands tightened around the slim bars, clenching. I felt my legs being widened and tensed again. I had no idea the bench could do that so it shocked me. I was spread wide and knew he could see everything while standing over me. I gripped the bars tighter.

"So fucking beautiful. I could tie you up this way but I like knowing you'll stay still for me because it's what I want." His hands moved to my back and caressed over it softly. "Now that I can think, what should I do with you?"

I wasn't giving my opinion because I was still trying to get used to the idea of laying over the strange table.

Oddly enough it was very comfortable. Had I known what he had in mind I might have relaxed more. His hand fell upon my ass and I gasped, not expecting the slight sting. "Don't think I'm upset with you baby, I just like seeing some color on those gorgeous mounds."

Apparently he did because several more fast slaps landed there, leaving me tensing waiting for the next to fall. I waited for his hand to caress like the last time he spanked me but instead his fingers slid between my legs proving how much my body liked this because I was drenched in my own juices.

"I want to try something. Don't move." His fingers slid free and I groaned. I wanted him to try something too, like taking me from behind and stopping this ache that now left me throbbing and craving something to fill me up.

He walked back in front of the table and showed me a device. It had a small phallus and straps and I understood immediately what its use was. "I'm going to turn you on then paddle that gorgeous ass for no other reason than the pleasure it will give me." Lowering his lips to my cheek he dropped a quick kiss there before moving behind me again.

I was all about the strap on toy, but the paddle. It made my butt cheeks clench just thinking about it. Biting my lip to stop from saying no, I decided a little benefit of the doubt was fair since I didn't have to sign the dreaded contract.

A few seconds later I was thinking I'd made a smart choice as the little phallus pulsated over my clit. He made me crave insertion as he teased me mercilessly with it before slowly inching it inside. The straps felt strange but I didn't care as long as the vibrations continued. Before long my toes curled as I felt release on the horizon. Samson immediately turned the vibrations off.

"Oh no, baby. I'm not ready for you to come yet." He chuckled and I felt something cool caress my ass. It didn't take long to figure out what it was as the paddle came down with very little force. It didn't hurt at all and I relaxed knowing I could handle this.

He brought it down a little harder and I gasped. It still wasn't painful but not exactly the most pleasing thing I'd ever felt either. I whimpered at the next downward stroke of the paddle, ready to tell him to stop but he turned the vibrations on again and my mind focused on the pleasure instead.

The paddle fell again and I was caught between the increased force and the clenching of my core against the embedded toy. It was a unique sensation to feel both pain and pleasure and I wasn't sure which one would win. He brought it down with a resounding slap against my ass and I'd almost decided when he turned up the vibration of the vibrator and it hit my g-spot. Fuck that felt incredible making the pain almost non-existent.

My body tensed again, on the edge of orgasm and I cried out loudly. He didn't stop the pleasure instead he brought the paddle down with several hard smacks against my ass cheeks and I still came undone.

"I knew you could handle the pain if you weren't thinking about it." My ass was definitely on fire, but my release left me more breathless than the ache there. I moaned as he slid the tiny phallus out and unstrapped it, leaving me empty. "That was so beautiful baby." He lifted me from the table and cradled me in his arms.

I clung to him not sure how to feel about what he'd done. My cheeks were still stinging and I tried to resolve in my mind that I'd just allowed him to spank me that way. Not only had I allowed it but when the vibrator had been added in, I'd almost craved the stimulation from that paddling.

"You okay?" Samson stroked my hair as he walked over to the couch still holding me like a child.

"I'm not sure I was supposed to like that." The confusion spilled over into my voice as I rested my cheek against his chest.

"My sweet, sweet girl." He chuckled softly. "If I didn't think you'd enjoy it I wouldn't have done it. It's okay to find pleasure in anything I do to you."

His words made me feel better. Rubbing my face against his chest I felt like a kitten longing to be petted. "I want to please you." What did that say about me? I guess what it said was that I could easily get lost in doing whatever he wanted as long as it made him happy. That was a terrifying thought.

"You already do." His hand moved from my hair, down my back and using slow soothing motions gave me the petting I craved at that moment. I felt how hard he was under me and I knew how to show him how much I meant those words.

"Let me taste you?"

"Did I ask you to do that?" His hand moved from my back to my chin, forcing me to look in his eyes. He wasn't upset because he was smiling but I didn't know how to read his question.

"No. I just don't know how else to show you that I want to please you." I nibbled my lower lip not sure if I was explaining things right.

"Don't try to guess what I want baby. It pleases me when you let me control what goes on here." He lowered his lips and kissed me and I tried to understand his words. A few minutes of our tongues dueling together and I didn't care. If he wanted to make the decisions here then I wasn't going to worry about anything else.

"You need a bath and some ibuprofen. I don't want that beautiful ass hurting later on." Lifting me off his lap, I stood and he joined me. My clothes were left in a pile as we walked back upstairs and we didn't stop until we were in his room.

He started the water in the tub, then helped me out of my heels and stockings. "Soak while I go downstairs. I'll be back soon." With a kiss to my forehead he left me standing there alone.

I stepped into the warm water and sat down, shocked at the throbbing pain of my backside. I knew he'd paddled me but until that moment I wasn't aware of how hard. I guess he was right about needing the pleasure to mix with the pain because without it I finally felt the aftermath of what he'd done.

Resting back in the tub, the soft throbbing was annoying. He walked back in the room with a bottle of water and two tiny pills. "Take these." He gave me the pills then held the bottle to my lips so I could drink. When I was finished he put the bottle on the floor beside him and those gorgeous hands bathed me like I was the most precious thing on earth. When his fingers slid between my thighs the last thing I was thinking about was the slight pain.

"Let's get you out of that tub." Reaching under my arms he pulled me up, soaking his pants in the process. He didn't seem to care as he grabbed a towel off a shelf and dried me carefully. "On your knees baby."

I followed his command and lowered down to the cool tile floor. He unbuttoned his pants, slid down the zipper, and pulled them down along with his underwear. "You've got such a gorgeous mouth and I can't wait to fuck it." Grasping his cock, he began stroking it.

I didn't think, since it was now at eye level I reached out to add to his pleasure and he quickly stepped back. Looking up at him in confusion, I noticed the sexy smirk on his face. "Those hands need to be restrained." He kicked off his shoes and the clothes around his ankles then pulled me up to stand. I was led to the bedroom still not understanding why he wouldn't let me touch him.

"I want you on the bed. Scoot that sexy little ass to the edge, and put your hands behind you." Having no idea what he was planning, I did as he asked and watched him open a drawer on the bedside table. He pulled out a pair of metal handcuffs, then moved behind me to enclose my wrists. All I could do was look at him like he'd lost his mind.

I felt my hair being pulled up into two long ponytails and grinned. I hadn't worn my hair this way since I was a child and it just struck me as humorous to be sitting on his bed naked that way. My smile turned into a moan when he parted my legs and stood in front of me, that gorgeous cock only scant inches from my mouth. His hands tangled in my hair, pulling slightly.

"I want that hot little tongue to make me wet, don't take me into your mouth." Without hesitation I licked him from base to tip, and completed the action several times until he was covered in my saliva.

"Such a sweet girl. Now open that mouth." I did as he asked and he fed me a few inches of his cock before sliding out again. "Keep me wet baby." My tongue found him again and then he pushed back into my mouth a few inches again, riding me slowly. He retreated then inched further into my mouth keeping up that rhythm until I was almost taking his full length.

His hands tightened in my hair and he increased his pace, almost gagging me as he pushed in deeper. "Relax your throat." He demanded on a growl and then unleashed his thrusts until I was gasping for air with each retreat. I couldn't believe he was actually doing exactly what he said he wanted, fucking my mouth.

My eyes lifted to his face and I saw the ecstasy written there and decided he could fuck my mouth whenever he chose. It wasn't exactly comfortable for me, but knowing it made him happy made me willing to let him do just about anything. When he suddenly pulled free I wondered why he stopped.

"I'm not coming in your mouth." He flipped me over and my stomach rested on the edge of the bed, my legs finding the floor. My hands were still encased in the handcuffs and rested on my lower back. I felt my legs being spread then stopped thinking as his tongue speared deep into my core. God, that felt amazing!

I was so close to the edge when he stopped tasting me, I groaned in disappointment. I didn't have long to feel that mentality because he filled me with his cock and began riding me with a force that left me gasping for breath. I came so hard I almost saw stars, and still he pounded into my body.

He pulled from my clenching core as my orgasm receded and I couldn't move, only attempt to breathe again. I felt fingers drift through the wetness and then press against my ass. Slowly his finger inched inside, coated by the honey my body was still flooding. Another finger joined and he stretched me deliciously.

"I'm going to fuck this perfect ass, Zoey." His cock nudged against the tight opening and slowly pushed forward. He was so much bigger than Leon that I knew he wouldn't fit. I tensed instantly.

"You can take me baby, just relax. I promise we'll make this work." Make it work? For him maybe, he was going to tear me apart. Still it was Samson. Forcing every thought in my mind away I made my body unclench and felt his large mushroom-shaped head push in.

I gasped at the size of him, not to mention the burning pain as he pushed forward with more strength. His fingers moved around to my clit and rubbed in tiny circular motions. Holy shit that felt good. Groaning for another reason all my attention focused there until his length embedded deeper. Just like he'd done downstairs with the paddle, he used his fingers to focus my mind on the pleasure aspect. My body began spiraling again toward release as his fingers worked their magic and he gave a strong thrust until I felt his groin against my ass.

"That's it baby I'm all the way inside you. I wish you could see the view from here." He gyrated his hips slightly and I felt him filling up my body completely.

Inching out part way he slowly filled me again and I felt the burn, but it wasn't nearly as bad as I thought it would be. Each pull and push slowly opened me up to accept him and before long I felt no pain at all. Then he really rode me.

His hands grasped my hips and held on tight as he fucked me masterfully in a way I'd never imagined I could take him. All I could do was feel as he took control and continued to pump into me with strokes that left me breathless. Then he exploded within me and bathed my walls with his essence. It was the most incredible sensation I'd ever felt!

Slowly pulling from me, he undid the cuffs and led me back to the bathroom. We showered together. I was sore but in a delicious way and reflecting, I wouldn't have changed a thing. We walked back to his bed, and I was smiling.

"I love seeing that smile on your face sweetheart." We slid into bed together and he just held me in his arms. After we recuperated, he made love to me several more times and I was convinced that he was the best lover in the world.

CHAPTER EIGHT

Amber

After an incredible weekend with Samson, I almost regretted having to go to work Monday morning. We kept ourselves entertained in the bedroom, forgoing the dungeon at his request until I felt a little more comfortable there. It was definitely a weekend that would remain in my memories for the rest of my life.

I didn't have time to really think about what we'd shared because my client list was overwhelming today. Miles was joining me before lunch for the interview with the young virgin who wanted a fantasy and she was just one of the concerns piling up on my to-do list for the day.

The only time I could breathe long enough to focus on Samson was during our morning board meeting. His normal temper was cooler than usual and I liked to think it was because I couldn't keep my eyes off his body. He was discussing business, but all I could think about was how wonderful each part of his anatomy was and the feelings he'd brought to life at his house.

"Fuck Zoey, could you get your mind focused for a minute." Leon's words were harsh but he was smiling. That made me embarrassed as hell.

He didn't stay on the subject but launched into the issues dealing with the island which were growing by the day apparently. The contractor was not living up to expectations and new ones were being interviewed for the position so my mind came out of fantasy land for the rest of the meeting.

Keeping things platonic at worked sucked, and I was amazed that it was me that felt that way. Samson had full control and outside of a knowing smile here and there you'd never imagine we spent the weekend enjoying so many different positions I couldn't keep up. Being back in my office helped me concentrate again.

I interviewed the first few clients, and the fantasies were so dark that it forced me to pay attention. One I had to dismiss outright because we did nothing here that wouldn't be considered legal in the bedroom. That ended up causing a disagreement that forced me to pull Leif into the room to calm the client down. Snuff fantasies were a big no-no at Fantasy's and the irate member was told point blank that if he couldn't agree to those terms then he needed to forfeit his membership.

By the time Miles had joined me for the interview I was glad that this fantasy would at least be easier to manage. Amber's soft knock on the door alerted me to who was on the other side. Everything about the young woman was quiet.

"Hey Amber." I led her into the room sensing immediately how nervous she was. Part of my job was to make the client feel comfortable and I offered her coffee, hoping keeping things as normal as possible would help.

She shook her head and gave me an insecure smile and I just wanted to hug her to pieces. She really did look like a little pixie with her short bob haircut and pale blue eyes. The contrast of her dark hair and eyes was just beautiful. Pair that up with porcelain skin and a tiny little frame and again I wondered how she waited so long to experience a lover.

"Okay then well let's get started." I motioned to the desk and the empty chair beside Miles. "This is Miles Dresdon. He wanted to meet with us today so we could go over a few ideas about your fantasy."

Her eyes widened as she sat down beside him and I could tell instantly that she found him attractive. This pleased me deeply. Miles, being the sweetheart he was, gave her that gorgeous smile that made most women swoon and apparently, Amber wasn't immune either. She blushed and the rosy tint to her cheeks made her even more doll-like.

"I'm Amber," she whispered the words looking up at him almost like she was in awe. This meeting was starting out very well, I thought to myself.

"Pleasure to meet you love. I hope you don't mind, but I wanted to fulfill your fantasy personally, unless you object?" He kept his tone soft and non-threatening, which he usually did anyway, and I could see the visibly relaxation in the women's form.

"I think I'd like that." Immediately she pulled her eyes to her lap and I knew she was embarrassed. She'd learn soon enough with Miles that he wouldn't allow that.

As expected, Miles reached down and lifted her chin in his hand. "I'm glad. I really want you to have a memory that pleases you Amber. I can read more in your eyes than I can by looking at the top of your head. Besides you have lovely eyes." He smiled again and I bit back a grin at how lovely she was when she returned the gesture.

"Thank you." Her words were whisper soft but the genuine smile she gave him showed how much it pleased her to be complimented. I wanted to hug her again. People in her life hadn't given her confidence obviously and it made me wonder what type of people she surrounded herself with.

I sat down behind the desk and almost hated breaking up the looks the two of them were giving each other. Miles was the perfect choice for this fantasy. "Why don't you tell Miles a little more about why you've chosen this fantasy?" I truly hoped that he could change her mind because she didn't seem like the type that needed to be forced, maybe given the right persuasion, but not forced.

"I'm not really good with men." She attempted to lower her eyes, but Miles wasn't about to allow that. He lifted her chin again giving her a charming grin. "It's just that I've froze anytime it gets to the point of someone taking off my clothes. I just thought maybe it would be easier if I wasn't given a choice?"

"Talk to me about that. What goes through your mind when it's time to undress?" Miles caressed her cheek with his fingers and the way she leaned into the caress showed she was aching for affection.

"I don't like my body very much. I guess I just think a person would be turned off because I'm, um, not very big up top." Amber fidgeted in her seat, but she kept eye contact with Miles. I was more than pleased that she was willing to try and please him.

"I happen to like a woman with smaller breasts." She gave him a 'yeah-right' look and he chuckled warmly. "I've found that smaller breasts are more sensitive, it makes me want to worship them more."

Her eyes widened again at his words and I could see the hope flitter across her face. Glancing down at his hands she frowned again. "I'm not sure mine are big enough to fill your hands."

I didn't expect miles to reach over and cup her through the thin shirt she was wearing but her soft gasp showed she wasn't against what he was doing.

"I think you fill my hands just right." He winked at her and she blushed, but instead of pulling back, she pressed against his touch. I almost felt like I was intruding as his fingers rubbed over the thin material of her shirt until her nipples were pressing against it. He pinched those peaks forcing a cry from her lips before releasing her. "Nothing wrong with those beautiful breasts sweetheart."

Clearing my throat, I knew I had to get this meeting back on schedule or find the bathroom to please myself. Watching them together was turning me on a little too much. "So outside of not liking to be nude, what other reasons do you feel have stopped you from enjoying a sexual encounter." I was clenching my thighs together to stop the ache that now consumed my mind.

Amber was a little breathless when she focused her attention on me. "I just don't have a clue what I'm doing. By the time a woman reaches my age, I think men expect her to know how to please them. Since I haven't had that experience, I guess I feel awkward?"

"I think you'd be amazed how many men would love to teach a woman how to please them." I know my Samson seemed to get off on it.

"She's right. There's nothing more exciting to me than knowing I'd be the first person to pleasure you. Tutoring you would be almost as much a fantasy for me." The hungry look in Miles's eyes spoke volumes and I admit there was a little jealously knowing how much he wanted this experience.

"Really?" Amber looked shocked that he could want to be her first. "I thought guys liked women with experience?"

He smiled before taking her hand in his and placing it between his legs. "I think you can feel how exciting the prospect is for me."

This interview was turning more into a show and tell and that was definitely a first. I always kept interviews professional but there was little of that happening in this room at the moment. I sat back in my chair not sure how to get it back on the proper level.

"I did that?" Amber's mouth fell open and even a blind person could see how good it made her feel to know she might be responsible for his body's reaction. Men were obviously idiots. This woman was longing to be someone's lover and none of them had figured out how to be the one that had her. Miles was having no problem.

"You did." Covering her hand he encouraged her to massage him and I was amazed as her little hand worked him over, knowing I was still in the room. "I think we'll have an incredible time together. Are you sure you want me to force you?" He chuckled softly, lifting his hand that sound turning into an aching groan as she continued to caress him.

"No. I think with you there be little forcing involved." The sweet smile on her face as she continued to stroke him was really something to behold. Amber had a little vixen in her, she just needed someone to help her bring it out.

His hand rested on hers again, stopping her motions. "Sweetheart if you don't stop that I'm going to have you on your knees and I'm not sure you want to do that with Zoey watching."

I knew Miles was at the edge of his control and it really seemed to make Amber happy knowing she had that ability. Lifting her hand from his crotch, she smiled and blushed again before turning to me. "Sorry."

"Don't be hon. Watching the two of you together is really amazing." I didn't mention that I was so horny now that I had no idea how I'd make it through the rest of the day.

Her blush intensified but she didn't look uncomfortable really, more pleased than anything. "I think we should rethink this fantasy."

"How would you like to change it?" Miles was shifting uncomfortably in his seat and I felt pity for his situation.

"I don't know. I've never gotten past the point of just wanting to have sex." She laughed softly and even her laugh was infectious. Miles was going to really enjoy having her.

"Why don't you take some time and think it over then?" Miles forced a smile, and if I hadn't known him as well as I did, I'd never have guessed it wasn't genuine. He was seriously needy at the moment.

"I don't want to wait." Pouty lips on a pixie doll, something told me that was every man's fantasy and from Mile's groan I was right.

"Neither do I but I want to give you the best experience of your life sweetheart. When we're together I want to make sure that it's an evening you'll never forget. Do this for me. Go home tonight, and think about the perfect setting. Leave all those insecurities out and truly ponder how you want me to love you. Can you do that for me?"

Amber nodded and stood up. "I don't think anything else will be on my mind." Miles stood with her and the noticeable tent in his pants said he still wasn't in control.

"I can't wait to see what you come up with." Lowering his head, he kissed her cheek then walked her to the door. "Just call Zoey when you've decided and we'll put this all together."

Amber was smiling as she walked away and I couldn't stop grinning myself. "I think she was just waiting for someone like you."

"There's a lot of passion in that little lady. I'd admire that but at the moment I'm so hard I feel like I could split bricks." He chuckled self-derisively.

"Um. Yeah I notice that she left you a little turned on." I didn't mean to joke, but there was no way he could walk out of the office without someone noticing how hard he was.

"If you don't have another interview maybe I could hang out here until I have a little control?"

I don't know why I let the next words slip out of my mouth. "I could help you out if you wanted?"

He shut the door. "Zoey don't say shit like that to me right now. You have no idea how easy it would be to fuck you over that desk at the moment and Samson would be livid."

It pissed me off that he thought about Samson first. "Samson's already told me that we'd all be together eventually, so this is about you and me." I walked away, turned my attention from him and back to my computer. I knew we'd agreed to keep things professional in the office but it was my decision, not Samson's.

"So you signed his contract?" Miles walked back over to the desk and sat on the edge, staring into my eyes curiously.

"No. We decided a contract wasn't something I was ready for but we're still a couple." At least I assumed we were after our discussion.

"So no contract. Did he say that you couldn't be with anybody else?" I wasn't sure why but Miles seemed really pleased that I hadn't signed anything.

"We didn't talk about that this weekend. I know that we're not allowed to be with anyone outside of the club. Even if I had signed that contract being with you wouldn't have been against the rules, I'd just have to get his permission." Why I needed it was beyond me, outside of my guys I had no desire to sleep with anyone else.

"That changes things. I won't fuck you without his blessing but we can fool around." Miles waggled his eyebrows and I giggled.

"And what did you have in mind?" Miles being a flirt was such a different persona for him that I admit I was excited about the prospect.

"Well first of all this has to be mutual. I don't want you to walk back in here tomorrow and worry that I'll expect something when we're at work." He was smiling and I couldn't help but return it.

"I'd say we both got turned on with Amber, so it's mutual."

"How turned on?" He lifted his eyebrow again and I shook my head.

"My panties are soaked at the moment." I flushed at the admission but didn't feel I had to hide things with Miles.

He turned back to the door, locked it and then held out his hand. Helping me to my feet, he lifted my skirt until it was bunched around my waist, and his fingers slid under the elastic of my panties. "So it turned you on watching me pet another woman. That pleases me. A lot."

His fingers were sliding over my clit and against the slick flesh of my pussy which pleased me more than a lot. I moaned softly. When two long, thick fingers entered my core I almost lost my balance.

"Hell Zoey, I could get you off like this couldn't I?" He didn't wait for an answer, instead he began riding me with those magical digits until I had to put my hand over my mouth to stop the sounds of pleasure.

He added a third finger and I grasped his shoulders as he fucked me that way. Within seconds I came undone and melted against his hand. He slowly slid out and brought those fingers to his mouth sucking away the juices. "Delicious."

Sitting down in my chair I pulled him over to me by his belt and had his pants and underwear at his feet before he could catch his breath. Taking him deep in my mouth I wrapped my lips around his huge width and pleasured him until he tensed.

"I'm going to come Zoey." He warned me like that wasn't the end result I wanted. I tightened my lips and took almost all of his impressive length in.

His pleasure slid down my throat and I drank in deep gulps, not wanting to miss a single drop. When he pulled from my mouth I grinned at him, pretty satisfied at my new oral skills.

"That was so fucking hot!" Grinning, he pulled up his pants and adjusted his belt. I licked my lips and he groaned. "If I stay here I'm going to want more than your mouth love. You tell Samson we need another night together soon."

I stood up and adjusted my now wrinkled skirt and giggled, seriously giggled! Grabbing a tissue from the box on my desk, I swiped at my face knowing I probably looked like a hot mess now. "I'll do that."

If he needed Samson's permission I'd make sure he had it, but I didn't mind breaking office protocol at all today.

CHAPTER NINE
Ethics

I didn't see Samson until we were ready to leave the office and he didn't seem very pleased to see me then. "I think we need to talk."

I had no idea what he was pissed off about, but after the day I'd had I was in the mood to let off some steam. "Fine. Where do you want to go?"

"My office. Everyone else is leaving so we should have some privacy there." He didn't wait to see if I followed, just walked off with long strides and I knew he was really angry about something.

"Close the door behind you." His voice was commanding as I finally caught up with him and I was starting to get pissed. Closing that door I stood, hands on my hips and glared.

"What the fuck were you thinking Zoey? We agreed to keep anything sexual out of the office and you're giving Miles head?" He looked ready to pounce and it made me even angrier.

"Why are you so damn mad? We both wanted it! " I couldn't wrap my mind around why it was such a big deal because he obviously expected me to sleep with the other men from our discussion.

"I'm mad because this is a place of business and if any of us start seeing it as anything else the clients will be the ones who suffer." He threw up his hands in exasperation and looked at me like I was a stupid child.

When he put it that way I understood, but I still didn't like how high and mighty he was acting. "Fine, I'll keep things professional here." Miles must have told him what went on and I had a few words for him when this was over.

"You have no idea how I want to light that ass up at the moment." He crossed his arms over his chest and I could see the anger in his face.

"Then do it. I'm sorry I pissed you off but we were both horny and just wanted some relief." When I thought about my words I felt bad for saying them. I was becoming as deviant as they were!

"Don't tempt me." Shaking his head he walked out of his office and after a few seconds I ran to join him. He wasn't ending our conversation that way. Hell no. I slid in beside him in the elevator and only Dean being there with us kept my anger at bay.

I followed him out of the club and grabbed his arm on the sidewalk before he could get into the waiting car. "You don't get to throw out words like that and not talk about it!"

"Get in the damn car, Zoey. I'm not about to have a shouting match with you in public." He pulled his arm from my grasp and slid into the backseat. Informing the driver that we were going to his home, he waited until I got in the car, slamming the door before he looked at me again.

"That won't ever happen again." His voice was quieter than it had been in his office but his eyes were filled with steely reserve.

"Fine." I didn't really want to argue with him but I hated his asshole attitude when he delivered ultimatums.

"I'm taking you up on that spanking. Over my lap. Now!"

The controller in me wanted to tell him to go fuck himself, but the woman that still cared awkwardly draped over his lap in the small confines of space. He struggled with my skirt until he had it at my waist and my mouth was open in shock that the driver could see what he was about to do.

I had no time to think about that as his hand landed smartly on my ass several times leaving me squirming to get away from the punishing strokes.

"Be still." He demanded harshly still reigning down terror of my backside until I was ready to scream. His free hand splayed over my back holding me down as he continued to spank me. There was nothing erotic about this at all and at the moment I hated him.

Then it was over and he readjusted my skirt and sat me down on my sore ass beside him. I refused to look at him, instead I stared out the window as he rode. I felt chastised and pissed, the throbbing reminding me with each bump of the car that he hadn't attempted to soothe me after.

"Still want to come home with me?" His voice was now tender and I wanted to slap him for being such an ass to now considerate.

I shrugged, continuing to look out my window. This man confounded the hell out me with his dual personalities. I knew I'd crossed the line today, and maybe I even deserved to be punished, but it didn't mean I had to like him for it.

My eyes filled with tears because I couldn't understand how I could still want this man when he'd treated me like a naughty child. Those tears eventually trailed down my cheeks.

He pulled me into his lap and I struggled, not sure I wanted to like him. "Stop it Zoey." His words were whispered which made me feel like crying even more. I did relax in his lap and allow him to stroke my back.

When we arrived at his house he helped me out of the car and lifted me into his arms after opening the front door. He took me straight up to his bedroom and put me down on the bed. I flinched as my sore ass hit the duvet.

"This is what it means to belong to me Zoey. I'm not going to apologize for who I am." He sat down beside me, not touching.

My tears had dried and I looked up at the man that I knew owned my heart. "I just don't understand why you're so mad that I was with Miles."

"I'm not upset about you pleasing Miles, baby. I'm pissed because you did it on office time. Hell. Fuck him if you want, just make sure to do it somewhere else."

The anger from earlier was completely gone, but I think that confused me more.

I couldn't argue with him about keeping sexuality out of business, but did he really not care if I slept with Miles. "So you don't care who I sleep with?" I knew I'd be pretty pissed if he slept with another woman and didn't that make me a hypocrite?

"I didn't say that. Miles, Leon, Leif? If you want to fuck them then I have no problem with it. I told you what we all wanted."

"What about when they have partners. Will you sleep with them?" Jealously was a green-eyed bitch, and at the moment her name was Zoey.

"Yes, and so will you."

Didn't that just throw shit right into the fire? "I don't do women." It was bad enough thinking about him sleeping with another female, but me? That wasn't something I'd ever been interested in.

"You didn't do four men before we met, baby, you'll learn." The smirk on his face said he was looking forward to it too.

Okay so I hadn't exactly been sexual before them, but a woman? "I don't think I'd like touching another woman that way." I'd just gotten confident enough to enjoy having my own body pleasured.

"I think with the right incentive not only will you like it you'll beg to do it." That smirk was more pronounced and I wondered what devious plan he had in mind.

"So you'll bribe me, huh?" I wasn't even mad anymore about the spanking, even though my ass still throbbed slightly.

"Oh I think I can come up with a few ideas that will make you willing to try anything." He reached over and pushed a strand of hair away from my face tenderly. "Besides remember what Leon said, until you've actually tried it you don't know if you enjoy it."

Until recently I'd hated the thought of anal, so what could I really say? "Maybe." I wasn't giving him a definite agreement, not that he was asking in the first place.

"Why don't you get undressed and let me see if I can get a more pleasing response?" He stood up and began undressing and all earlier thoughts flew from my head. Samson was so damn beautiful naked that I wanted to agree to do anything he asked.

Without hesitation I stood and began losing my clothes. When he had me back in bed, my thighs spread wide, his mouth and fingers driving me insane? Any thoughts of denying him were impossible. He knew my body so well already and we'd only just begun. I couldn't imagine what he'd open my eyes for later on.

Consumed

Fantasy's Bar & Grill – Book 3

Michelle Hughes

Tears of Crimson Publishing

"Sex is one of the most wholesome, beautiful and natural experiences money can buy."
– Steve Martin

CHAPTER ONE
Second Thoughts

The last two months with Samson had been a learning experience. That's the only way I could classify our relationship. I wasn't sure I'd ever come to grips with his dominant side. The more I discovered the less submissive I felt. Don't get me wrong the pleasure was off the charts, but the discipline? I drew a line that I refused to back down from for my own sanity.

To be honest I wasn't even sure that I was the right woman for him. The only thing that made that bearable was Miles. I was spending more and more time with him and our talks sometimes lasted long into the night and it wasn't just about sex with him. I knew this fantasy with Amber was something he truly wanted, and I admit that I had trouble dealing with the jealousy of knowing he wanted another woman.

I knew getting over my possessiveness was the only way we could all have the relationship they wanted.

Miles was taking me out with him and Amber tonight to help me work through that issue. He'd decided before their fantasy took place they'd spend time dating. Believe me I didn't like the idea of them dating much more than the thought of what would happen during their fantasy.

I'd dressed to please Miles tonight, and Samson was in a pissy mood because of it. We'd been having a lot of those nights lately. A huge part of me understood he was unhappy because I refused to relinquish control. I couldn't help it. I just didn't want to be 'owned' by anyone.

The guys had changed my entire perspective on life in the months I'd known them, and I wanted to have the freedom to explore at will. I left Samson sulking, seriously he was sulking, and took a cab to meet up with Miles and Amber. They were deep in conversation by the time I made it to their table in the restaurant. I felt almost like an intruder and that did little to help my mood.

"Would you two rather be alone?" I knew how snarky I was being, but damn it I hated feeling like a third wheel.

"Of course not sweetheart." Miles stood and held out my chair for me. I felt like the bitch I was being at his sweet gesture. Even more so when he ordered my favorite glass of wine and smiled warmly. Fidgeting in my seat, I was more uncomfortable than I'd ever felt before in his presence.

Amber looked beautiful tonight and I had this overwhelming urge to scratch her eyes out. Frustrated.

That's what I was. I returned her smile with a glare and excused myself to the restroom. I should have canceled tonight. After dealing with Samson's sulking, my mood was in the gutter and jealously was not a good companion. Her following me into the bathroom was the last thing that should have happened.

"Are you okay?" The concern in her voice should have made me feel even guiltier, instead I wanted to go Rambo on her ass.

"No, as a matter of fact I'm not." Reeling in my temper, I decided to get the hell out of there before I showed my true colors. "Please tell Miles I'm sorry, but I need to leave." I shook my head and began walking toward the door.

"Maybe you need to talk about what's bothering you? I'm a good listener."

"You wouldn't understand." Scoffing I allowed my eyes to roam over her perfect little body. The guys would have a field day with her if Miles decided to keep her. That just pissed me off even more. I wanted to push her away and my mouth just overloaded my ass. "Maybe we'll talk after Miles and the guys initiate you into their games."

Her pale blue eyes widened, and I felt like shit for taking out my jealousy issues on her. This woman hadn't done anything to me, and she just happened to be the sounding board for my bad mood. "I'm sorry." Walking past her I left the bathroom, stopped by the table to pick up my purse, and refused to look at Miles as I exited the restaurant. My feet made it to the sidewalk before he caught up, lightly grasping my arm as I hailed down a cab.

"Zoey, what's going on here? I hate seeing you so unhappy." The tenderness in his voice made me want to cry which in turn made me angry.

"Go take care of your date. I'm just tired of all this." Pulling my arm from his grasp I almost sighed in relief when the taxi pulled up. Sliding inside I didn't spare him a look as I drove away.

Tears streamed down my cheeks as I rode back home and I knew something had to give. I swiped at my cheeks, angry at the emotion, and wished for the first time I'd never met any of the guys. Arriving back at my apartment, I was a complete mess when I walked through the door.

Rachel was sitting on the couch with her friend Brandy, and it looked like they were having a girl's night in from the stash of snacks on the table and casual wear. Her eyes lifted as I walked into the room, her smile fading as she saw my expression. "You okay?"

Putting down my purse, I walked over and sat down on the oversized couch with them. "I hope you have more of this." Picking up the half-eaten bowl of popcorn I began munching, ignoring her question.

"I'll go make some more." Brandy stood up and walked into the kitchen giving me and my best friend a little space.

"Spill it baby girl. You look like you've been crying. Whose ass am I kicking?" Rachel took the bowl, sat it on the table, and gave me the best friend stare, the one that said she expected answers and not to offer any bullshit.

I couldn't keep it inside any longer. "What the hell was I thinking? I can't have an affair with four men!" Picking up the bottle of wine they had opened, I took a swig of it without any thought of manners.

"I'm surprised it took you this long to fold." Rachel grabbed the bottle and took a long drink while shaking her head. "Don't get me wrong, they are all fine as shit, but holy hell girl, even I couldn't sleep with them together."

That was saying a lot because Rachel had never been shy about her sexual encounters. "It was only the one time but I know they want a relationship that centers around all of us together. Fuck! I can barely deal with Samson's mood swings lately."

"I worried that might happen. He doesn't deal well without being in control." She handed me back the wine and I drank again.

She knew everything. I'm sure Rachel was tired of hearing me bitch about what an asshole he'd been lately. On a good day Samson could be a control freak, but deny him what he wanted? It was like walking on egg shells his moods had become so volatile. "He wants some sweet little submissive that will yes Sir him to death, that's just not me."

"You and submissive don't even belong in the same sentence together." Rachel laughed and the dark cloud that had been hovering over me for the last month seemed to dissipate.

"I know, right?" Joining in her laughter, I managed to smile as Brandy joined us on the couch with fresh popcorn.

"So you're sleeping with all four of them?" Her beautiful brown eyes almost popped out of her head as she followed along with our conversation.

"That's not public knowledge." I warned without malice and gave a half-hearted grin. "But we have a relationship. I'm not sure you can even call it that though." Rolling my eyes, I took another gulp of wine.

Brandy was filling in for one of our waitresses while she was out on medical leave, and I really liked her attitude. She was very outspoken but did it in a way that was respectful. Basically she said what was on her mind with a matter of fact attitude. She and Rachel had been friends for the last few years and I'd gotten to know her pretty well.

"If you're not happy, then call things off. I know it's none of my business, but life is too short to fill it up with things that make you second guess your needs." She took the bottle from me and winked before taking a drink.

"She's right you know. The way you've been acting the last few weeks doesn't show a person who's getting what she needs from a relationship." Rachel pulled her feet up under her on the couch and smiled at me sadly.

"Don't get me wrong, the sex is great, but it's all the other stuff. Maybe putting an end to this is the right thing to do." I was still so confused. I hadn't had the foursome with the guys since that one night, but I'd enjoyed each of them separately. I felt guilty for finding pleasure with anyone but Samson after the way he'd been acting lately.

"Well you've made up for lost time, that's for sure." Rachel grinned and I knew exactly what she was talking about. Before the guys I'd only had one lover and he'd sucked beyond belief.

"Lost time?" Brandy looked at both of us in confusion and I couldn't help but laugh.

"My only lover before the guys was a one night stand who made me hate sex." That definitely wasn't the case any longer. I loved the sex, just hated the insane relationship that came with it. To be honest, it wasn't even the relationship but the way Samson wanted to control me that was driving me nuts, and my new jealousy issues with Amber.

"Shit girl, how in the hell did you go from that to sleeping with four men?" Shaking her head, Brandy got comfortable on the couch.

"Just lucky I guess." I made a joke out of it, because I honestly wasn't sure what I was thinking when I decided to follow through. Thinking wasn't really a part of the plan after our island getaway. I enjoyed feeling desire for the first time in my life and got lost in the sensations.

"I know exactly how it happened. I mean you know the club owners. There's not one of them that a girl wouldn't drop her panties for if they asked. But all together? Hell that's like any woman's fantasy come to life. Maybe that's what it should have been though, just one night. Making four men happy is pretty much impossible." Rachel looked at me, almost seeming to contemplate.

"And they say women are hard to please." I didn't know where this thing with us was going or even if it should be going at all. The idea of walking away from them made my heart ache though.

"I've only worked for them a short time and I couldn't imagine trying to have a relationship. Samson and Leon especially, those guys are like drill sergeants." Brandy cringed and it made me feel a little better. Maybe I was asking too much of myself.

"You've just got to decide what makes you happy." Rachel shrugged. "Why don't we just enjoy some girl time tonight and forget about things."

I nodded and the subject was dropped. The truth was no one could make this decision but myself and I wasn't in a place right now that was ready to make that kind of choice. We stayed up watching sappy movies and snacking and ignored the ringing of my cell phone. I wanted to be normal for a change and tomorrow I could deal with the serious life choices.

CHAPTER TWO

Decisions

I awoke in my own bed Saturday morning which was a first since meeting the guys. Usually I stayed over with Samson, but I'd had nights at Miles's and yes, even Leon's and Leif's. It was almost refreshing waking up at home. Taking a quick shower, I dressed in shorts and a tank top and traipsed into my kitchen putting together a small fruit salad.

There's something to be said about being at your own place. No matter how much someone tells you to make yourself at home, I'm not sure you ever really do. I tried to keep quiet since Brandy had passed out on our couch last night, but still I was in my place.

After eating I went through my messages and scoffed. Not only had Miles left me a dozen texts, he'd apparently told the other guys I wasn't in a great mood

because I had several from them as well. I knew they all
cared about me and it wasn't fair to not let them know
what was going on in my mind. Making a quick decision,
I sent them all a text asking them to meet me at
Samson's for lunch.

They'd all replied within minutes, agreeing. I had to
make a decision before I arrived there today. Since I
hadn't spent a full night at home in months I decided to
catch up on clothes and do some serious soul searching.
Something about cleaning always helped clear my mind.

Three hours later I'd put away all the clothes and got
dressed for a confrontation. I dressed in office wear, a
pair of dress slacks and silk shirt, with a lightweight
blazer. This wasn't about turning them on, and I wanted
to go about this professionally. Was that even possible?
Could I talk about our sexual relationship in a
businesslike manner? I was about to find out.

Rachel and Brandy had left half an hour ago to go
shopping and I wished she was still here so I could
bounce ideas. Seriously, I had no idea how to go through
with this. Driving over to Samson's made the tension
even worse and by the time I walked up to his door I was
nothing but a pile of nerves.

Samson opened the door looking too damn sexy for
what I had in mind and I bit my lips to stop the groan
that threatened to escape. That man could sure fill out
a pair of khaki shorts and a t-shirt. He held the door
open for me and as I walked past, his cologne filled my
senses making me wonder why I was about to ruin
everything.

Closing the door behind him, he walked into the living room where the other men were seated. Surrounded by all this delicious eye candy, I could almost forget why I'd come here and just give in to being surrounded by such delicious men. I gave a tentative smile at the looks of concern being thrown my way.

"What's going on Zoey?" The tick in Samson's jaw gave me a quick trip back into reality. He was obviously pissed and I was tired of that being the response I got from him lately. Everything was a freaking argument!

"I don't want to do this anymore." The words just leaked out. No mouth filter whatsoever. All it took was his caveman stare to make me decide that no matter how beautiful the package, it wasn't worth dealing with the animosity.

"Do what? Me, your job, all of us. You need to be a little more specific." Oh hell yes he was in asshole dom mood and it was yanking my chains in the worst way possible right now.

"First of all you can drop the dick attitude. I didn't come here to fight and I'm pretty fucking sick of feeling like nothing I do with you is right." Just saying the words pulled the anger out of me and left me depressed. "I can't do us anymore Samson. You obviously want something different than what I'm prepared to offer." Hanging my head in defeat, I hated that he had the ability to make me feel this way.

"Shit baby." He walked over and pulled me into his arms and held me so tight I could barely catch my breath. "I didn't mean to make you feel that way."

I wanted to believe him, honestly I did. But I knew he was just who he was and if I didn't become his little perfect submissive things wouldn't change. I felt tears cascade down my cheeks and wanted to kick myself in the ass for being such a weak bitch.

"I knew this would happen." Miles stood up, walked over and pulled me out of his arms. Wrapping me in his I clung to him, trying to get my emotions back under control. "I love you like a brother Samson, but I told you she wasn't a submissive."

"Let's not go laying blame right now." Leon warned in his best 'don't fuck with me voice'. "It's apparent Zoey's not happy so instead of getting stupid, we need to figure out how to fix that."

"Give her to me." Miles said, caressing my hair like I was a child. The sweetness of his touch didn't cross out the fact that he'd just basically said I was a piece of property to be handed around at will.

Pulling out of his embrace, I swiped at the dampness on my cheeks. "I'm not anyone's to give." I stated angrily. Glaring at him, then at the other men I wanted to make damn sure they got my point.

"That's not what I meant sweetheart." Miles was backtracking and from the expression on his face I could tell he regretted his words.

"Maybe you should explain what you did mean then Miles. This is such a cluster-fuck. Why do I have to belong to any of you?"

"I explained to you what we were looking for baby." Samson was running his hand through his thick hair in exasperation. Hell I was exasperated too.

"I know that you want all of us to have a relationship but why does it have to be exclusive with me belonging with one of you." I'd never understood that mindset. "I love being with you Samson, when you're not being a total jerk, but if I'm sleeping with the other guys too how can I truly belong to you?"

"Because you're mine and I can choose when to share you, or at least that's how this was supposed to work." He looked so utterly defeated that for a brief moment I felt sorry for him. "At least if you'd completely submitted to me that's the way it would have worked."

"It's just semantics then. Either I belong to you or I don't but sharing me means you don't get to control who I sleep with because you've already taken that option of exclusivity away."

"If you were a true submissive you'd understand that it doesn't really work that way in our relationships." Shaking his head, Samson sat down on the couch.

I shrugged and sighed deeply. "Then I guess I don't want to be a 'true' submissive because that line of thinking doesn't work for me." And that was the problem. He wanted a person to share that type of relationship with him. I was not that woman.

"So you're breaking up with me." He lifted his eyes to mine and the hurt that filled that beautiful gaze tore at my heart. Granted the terms he used reminded me of something people said in high school, but I knew what he meant.

"I guess so." I felt like shit after saying those words, but also a bit relieved. There was no doubt in my mind that I couldn't be the type of woman he needed after this conversation.

"What about us, Zoey." Miles, my tender-hearted hero. How could I look into those compassionate eyes and just walk away. My heart was seriously going to break here.

"I don't know what else to do here. You know I love being with each of you and hell, even all of us together, but I can't pretend to be something I'm not." I sat down in the oversized chair facing the couch and slumped.

"We love you too Zoey." Leif stood up and walked over to my chair, kneeling down he rested his head in my lap. Instinctively I reached down to caress his hair. I couldn't imagine a life without all of them in it.

"You could agree to be mine." Miles knelt beside Leif, and lifted my free hand, his fingers rubbing softly over the top.

"What about Amber?" I knew how much he wanted to give her that fantasy, but it was more than that. Over the last few months they'd become really close friends.

"I'm not going to lie to you. I really like Amber. She's a sweet girl and I am going to live through the fantasy with her, but long term? I honestly think she's looking for a more dominant male."

I found it ironic that judging from his words Amber would be a better match for Samson than I was. "I didn't get that vibe from her." Lifting my confused gaze I studied his face.

"She's nothing like you, and I don't mean that in a bad way. Amber craves someone that will tell her what she's supposed to feel and lead her in the direction that will help her fulfill her needs. I'm not that person. For me I want a strong woman who's already confident in what she needs in life. That's why I was so upset when I knew you were considering signing Samson's contract. I wanted you to be mine."

"Apparently you were right and I was wrong." Samson's attitude while less pissy than usual was still shining through. "Maybe Miles is the perfect partner for you."

If he didn't look so dejected at the possibility I might have been angry. Instead I wondered if he was right. I'm not sure that said anything good about myself, but I was seriously considering the option. Miles made me feel cherished and seemed to really care about what I needed versus what he wanted. That was one of the things I truly loved about him. "I'm not sure I'll ever be comfortable with sharing."

"I thought you enjoyed being with all of us." Leif lifted his head from my lap and gave me a pitiful little look.

It was so comical that I had to laugh. "I do love sleeping with all of you, it's the thought of sharing you with another woman." I knew it was petty, and considering the relationship we had pretty stupid, but I couldn't lie about how I felt.

"So you're having trouble dealing with the fact that Miles wants to bring another woman into our relationship." Leon grinned and gave me a look that said it all. "Baby girl it's not fair for us to all share you and you get your pride pricked at the thought of us asking you to share another woman."

"I know it's not fair, and I'm willing to try and suck it up." My mouth lifted in a smirk. Leon always knew how to call me out. "Never said I was perfect."

Leon chuckled loudly at my comment. "I think you'll enjoy this if you stop over thinking things. I agree that you and Miles make more sense. If this Amber is a true submissive maybe she and Samson will be a better fit."

"I'm still acting out her fantasy." Miles glared at Leon and I couldn't help but joining in the laughter.

"Virgins aren't my thing." Samson sneered. "Get a little experience under her belt and then introduce us."

I probably should have been hurt that he was so ready to cast me aside, but the truth was I knew we would never work as a couple. Still it made some of my insecurities rear their heads. "Glad to know I'm so replaceable." I did manage to smile as I said it.

"Damn it Zoey, I'd love nothing more than to tell you to get your head out of your ass and make this work with me, but that's not what you want. If you were my submissive I'd beat that stubbornness out of you!" He glared at me, actually glared, before standing up and walking over to the bar and pouring himself a drink."

"Then it's a good thing I'm not because I might just beat the shit out of you in response." Crossing my arms over my chest I wanted to take one of his beloved crops to his ass at the moment.

Leon tossed back his head and bellowed so loudly it nearly hurt my ears. "Yeah I think it's safe to say our Zoey is more dominant than submissive."

I couldn't help it I laughed too. "I wouldn't say dominant but I don't like the idea of anyone trying to control me." I shrugged and decided if I was going to be honest, it needed to be all of the truth, not just what I thought they needed to hear.

"I can't believe I was so damn wrong!" Samson eyes had widened and he was shaking his head.

"You can't always be as perfect as me." Leif, in his egotistically fashion, chimed in with a soft chuckle.

"Yeah babe, you're perfect as long as you're under me." Leon winked at him and I almost fell out of my chair. These two were meant for each other.

"I prefer having someone between us." Holy crap was Leif sulking? They way Leon looked at him when he said those words showed he wasn't pleased.

"There's nothing wrong with how we make love." Leon barked out those words and I felt like cringing myself, Leif stood up and glared at him with such anger I thought they were going to come to blows.

"Don't go getting all possessive on me! I've explained that I need the female love too and if you want this to work, you're going to have to pull your head out of your ass and accept it." This was a side of Leif I'd never seen, and it appeared that Leon was taken back too.

"We have our Zoey, and if Samson decides to take the other woman then I don't see why we need to add another female into our permanent mix." Leon was sulking? The world was going to explode at any moment. This was definitely a day for firsts.

"You bitch at Zoey for not wanting to share with another female, and here you are pulling the same damn shit. I'm not backing down on this one Leon. I love your ass but you will not be walking over my needs just to make yourself happy. I need this in our relationship!" Leif was shouting now and all I could do was stand there with my mouth hanging open.

"Apparently we've all got some issues to work through." Samson chuckled softly and it broke some of the tension in the room.

"We can discuss things like friends that love each other, instead of Neanderthals." Miles rolled his eyes and gave a look to the guys that made me grin. It was pretty obvious that he didn't enjoy confrontations.

"Miles's is right." Leon sat back down on the couch and looked to be deep in thought. Leif and Samson joined him, and tempers cooled down rampantly.

"You find the woman and I'll deal with my possessiveness issues." Leon gave in easier than I thought he would and the relief on Leif's face was exactly how I felt after I ended things with Samson.

It was crazy how things had changed in one meeting, but I couldn't help but think all of us were going to be happier knowing we'd explained what we wanted in this relationship. I was almost convinced this could work out still. I just had one concern.

"So you're doing the fantasy with Amber tomorrow night?" I couldn't believe that much time had already passed.

"That's one of the reasons I asked you out last night. She wanted you to be in the room with us." Miles was looking at me searchingly, obviously trying to get a read on my thoughts.

"Why would she want that?" If I was making love for the first time, and with Miles it would be nothing less, I definitely wouldn't want someone observing.

"Apparently it was a huge turn on when we interviewed her that you were in the room. She said it made her feel safer too." Miles chuckled softly at that, and I could only presume it was because he had no intention of doing anything that made her uncomfortable.

"I'm not sure I'm the best person to be in that situation with you. I'll be honest, watching you together may make me want to kick her ass." I knew I had jealousy issues.

"To be honest sweetheart, it's the reason I agreed to talk that over with you. Yes, I want this fantasy and the thought of being a woman's first turns me on a great deal, but I truly love you Zoey. I wish I had been your first, but since I wasn't this is something we can share together." The compassion in his eyes proved his sincerity and I couldn't turn him down. Honestly, I really didn't want to.

"How much a part of this fantasy do you want me to be though, Miles? I can watch, that I'll give to you, but as far as anything else, I'm just not ready for that yet." Being honest with him was easy. There would never be any pressure.

"Then there won't be anything else. Just be in the room with us. If it gets to awkward, you can leave. All I ask is that if you need to do that, keep it inconspicuous. I know a woman's first time is overwhelming so I don't want to break a mood after we begin."

I nodded at him. The way he was going about this made me a little more secure. To me, it felt like he was just talking about a business transaction, and that I could deal with. Of course seeing his hands on another woman might change my mindset, but I was willing to try. "Then count me in."

"I don't know about the rest of you, but I've had about as much seriousness as I can deal with on a weekend. What's say we get some lunch and just enjoy each other's company for a little while?" This was from Samson and I was amazed at how laid back his attitude was after everything that transpired here today.

We all agreed. The tension level was down, and all of us wore some form of relief in our expressions. This talk had done a world of good for all of us. Leon suggested we visit our favorite restaurant and everyone fell into agreement. Just like that the trials of our new relationship were fading away, and we went about our lives.

CHAPTER THREE

Amber

Tonight was the night that I discovered if I could put my jealously in the past and I wasn't sure of the outcome. Rachel and I had talked about this all afternoon, and she was the only reason I wasn't a big jumble of nerves at the moment. I had about twenty minutes before I needed to leave and she was still hanging out in my bathroom as I finished up.

"At least you know that the first time really sucks and she probably won't enjoy it much." Rachel's grin was devious and I had to laugh.

"You're such a bitch." I said the word fondly and shook my head trying not to wish that on Amber. "Knowing Miles he'll make it absolutely perfect." And he would do his best, he never did anything half-assed.

"From what you told me about his package, the man needs to have his own warning label." That definitely made me almost smear the lipstick across my face that I was putting on, I laughed so hard.

"I sure as hell wouldn't have wanted him for my first, that's for sure." I shivered remembering how well he stretched me.

"See this is going to be easier than you thought." Smirking, Rachel pulled her hair up into a ponytail as she stared back into my reflection in the mirror.

Outside of the jealousy I felt for Amber sleeping with Miles, I really did like her. Maybe I was being petty about this insecurity I had? "I really don't want him to hurt her, Rach." I'd been caught up in my own thoughts and hadn't stopped to consider how she'd be feeling tonight after sleeping with Miles.

"I know you don't honey, I was just trying to make you feel better." She lowered her chin to my shoulder and peered into my eyes through the mirror. "I'm sure he'll make this as good as he can for her."

"Well hopefully not that good." Yes I was being bitchy, but I really didn't mean it. The last thing I wanted was for Amber to walk away from this experience with a jilted view of sex. I'd done that before and it wasn't fun.

"On a positive note, he'll be raring to go after he completes this fantasy, because he'll have to treat her like something fragile." Rachel was right, knowing Miles the way I did, he would take every precaution with Amber tonight.

I giggled at that thought. "Yeah we can swing from the rafters or something when he's done." Now that I could envision with humor. "I guess I should get my ass in gear. The sooner this shit is over, the faster I can have him to myself."

"Now that's the power of positive thinking!" She lifted her chin from my shoulder and glanced over my appearance. "You look incredible tonight by the way, I'm so borrowing that dress."

I'd picked up the little red dress as a mood enhancer after lunch with the guys yesterday, and even I had to admit it looked great. It had a baby doll feel to it, clenched under my breasts before falling about mid-thigh. Paired with a pair of two inch heels, even with my short stature, I had nice looking legs in this outfit.

"I just wanted to wear something to make him remember who he loves." Grinning widely, I walked out of the bathroom with Rachel following, and found my purse. "Wish me luck." I didn't need it because after our talk today I felt like this was something I could do without having a bitch fit.

"I'll wish him luck instead. You'll do great babe, and I want to hear all the dirty details of how your night ended when he's done with her."

I kissed her cheek, nodded, and walked downstairs to where the car was waiting. I had to look at this as just a fantasy for Amber or I'd never make it through the night. Thanks to Rachel, I felt like I could do just that. It was just sex after all, he wasn't making a long-term commitment with the woman. My confidence level shot up a few points when I reminded myself of that and I made the drive to his home feeling pretty secure in my own skin.

That confidence stayed with me as I finally arrived at the CitySpire building. Miles owned a penthouse that overlooked Central Park and was one of the most impressive properties I'd ever been inside. The doorman smiled as I walked up, and I returned it. The older man was a real charmer, and I bet he'd seen his share of action back in the day.

He held the door and I walked down the long hall to the elevator. When I finally reached the top floor, I quickly made my way to Miles's door. He answered himself so I assumed he gave his servant the night off. Being embraced in his arms gave me even more confidence, and I returned it quickly.

"Amber's in the restroom, a little attack of nerves I think." He looked worried, and my thoughts about what I was going to deal with suddenly disappeared at his concern. I knew this was something he wanted, and I hoped she wasn't having second thoughts. I know, that was very generous of me.

"Should I go talk to her?" Seeing this gorgeous man with that frown on his face was not making me happy.

"I know it's asking a lot but would you? No idea what goes on in a woman's mind before something like this." I gave a subtle nod, and walked back to talk to her. I could only imagine what she was feeling right now and that made me have a little pity.

Knocking on the door, I waited for what seemed like forever before she answered. It didn't take long to figure out that she was terrified. Any thoughts of animosity I had against this woman evaporated. I pulled her into a tight hug. "Everything will be fine." Hell, she was shaking like a leaf and it was hard not to have a little human compassion.

"What if it's not? I mean I obviously suck at this or I wouldn't be paying for someone to do the deed. Maybe this was just a stupid idea." She was clinging to me and my heart seriously just bled for her.

"You don't suck at anything hon, you just haven't experienced it yet. Miles doesn't expect you to do anything except enjoy yourself. So don't worry about it. All you have to do here tonight is let him take the lead." I pulled back so I could read her face and smiled warmly. "Besides I'll be here with you and I promise that nothing that you don't want to happen will even be thought of."

"You probably think I'm the stupidest person in the world right now." She glanced down and I could see that she had no self-confidence whatsoever. I'd been so jealous over her pixie-doll looks that I'd overlooked how completely insecure she was. Yes I felt like shit at the moment.

"No I don't Amber. What I see is a beautiful woman that has never been shown how incredible she is. Seriously, I'm so jealous when I look at you." Her eyes widened at I grinned.

"That's crazy. Come on Zoey, you're freaking perfect. I'd give anything to have your confidence, not to mention your boobs." She blushed deeply. "I mean at least you're not stuck with these tiny things."

"Would you stop doing that to yourself? You're perfect just the way you are. Hell I know guys that would foam at the mouth to sleep with a living doll. That's what you remind me of, a perfect little china doll." I hugged her again and then stood back. She did too. Her sweet little body was a little under five feet tall. Amber's hair was jet black and cut in a little bob that just reached her chin, and her eyes were this amazing pale blue that seemed to be almost too perfect to be real.

I was shocked to find myself wishing I could kiss her. That was definitely a first. "We need to get you out to Miles, before I do something that makes you uncomfortable." Leon was right, I didn't know what it felt like to be with a woman until I tried it, well now I was curious.

"Like what?" Her words were whispered but those pale blue orbs were filled with curiosity.

I probably shouldn't add more to this night than she was already going to deal with, but I couldn't stop myself. "Maybe like this." I lowered my lips to hers, kissing her tenderly. Her soft gasp, then the feel of that tongue darting into my mouth was all it took to change my opinion completely about having another woman in our relationship.

I pulled back first, shocked that I'd done that. From the surprise in her eyes, she was a little shocked herself. "See, even I can't resist you." Giving her a grin, I backed up, knowing I needed to put some space between us before I decided to venture into the sensations a little more. Kissing a woman was not the horrible experience I'd thought it'd be. The smile that broke out over her angelic face did something to my heart.

"Thank you." Her fingers reached up to her lips and her smile never faded. "I think I can do this now."

She was thanking me and all I wanted to do was kiss her again. Pulling my head out of my own fantasies, I winked at her. "Let's go to Miles before he worries you've run away." Grasping her hand in mine, I walked her back into the living room where Miles was standing with a concerned look.

"Everything okay?" Bless his heart, he was really worried that Amber was going to change her mind. I could see it from the tension in his body and in his eyes.

I turned to Amber and was pleased to see she was still smiling. "I think we're good to go here. She just needed a little girl talk." I winked at Amber and was pleased at the soft blush that found her porcelain cheeks.

Miles walked over and took her hands in his smiling down into her sweet face. "All you have to do is trust me tonight sweetheart. We're going to have a beautiful evening and I promise it will be an experience you'll never forget. Can you do that for me?" He kept his tone soft and cajoling, bringing out all the compassion that he was known for.

She nodded her head softly and the smile he gave her warmed my heart. Amber had no idea how lucky she was to have Miles initiating her into lovemaking. There was not another man that I would want to be a woman's first. I was the observer here tonight, and I planned on being as much in the background as I could.

Miles and I had discussed what would happen on this night for months. Certain things had been altered after he'd gotten to know her better, like me being present, but I knew from his plans that she wouldn't be able to ask for a better fantasy.

I was going to sit in a chair that was at the back of the room. Miles's bedroom was huge so there definitely wasn't any worry of feeling crowded. Our conversation this morning on the phone had put everything into perspective. I know it sounds petty, but I secretly wished now I was joining in their little fantasy.

I knew his focus would be completely on her the moment we reached the bedroom, so I walked in behind them and sat down in the oversized chair. I'd never watched anyone make love except Leif and Leon, so this heterosexual experience was going to be an experience for me as well.

Miles had the lights in the room dim, and I knew it was to make Amber feel more comfortable. He stopped at the side of the bed and gave her a look so tender that it melted my heart. "Trust, sweetheart, I'm going to love you completely and I want you to do nothing but feel for me. Okay?"

She nodded slightly, and I could only guess that it was hard for her to talk. I watched as Miles unbuttoned his shirt then slid it from his shoulders, giving her a chance to study his beautiful form. The wide width tapered down to muscled arms, and a smooth chest that was surprisingly tanned. Most redheads didn't tan well, but Miles was the exception.

Amber's eyes roamed shyly over his body and I could tell from the look on her face that she was pleased at what she saw. How could she not be, he was perfect. I was a little surprised when her dainty hand reached out to rest on his chest, then removed it quickly like she was afraid to touch him.

He quickly grasped her hand before it could fall to her side and placed it back. "I want to feel those beautiful hands on me sweetheart. Don't be afraid. I promise you won't break me." He laughed softly and her answering blush was just precious.

Experimenting, she allowed her hand to trace across the expanse of his chest and then brazenly followed the trail of hair that led from his navel down to the buckle of his belt. Miles's quick intake of breath showed that he enjoyed that a lot.

"I think to be fair, we should get you out of this shirt." With a tender smile, he moved down to the hem of her silk top and then met her eyes, waiting for approval. When she nodded he slowly lifted it over her head, leaving her top half bared except for the small lacy, white, bra she was wearing.

I could see her tense as his fingers moved behind her to unclasp the flimsy garment. He gave her little time to be concerned as he unsnapped, slid it from her shoulders and let it pile on the floor. His hands immediately cupped her small breasts and his fingers rolled over her nipples. "These are so beautiful sweetheart. I want to taste them."

Lowering his head, he followed through his words with actions and his mouth suckled in one gorgeous peak. Ambers head fell back with a moan at the sensation and I crossed my legs almost sharing in the moment with her. Miles knew how to use that mouth well and it was no surprise that she cried out as he bit down on the tender flesh lightly. It felt so wonderful to be worshipped that way.

Her small hands tangled in his thick red hair as he moved to the other breast, and held him tightly against her chest. He released her nipple with a popping sound and I watched as the ecstasy crossed her face.

"Sit down on the bed for me." When she complied he lifted one of her feet, and slid off the heel. Slowly he inched that leg to the floor and picked up the other, doing the same thing before lowering it as well. Spreading her legs he knelt down between them and cupped her breasts again.

"They are beautiful sweetheart. And just like I knew they'd be, so very sensitive." He pinched one of the coral-colored nipples between his fingers and grinned as she gasped at the pleasure. His hands dropped from her breasts, and rested on her thighs. Inching up her skirt he smiled at the discovery that she was wearing thigh-high stockings.

"We can leave these on for now." With slow movements he inched up her skirt until it rested around her waist, giving him a perfect view of the small little scrap of lace that covered her core. "I wonder if the rest of you is as sensitive." One long fingered hand trailed up between her legs and traced over the covered slit.

Rubbing softly, he smiled. "I like that a lot sweetheart, you're already wet for me."

She blushed and looked down, but Miles wasn't having any of that. His free hand lifted her chin. "I want you wet for me, and I plan to make you even wetter."

"How?" Amber was leaning into his caress and I grinned at the innocent question. Knowing how wonderful his fingers felt personally, I could imagine she was already drenched with passion. Again I clenched my thighs together, aching.

"Well sweetheart, I could keep doing this." I watched as his fingers pushed harder against the silk of her panties. "Or." His words trailed off and he lowered his head between her legs, pushed the elastic to one side and gave one long swipe of his tongue to her glistening pink flesh.

"Oh God!" Amber's hips bucked off the bed at the first contact and her body fell back. I knew Miles had intended just that, breaking her into oral without giving her a chance to deny it.

Miles feasted on her flesh until she was bucking her hips upward to meet each swipe of his tongue. There was something so erotically beautiful about watching the pleasure on her face, seeing her neck arched back in ecstasy, as her body succumbed to the release of his wicked lovemaking skills. My own core throbbed with need at the soft mewls of pleasure escaping Amber's lips.

The whisper soft sound turned into a scream of fulfillment as Miles drove her over the edge. My fingers slid underneath the waistband of my skirt, then drifted down to my throbbing clit, for some much needed relief. He lifted his head, that gorgeous face glimmering with her passion and for a moment our eyes met. That magical tongue licked his lips before turning back to the woman he'd unraveled.

Giving Amber no time to come down from her high, he lifted her hips and managed to slide her panties off before she had even caught her breath. "Your sweet little pussy tasted delicious I can't wait to feel myself embedded inside that tight paradise."

She took in a deep breath at his dirty bedroom talk and held it, still seeming to be in shock at what they'd just done. His hand moved between her thighs and I watched as he slowly introduced one long digit, forcing her breath to escape as he rode her slowly. I mimicked the action of his finger with my own, so close to finding some relief at the delicious torment of watching him love her.

He added another finger, stretching what I knew was her tight virginal entrance, and I followed along again. It was like living through this fantasy with him as I became part of the game. The rhythm was so slow that I almost cried out wishing he'd fuck her with those beautiful fingers so I could unleash my need to be penetrated. He continued the sensual torture though, and I forced myself to keep his pace.

Her hips were raised slightly off the bed again and I knew it was because he was holding her right on the edge again. When he slid free, and stood up Amber's soft cry of disappointment had me biting my lips to stop my own since I slid my own away to mimic him.

Miles kicked off his shoes, then his hands slowly moved to the buckle on his belts. He was giving her time to prepare, but I just wanted him to rip that thing off and take her savagely. With practiced ease he unbuckled, then slid the leather from his pants, and then with tormenting nonchalance, undid his pants. By the time he finally stepped out of them I frantic with the need to come.

Amber rested on her elbows watching him with wide eyes and I could read every emotion there. Desire, fear, but most of all curiosity. There's something really exciting about seeing your lovers cock for the first time. You wonder if it will be everything you'd hoped for or maybe fearful that you'll feel disappointment. As he inched his briefs down and that gorgeous appendage stood large and proud, I knew how overwhelmed she felt. If it came to a cock of the year award, it would certainly go to Miles.

Amber wasn't as impressed since she sat up in the bed, staring at him like he was out of his fucking mind. "This is so not going to work." Her eyes were glued to his anatomy, her mouth opening to say more but nothing would come out.

"We'll work beautifully together sweetheart." He chuckled softly and moved back to sit on the bed. Amber wasn't buying it because she crossed her arms over her breasts, as if finally remembering she was sitting there nude.

"You're hung like a horse, there's no way it's fitting and I want to walk tomorrow." Shaking her head, she lowered her eyes, and I could feel the disappointment drifting off her as her shoulders slumped.

I knew she'd felt the size of him in my office that day, but until you glanced on the full glory that was Miles, you just didn't understand how well-endowed he truly was. What she didn't know was how gentle he could be. I'd had the same fear the first time we'd made love, but then again I wasn't a virgin.

"Do you remember how you promised to trust me sweetheart?" His deep baritone voice was seductive and it was filled with just the right amount of tenderness that her eyes lifted to his. She nodded, but still nibbled on her lip in concern.

"I'll make this good for you." His long fingers reached out to caress her cheek and that heartbreaking smile lifted the corners of his lips. "Just trust me." It was a plea and I knew personally that he was begging her for the opportunity to prove he could fulfill her fantasy.

I wanted to walk over and wrap my arms around him. This was my Miles, and if he made a promise he'd move heaven and earth to keep it. For the first time I wished Amber knew him as well as I did. She nodded again, and I let go of the breath I'd been holding. I hadn't even realized I was doing it.

"Can I touch it?" Her words were whisper soft again and I smiled at how her curiosity was winning the battle over fear.

"I'd love nothing more than to feel your sweet little hand on me sweetheart." To prove his words, he rested back on the pillows, and surrendered his body for her perusal.

I expected her to work up to touching his cock, instead her dainty hand circled his base, and squeezed lightly. His soft moan of pleasure made her smile. She obviously had no problem with this since she lowered her head and got a bird's eye glance, her hand moving slowly up and down his large shaft.

It was written on her face how entranced she was at the way his cock hardened even more with each stroke of her fingers. The pleasure it gave her to know she had the ability to turn him on put a sparkle in her eyes I'd never seen before. She was truly enjoying touching him.

Miles had to be using all the will he had not to come as that little hand grew more practiced, increasing the rhythm and pressure of her stroke. When her mouth lowered to lick away the small drops of pre cum though he'd reached his limit. Sitting up quickly he forced a smile while removing her hand.

"One more touch like that sweetheart and this is over before I love your body." He chuckled self-derisively and pulled her into his arms.

"I want to taste you." Amber was pouting. She had no idea that he was trying to make this better for her and I wanted to laugh. Remembering my place in this fantasy I sat back and watched instead.

"You have no idea how badly I want you to do just that, but I'll never last." Lowering her back on the bed, he parted her thighs and came between them. Resting his weight on his arms, his cock rubbed over her clit slowly.

"Don't tense up for me sweetheart," he cajoled while continuing the back and forth movement, sliding his engorged shaft over her most sensitive area.

Her small hands gripped his biceps and she took several deep breaths. As she exhaled Miles pushed forward embedding only a few inches before retreating again. "You're so tight sweetheart, it's like that little pussy is suckling my cock."

He repeated the same action several times, only giving her a taste of his size. She began lifting her hips to meet him but discovered quickly that Miles was in complete control, not allowing things to progress any further.

"Please Miles, more." Her soft words fell from those lips as he pulled back again and I knew she was close to going over the edge.

"Are you ready for all of me?" He was teasing her, and slowly inched forward only to retreat again before he'd barely begun.

"Yes. Now! I want all of you inside." Her hips were gyrating as he continued the teasing seduction and the frantic movements were those of a desperate woman seeking release.

"I'm not sure you do, sweetheart." I could see the tension in his shoulders as he held himself back, needing to build her desire to the point where nothing else mattered. Barely pushing forward, he allowed her to lift her hips for deeper penetration, holding himself fully in check.

She cried out as her body was stretched even more, but still she lifted higher. Amber lowered and raised her hips continuously, taking him deeper each time but still only enjoying half of his length. Then paradise found her. Miles waited until she came before thrusting deep and claiming her body for his own. Remaining completely still he allowed her body to grow accustomed to his cock, the small tremors of pulsing pleasure helping stretch her without all the pain.

"Oh God!" She held on to him tightly as the remaining tremors shook her frame then looked up at him with a smile. "You're inside me."

"Yes I am sweetheart." She wiggled her hips slightly and he groaned. "Are you okay?" Even though I knew he wanted to pound into her at the moment, he still held concern for her at the top of his list. I loved this man.

"You're really big, but it feels kind of good." She moved her hips in a circular fashion and moaned.

"Only kind of?" He winked and carefully inched out of her. "We'll have to work on that." With patience he slowly slid back in. "How's that?"

The man had to have the most self-control of any person I knew!

"More!" Amber was becoming a demanding little thing, but I knew that Miles was more than ready to accommodate her.

"As you wish." Lowering his lips he slowly began riding her body in an unhurried fashion. Watching them make love was nothing short of incredible. His well-rounded ass relaxed, and tensed with each thrust and I was enthralled. The symphony of two lovers striking a chord of passion as their bodies increased the rhythm, was almost magical.

Hands grasping, legs clenching, breaths escaping on the notes of passion. My heart raced right along with them until the finale that ended with two beautiful bodies resting against each other in fulfillment, overwhelmed by the act of love they'd shared.

It was almost too much. Silently fleeing from the room where they rested together on their stage, I found my way to the kitchen. My fingers grasped the cool tile of the island bar as I tried to catch my breath. Miles had just made love to another woman and I found pleasure in that act. I wasn't sure how I was supposed to feel.

For long moments I stood there gripping that bar. I needed to go home and think. My body was still aching for release, and the memories of how they'd loved so completely wouldn't release from my mind. Grabbing my purse I found my way out of the penthouse and waved down a cab.

CHAPTER FOUR

Acceptance

I rode back to my apartment, still trying to come to grips with how turned on their lovemaking had left me. It took everything I had not to find my pleasure in the back of the cab. Clenching my thighs together, I could only hope that this driver hurried and got me home before I made a fool out of myself.

The moment he pulled up to my curb, I tossed a bill at him, not caring about change. Faster than I'd ever walked before, I made it upstairs and through my apartment door. Thankfully Rachel was at work, because I wasn't sure I'd make it to my room. Walking over to the couch, I laid down, and spread my legs wide. My core was still soaked and without any thought my fingers slid under my skirt and over my throbbing clit. Closing my eyes I could still see them fucking on that bed and I pleasured myself to the memory.

Even after release, I was still hungry for more. I wished I was at Samson's so I could use one of his toys. Deciding then and there, I was going to have my own personal vibrator, I wished I'd thought about it before. A firm knock on the door pulled me out of my wishful thinking. I really wasn't in the mood to socialize, and walked over to answer it with a scowl on my face.

"Miles said you ran out on him." Samson was standing there with a concerned look on his face and I felt horrible that I'd made them worry.

"How did you get here so quick?" My ton was bitchy but I was still horny as hell. It only took twenty minutes to get from Miles's place to mine.

"I was parked outside." He shrugged like that wasn't a huge deal.

"Wow. Stalk much?" My thighs were drenched with my juices, and I wasn't really in the mood to make small talk. Making a face at how uncomfortable I felt I shifted my weight from one foot to the other.

"I wasn't stalking Zoey. Sorry if I was worried that you might not deal well with what happened tonight." He didn't look sorry at all, he looked angry that I was one again defying him. "Do you need to use the bathroom?" Obviously he noticed my shifting.

All I can say is the devil made me do it. "No. If you must know I'm horny as hell and wishing you would leave so I could do something about it." No mouth filter whatsoever. The truth was I didn't care if he knew.

"Fuck, Zoey, I can take care of you."

I should have told him to go screw himself, but the throbbing between my legs had other ideas. "Then stop talking about it and do something." Resting my hands on my hips I glared at him.

"Oh, I'll do something about it alright." Slamming the door behind him, he locked it and all but dragged me over to the couch. Draping me over his lap, his large hand landed on my ass several times, and there was nothing gentle in his touch. He wanted to punish me for my smart ass mouth. Oddly enough I had no problem with him doing it.

Raising my ass to meet each one of his downward swipes, I was getting off on this. Instead of demanding he stop, I wanted to scream, harder. Whatever demon had broken free in me tonight, she liked the feeling of his hand slamming down without thought. The sweet burn to my covered ass, making me hotter than ever before.

"Shit, Zoey!" His hand stopped the punishing strokes, and caressed instead.

I moaned in denial. "Spank me!" I didn't want his tender caress. It wasn't giving me what I needed right now.

Instead of answering me, he stood me on my feet, pulled down my skirt and panties in one motion then pushed me back toward the bedroom. "You don't get to make the rules with me. Suck it up, buttercup." He chuckled as I began struggling against him.

With no finesse whatsoever, he turned me in his arms and faced me down on the edge of the bed. "Keep that ass still. If you move I'm going to fuck it and the last thing you'll feel is pleasure."

A part of me wanted to tell him to fuck off, but another side liked this side of him that told me what I was going to do. Since him in my ass was not what I wanted at the moment, I decided to for once just keep still and let him take the lead.

I heard the slide of his zipper, and the rustling of clothes before I felt his legs pressing against me. "I should make you use that smart ass mouth before giving you what you need." His hand fell down on my bare ass again, and I gasped.

That was the last sensation I felt before he parted my legs and thrust into me without any diplomacy. I cried out as my core accepted him, stretching me beyond what I was ready for. His ass pressed against mine and he held completely still.

"This works better." His hand wrapped in my hair, pulling back harshly. "That sweet little pussy is filled up now, isn't it?" He yanked back on my hair, causing a whimper to escape my lips. "You want me to fuck you?"

He rotated his hips slightly, and I moaned in pleasure.

"Answer me Zoey!" Stilling, embedded inside me as deeply as he could possibly be, I wanted to scream back.

"Yes, you asshole, fuck me!" His answering chuckle should have surprised me, it didn't.

"I don't think so baby. You want me to give you what you want, you ask nicely." He pushed forward, grinding his ass into me and I gasped. Never had he been this forceful with me before, and I loved it!

I was so full of him, I knew I'd come if he'd only pull out a little and push forward. I attempted to wiggle my hips for that relief, but he had me pinned with his body making any relief impossible. "Please, Samson!" Shit I could beg. This not finding relief sucked to hell and back.

"That's better but I want you to really beg. Tell me what you want me to do to this pussy and who owns it baby."

Everything in me was screaming to tell him to fuck off and I'd pleasure myself. Everything except my core which was throbbing around his width and knew he could do so much more than my fingers could. I broke. "I'm yours Samson, please fuck my pussy!"

"Like this baby?" He pulled out with agonizing slowness then slid back in, remaining completely still again.

I groaned at the incredible friction. "Yes, please baby, just like that but harder." I didn't want the sweet lovemaking I knew he was capable of.

His chuckle was the only warning I had before he began riding me slowly, like he had all damn day to tease the shit out of me and was enjoying it. It felt good, but I wasn't in the mood for slow and easy. I thrust my hips back, demanding he give me what I craved.

"Oh no baby. You're going to take it like I want to give it or not at all." His body inched out and slowly found home again until I was ready to scream in frustration. My hand clenched the sheets in my fists, feeling that sweet temptation calling on the other side, aching to fall over into mindless bliss. Each careful stroke made me cry out and each pull back made me whimper.

He was killing me with pleasure and I had no choice but to take the rhythm he was riding me with. I felt the tension mount as he teased me with his cock and suddenly it didn't matter how he was loving me, my body came undone. With a soft scream I found paradise, and could only lay there breathlessly as my orgasm controlled everything.

Only then did he unleash the power of his passion in me. Riding me with a savageness that left me breathless for another reason. His hand slid under my body, pinching my clit, making me long again for that unreachable pinnacle of pleasure.

I don't know how he lasted so long, but my pussy was aching as he punished it with his cock. For a moment I thought about how sore I'd be tomorrow, but then I found paradise again. He pulled from my clenching core, and slowly slid in the backdoor, stretching me to the point of pain. With a few deep thrusts he filled me with his essence before falling on me, leaving us both winded.

After several moments of our breaths echoing in the room, he slid from my aching flesh and pulled me into his arms. We scooted back to the head of the bed, and rested there in silence.

"I have no control with you." He clasped me against his chest, making it hard to breathe. Then he loosened his hold. He stroked my hair, and kissed my cheek, my nose then our lips found each other's. There was nothing sweet in this, we devoured, taking and giving and maybe a little begging for forgiveness on both of our parts in that kiss.

We were dynamic together, as much as we pissed each other off, in bed there was no doubt how compatible we were. "I don't think I'll be walking much tomorrow." I giggled as our tongues stopped dueling.

"I guess on the positive though you aren't horny anymore?" His soft chuckle had me flushing and I thought 'yeah there was that'. I shook my head grinning.

"I don't know. Even as sore as I am, I want you." That was the truth. The overwhelming urge to fuck was gone, but I still ached to make love to him.

"You'll be the death of me baby."

"Gotta go somehow?" I lifted my head from his chest and smiled into those sexy bedroom eyes of his.

His hand landed on my now sore backside and I flinched. "A little sensitive now Samson." Sliding from the bed, I winked at him and walked toward the bathroom.

He joined me and I turned on the shower. We bathed each other off and it was like the fire from earlier was now gone, so we had time for the tenderness. The way he took care of me made my heart ache. I knew he was capable of great emotion, and I loved this side of him. But even a stubborn bitch like myself couldn't lie and say I didn't love possessive Samson too, when he wasn't being condescending.

With our bodies completely clean, I wrapped myself in his arms, holding on tightly as the hot water still streamed over our bodies. "What are we going to do Samson?" For the first time in our relationship I was asking his opinion.

"I don't know baby." He held me against his chest and caressed my wet hair. "I wish I knew how to make us both happy."

That was the gist of the situation. We both cared about each other, but needed different things. When he was holding me like this though, I wanted to believe anything was possible. As the water started to cool, I broke our embrace and reached down to turn it off.

He stepped out of the shower and grabbed a huge bathing towel. Wrapping me in it, he dried me first before doing the same for himself. Dropping the towel on the floor, he lifted me in his arms and walked back to the bed. Placing me on it as if I were some fragile girl, he joined me and cuddled up next to me.

I fell asleep not sure where our relationship was supposed to go, but comfortable just holding on to him for the moment. During the night he made love to me several more times, but it wasn't the frenzy of before. It didn't matter that my body was a little achy, because I wanted him just as much.

The next morning when I awoke, he was gone. It did things to my heart that I can't explain knowing that we'd left things in such an uncertain place. Samson would always give me what I needed, but I wasn't sure what that was anymore.

CHAPTER FIVE

Composing

"Looks like someone had an interesting night."

I'd just walked out of my bedroom to make coffee as Rachel was walking in. My skirt and panties, along with my shoes were scattered over the floor. "Samson stopped in." I knew my face was flushed as I picked up the clothes.

"Miles and Samson? Some girls have all the luck." With a soft laugh, Rachel walked into the kitchen and started the coffee brewing.

"I didn't do Miles." I felt like I had to explain that, but wasn't sure why it made me so defensive.

"I wasn't bitching girlfriend. Maybe a little jealous, but hell you've been living a life most people only dream of lately so who could blame me."

"Trust me it's not all it's cracked up to be." That was the crux of the situation. Trying to find my place in this crazy ass relationship was driving me nuts. I'd been so pissed at Samson but after last night I knew I still wanted something with him.

"So I guess you and Samson had wild makeup sex." Pouring us both a cup of coffee, Rachel took them over to the island bar and we sat down together.

"He left without waking me up this morning, so who knows." I had no idea where things were with him and it was driving me nuts. "Then Miles. The way he was with Amber, I think he wants more there, even though he swears he's not right for her."

"I'm the last person to be giving sexual advice, Zoey, but maybe you need to stop seeing all of them." She took a sip of her coffee, avoiding my eyes. "Obviously it's screwing with your mind and I don't want to see you getting hurt."

Was she right? Trying to be everything to four men wasn't something I had been prepared for. I mean sure. The sex had been great, but that was never going to be enough for me. In the back of my head, all I really wanted these days was a normal relationship and there was nothing normal about sleeping with four men.

"If you had to choose one, who would you stay with?" Finally she looked at me and I could tell she wasn't comfortable bringing up the subject.

"Leon and Leif have their own thing going, so ruling them out wouldn't be a big decision." I could have argued with her but the truth was I needed to make a decision. Then there was always the 'what if' they weren't willing to change their original idea for one big happy love fest. "As much as I love Miles, and I do love him, I think he needs something different. He says he wants a partner, but the truth is I could bend him to my will and make him miserable in the process."

When it finally struck me that I was just as dominant as Samson, the laughter struck, and I couldn't contain it. He was my perfect partner. Granted he wanted to control me, but he couldn't, but he wouldn't let me control him either. "I think I've been an idiot."

"Nah, I've seen your IQ tests, nothing stupid about you." Rachel was grinning into her coffee mug, and I knew she'd figured out what I hadn't long before.

I left my coffee untouched, stood up and hugged her tightly. "I think there's a stubborn ass man that I need to have a few words with." Kissing her cheek, I all but ran back to my room. Within twenty minutes I had showered, dressed in casual wear, and raced to the front door. It was time me and my lover had an in depth discussion.

I flagged down a cab and fidgeted in my seat the entire way to Samson's house. Paying off the driver, I walked up to the front door, not sure what I was going to say to him, but damn sure that things were going to be hashed out. He answered wearing only a towel around his waist. Damn him!

"You and I have some things to discuss." I pushed my way inside, refusing to look at his delectable body because I needed my mind focused.

"By all means, come right in." He shut the door behind me, and gave me his exasperated look. "Do I have time to change before we have this talk?"

I nodded, making the mistake of looking down and knowing if he didn't put some clothes on this discussion would end up as pillow talk. "I'll wait for you in the living room." Not glancing at him again, I walked away before I jumped into his arms.

How long did it take a man to put on some damn shorts? Pacing the room in nervous anticipation, I went over in my head what I wanted to say to him. Worst case scenario, he could tell me that wasn't interested in what I wanted, and then I'd kick his ass. No. I'd accept that he was looking for something different and end this. Fuck! I didn't like that idea either. He better not tell me that what I wanted wasn't obtainable.

By the time he walked back in I'd worked my way into a panic. As per usual, the mouth filter slid completely off. "I don't want you screwing other women, and I think this thing between us needs to be one on one."

"Alright then. But you need to start giving a little more and allow me to train you as my submissive."

That fucker was negotiating with me! Holy shit, wasn't that a complete change from what I expected. "I'll let you play your little games occasionally, but I'm not kneeling at your feet unless I get something in return. And no damn whips. That shit is just fucking scary and I am calling that a hard limit."

"No whips. But when we walk into my dungeon you will kneel at my feet, but outside that room we're definitely equals." He crossed his arms over his chest, that sexy ass smirk I loved on his face.

"I'll kneel at your feet, but only because you're going to make damn sure that I find pleasure there. And outside the dungeon, damn straight we're equals. Turn about is fair play though, when we're in your bedroom I get to make the rules."

Samson tossed back his head and chuckled deeply. "You, my sweet little negotiator, drive a hard bargain. Fine. In the bedroom, I'll let you be on top."

"Oh no baby, it won't be that simple. In the bedroom, you will let me tie you up and do whatever my wicked mind can come up with to bring you pleasure." Just thinking about how much fun I could have that way made my core flood.

"And just what does that sexy mind of yours want to do with me right now." He walked forward until we were only a few inches apart.

My heart raced and I swallowed deeply. "This conversation is not finished, Mister. Stop trying to change the subject." Before I forgot why I needed to get things out in the open and tackled that gorgeous body on the floor.

He grinned and it made him even more devastatingly handsome. Thankfully he also backed up giving me a little breathing room. "You're right, let's talk instead of doing what we both want right now."

That damn smirk again. With a groan I launched myself into his arms, wrapping my legs around his waist as my lips met his. He didn't play fair. I was definitely going to have to get this overwhelming need for him out of my system before I could clear my head. Losing myself in his kiss, I decided that would probably only take a few years.

His hands gripped my ass as we kissed and he carried me upstairs. How he saw where he was going with our lip lock going on, I had no idea. He didn't break the kiss until we walked through his bedroom door. The significance of him taking me to his bedroom instead of the dungeon wasn't lost on me.

I slid to my feet and raised my eyebrow. "So we're playing in my world, then. Strip and put that gorgeous ass on the bed, Sir." Giggling at giving him the title he longed for while being in control was a huge turn on.

"Yes, Ma'am." He didn't hesitate in baring his body for me and I liked acquiescent Samson.

To be fair, I stripped out of my clothes and grinned as he gripped the headboard, giving me complete control. I had a gorgeous Samson buffet laid out for me, now how was I going to indulge? The ideas were endless.

I grasped one of his ankles, and spread it to one side of the bed. "Don't move that leg." My eyes roamed over his perfect body, and the huge erection he had didn't go unnoticed at all. I had plans for that soon, but not before I situated him the way I wanted. Moving to his other leg I spread it wide, resting it on the other side of the bed before lowering my mouth to his toes. I suckled the biggest one and enjoyed the harsh groan from his lips.

"Fuck baby, you're going to kill me."

"You have no idea." Giving an evil little laugh I trailed kisses to his foot, up to his knee on one leg, then moved to the other determined to drive him as nuts as he did me. My hands then splayed on his large, muscular thighs. With more patience than I had, I rubbed those beautiful muscles up to his hips, purposely ignoring his huge cock, which was jerking with the teasing I gave.

Skipping that begging appendage, my fingers traced over his six pack abs, and up to those male buds, circling them slowly. Lowering my head I nipped one, then the other, enjoying how his strong arms flexed to keep his hold on the headboard.

Straddling his waist, I allowed my wet heat to barely graze his cock, reveling in the deep growl of pleasure that escaped. My lips lowered to his neck, and I nipped him lightly beneath the ear. Then using my teeth, I gripped his earlobe and bit down softly before whispering. "You like that baby."

"Like? Baby you've got me so hard I'm about to come!" He arched his hips up trying to nudge his way inside me, and I lifted off him.

"None of that. If you're not good, I won't give you what you want." Kneeling up on the bed, I found my inner whore. My legs were spread wide, and my fingers rubbed over my clit several times, before lifting them to his mouth. "Taste what you do to me Samson."

My fingers were quickly suckled into his mouth and I gave my own moan of pleasure. I don't know where I got the bravery, but the feeling of him suckling my fingers wasn't enough. I knelt over his face, pressing my dripping core against his lips. "Fuck me with that beautiful tongue."

I liked this. A lot. Even more so when his mouth ravished my core, until I was sure my trembling legs couldn't hold my slight weight. I didn't want to let go yet, and I quickly moved off him again. "First I want to taste you."

I moved back down his body, and my hand grasped his cock tightly. So tightly that he took in a quick breath of air. Instead of going for that delightful proof of manhood I suckled his balls again. I liked that he kept them free of hair, it made licking him even sexier.

Without warning I lifted and my tongue trailed from the base of his cock to tip, before taking it deep inside my mouth. He was mine to command and that made me want to please him even more. I finally understood what the big turn on was for him being in control. Instead of taking time to ponder that I fucked him with my mouth until I felt the soft drop of his semen. Then I pulled back.

"I didn't tell you to come that way." Giving him my best glare, I knew this game couldn't last much longer. I wanted him too badly. Straddling his waist again, I slowly lowered down on his cock, stretching my still sore flesh until he was embedded as deeply as he could go. We both groaned.

"You wore me out last night Samson, so we're taking this slow." I don't know who was aching more as I slowly rode him, lifting my hips up to where only the tip of his large mushroom head was embedded, before lowering myself again with well-practiced ease. He felt so good this way and I tossed back my head, arched my neck, unleashing in the easy, laid back rhythm.

"I want to turn you over and fuck you like an animal right now, Zoey." He grunted as I continued to torment us both.

"Don't you dare let go of that headboard." My soft demand came out on a whimper of pleasure, because I had him positioned to where his cock rubbed against my clit and I was so close to losing control.

I couldn't hold back any longer. My release was so close that it demanded to be found, and I quickened the pace. I'd never known I could be so wild in bed, but I fucked him like the world would end if I didn't find pleasure soon. God it was good! Lifting and falling on him without any concern except my own need, it was sheer freaking nirvana.

My core squeezed and released as paradise flooded my world. "Come for me Samson, fill me up." I wanted him with me, and I couldn't move as my body trembled around him. His hips began arching upward, almost like he was pounding me from the bottom up and it just fueled my orgasm. Feeling him flood my body just made it even more beautiful, and I cried out in ecstasy.

Falling on his chest, our hips pressed against each other, I was sure I'd never loved this completely in my entire life. Only when we'd both been fulfilled did his arms encircled my waist, holding me against him. Tears filled my eyes at the beauty of our lovemaking, they flooded down my cheeks, soaking him.

"Fuck baby, you okay?" He lifted my exhausted head, forcing our eyes to meet. The love in those eyes, only made me cry harder.

I nodded then kissed him passionately. I wasn't sure I could explain how it felt to finally know this is where I belonged. If he could surrender so completely to me, how could I do anything less for him? I couldn't. He was my Samson.

He pulled back slightly, pushing the hair away from my face. "Baby, you're killing me here. Tell me what's wrong." I was drenched in sweat from our lovemaking and so was he. I laughed softly, even through the tears.

"Nothing's wrong. I just think I love you." His long fingers wiped away the salty wetness and he smiled at me like I was the most precious thing in the world.

"You only think? I've known I loved you from the moment you first told me to kiss your ass." He grinned and I couldn't stop from smiling back.

"Of course I love you baby. I just didn't know it was possible to love you this much." I kissed him again, and I knew that whatever shit we went through, this man was my forever guy. There's a lot of profoundness in knowing you've found the one person in the world that was meant to be yours.

"Marry me then baby. I know who I want to spend the rest of my life with. Fuck, maybe even have a few kids?"

"Kids? I can do the married thing, but kids? We are so going to have to talk about that for a long, long, time." I was not good at sharing. The truth was as much as I enjoyed being with all the guys, that wasn't who I wanted to be. One man, one woman, and okay maybe a lot of forever, but kids?

"We'll put that as a soft limit for now, but bring it back to the table later on. Deal?"

Always negotiating. I had to love my Samson. "I can live with that. And no fancy wedding. I hear that shit really screws with people's minds. Just you and me and a few of our friends."

"What about your parents? Don't you want to invite them?"

I hadn't even called home in the last few months. I really wasn't being the best daughter. "I guess that would be the right thing to do. Okay but a small wedding. I mean really small." The idea of dressing up in some formal gown might be some people's idea of perfection, but I had no such delusions of grandeur.

I felt him harden inside me, and I forgot that we were having a conversation this way. Grinning, I looked up into his eyes with a devious glance. "Maybe you need to control the next round." The truth was I wasn't sure I could move after last night, and the little tryst we'd just had.

He rolled me under him so quickly I barely had time to catch my breath before he started thrusting. I could really get used to this, I thought before I couldn't think at all as he rode me savagely.

CHAPTER SIX

The Guys

Samson arranged dinner with the guys at our favorite restaurant. We'd spent the entire day in bed, except for the shower and a brief lunch, and I was wincing as we walked to our table. Giving him a glare as he held out my chair for him, I wasn't sure I wanted to smack him or grin at how well my body had been used.

How the man could keep going for so long was still a mystery to me, but I knew we had to find some other outlet for his need if I planned on walking. That didn't mean other women, but maybe advancing my oral skills, or even some new toys. I was rubbed raw from his overwhelming need to make love.

Leon and Leif were the first to join us, and they were already bickering. I swear they argued more than an old married couple, but you could tell they loved each other. "Sorry we're late, Leif had to change outfits a dozen times before he was happy."

"Fuck you Leon, you were the one that kept making comments about how certain pants made my ass look fat."

"I didn't say fat, ass wipe, I said plump. I personally like the way your ass looks." Leon winked at him and I watched in fascination as Leif's cheeks flushed.

Miles walked in and to my shock, Amber was with him. I guess I shouldn't say shock, because I knew after last night he wouldn't be able to just walk away. That wasn't the type of man he was. Instead of being jealous, I was happy for him. She really was a nice girl, and now that I knew what I wanted, I could accept that he wanted someone else too.

"I hope you guys don't mind that I brought Amber."

He looked so miserable that I had to help him out. "Of course not Miles, we're glad you're both here." Amazing how jealously flies right out the window when you've been loved so completely sex is taken out of your thoughts.

"So." Leif drawled with a smile, seeming pleased to take his mind off the other issue. "She the one." Leif winked at Amber and I thought Miles was going to come across the table and bust his lip.

"Amber isn't ready to be a part of the game." He was clenching his teeth as he spoke, and his arm went around her waist protectively. I knew instantly that he had no intention of sharing. My night just go much either.

"That's sort of why Samson and I asked you all here tonight." Now that the time had come, I wasn't sure how to say what I needed. Looking to Samson beseechingly, I hoped he knew that I needed him to break the news.

"Zoey's agreed to be my wife." The smile that filled his face made him almost glow, and I'd never seen him more beautiful than in that one moment.

Congratulations were passed around and Mile's looked so relieved that I couldn't help but laugh softly. "We've also talked and decided that we want to be exclusive." I was almost afraid to look at their faces but refused to be a coward now.

Leon and Miles looked really happy about the decision, and Leif was the only one that seemed not on board.

"So that's it then." The defeat in Leif's voice almost broke my heart.

"I loved being with you guys, but that's just not who I am. I thought I could be, but some things, I think are better in the fantasy world."

"That's just great then." Leif stood up and threw his napkin down on the table before walking away.

I looked to Samson, my heart breaking that he was unhappy. Leon stood and shook his head.

"It's not your news that has him upset Zoey. He'll be happy for you, there are some issues about our relationship that he's not dealing well with." Leon lowered his head to kiss my cheek, then walked off in the direction Leif had.

"I'm completely lost." And feeling some of my euphoria leaking away at how he took the news. I never wanted to hurt any of them.

Samson wrapped his arm around my shoulder and lowered his lips to my ear. "I think what's going on is Leif could accept Leon's pleasure as long as there was a woman involved. He doesn't want to be considered homosexual."

That floored me. I didn't understand why it made a difference who he wanted sexually, but I'd never had a relationship with the same sex. "I don't want him to be miserable."

"Sweetheart that's not your problem. Leif is going to have to find his own way in this. All we can do is be his friend as he decides what works for him in his life." Miles winked at me but his arm snaked around Amber.

I realized how uncomfortable it must be for her to be dealing with all our problems and gave her an encouraging smile. "So how are you feeling?"

"I'm just amazed that you guys care so much about each other. When Miles explained the type of relationship you all had, I was shocked." It was amazing seeing the change in her after only one night with Miles. He was really good for her, obviously.

"We all love each other." I could only imagine what it must look like to her. Actually I couldn't imagine. If I'd been in her shoes I would probably think we were all a bunch of oversexed deviants.

"I can see that." She turned to Miles and the devotion in her eyes was enough to make my heart sing. I hoped he felt something for her too, because even a blind person could see she was more than enamored with him.

Miles smiled back at her and I knew he felt something. I guess we were both fools to think he could be a woman's first and not have strong feelings for her. He was the type of guy that thrived on emotions. It was one of the things that made him such a great person.

"So when are we having a wedding?" Miles turned away from Amber and glanced at me and Samson.

"Zoey wants a small ceremony, but I'd like to have our parents there and our friends from the club." He turned from Miles then back to me. "What do you think baby?"

"I've never put a wedding together, so I don't know?" We were getting married! Holy crap! My heart fell into my stomach.

"If you don't mind the help, I've planned a few." Amber broke into my train of thought and I turned back to see her smiling.

I knew that was her profession since I'd interviewed her, but I wasn't sure how she'd feel about doing that since I'd slept with the guy she was now? Dating? Sleeping with? I wasn't sure what their relationship was. "If it wouldn't be too awkward?"

"Are you kidding me? Knowing that you're wanting a one on one relationship with Samson is probably the greatest thing ever." Her cheeks flushed as she realized what she'd said, and I smiled. "I didn't mean anything bad by that."

I could tell she was flustered and I had to save her. "Believe me I understand. I'd really appreciate the help and since I have no clue how to plan a wedding, you're a godsend."

Everything was working out just the way it should. I couldn't believe how easily things were falling into place. We ordered our meal, and enjoyed small talk for the rest of the dinner. Leon and Leif didn't come back. I hoped that whatever they were going through wouldn't affect their friendship.

CHAPTER SEVEN
A Wedding

Amber turned out to be more than a godsend. She'd managed to pull off a beautiful, yet simple ceremony in less than a month. I had no idea how she did it, but we were on the island with thirty of our closest friends and family. Samson's splurge on the yacht had paid off since we were able to bring our entire wedding party in one trip from the mainland.

The resort was still being built, but it was the perfect spot for our wedding. Giving in to my desire for a casual ceremony, I was dressed in a strapless, A-line dress, made of organza that billowed in the slight breeze coming off the ocean. My mother had laced my hair with tiny white flowers, and left it hanging loose.

Walking off the pier long after all the other guests had departed, I was stunned by the full effect of Amber's skill. A gazebo of palm trees, surrounded by sheer white curtains was made breathtaking by the view of the blue-green ocean and sugar white sand backdrop. White fabric covered chairs dressed in pale yellow silk with white tropical flowers were perfectly lined on each side of the yellow rose petal aisle. Standing at the end was my beautiful Samson, dressed in a white dress shirt and khaki casual pants. He looked delicious standing there with that gorgeous smile on his face as my father led me.

I saw the other guys dressed in casual white pants and shirts, and they were delectable, but Samson had my heart. Rachel, Brandy, and Laura, another friend of ours from college, were stunning in their pale yellow organza dresses. This was the perfect setting to give my life to the one man I knew I could never live without.

Squeezing my father's arm for support as I walked to my fate, I realized how truly blessed I was. Some people wait a lifetime to find their perfect partner, and here I was about to marry mine. I hoped my makeup didn't run because my eyes were filling with tears.

My father gave my hand to Samson and the next minutes passed in a complete blur. I know I said the words agreeing to join our lives together, but until our lips met for that kiss that sealed our fate, I wasn't even sure I was still living in reality. The touch of his lips proved that this wasn't a dream and I kissed him back with all the passion I felt.

"This island was the first place I made love to you." Samson lifted his lips from mine, and whispered the words in my ear. His hand gently pushed away a long strand of hair from my face and the smile he gave me melted my heart in so many ways.

"I wish we could stay here forever." I spoke the words softly, lost in this magical moment that I knew I wouldn't forget as long as I lived.

"Whatever wish you have Zoey, I promise to do my best to make it come true." He kissed me again and our friends and family began to clap. Of course Leif had to do the whistle as we got a little carried away in our own world. Breaking apart slightly we turned to face them as Mr. and Mrs. Samson Harold.

Amber had put together a small feast, and the most beautiful cake, three-tiered and surrounded by edible tropical flowers. I really owed her for how well planned out this event was, because all I could think about was joining my life to Samson.

We cut the cake and I admit I enjoyed smashing the first small piece into Samson's face. He wasn't one to be undone so he returned the favor and we laughed like teenagers. After we ate he told me he had a surprise gift and we left the party by way of a golf cart that was decorated to match the ceremony. I grinned as we drove away, having no idea what gift he could have for me on the island.

"It's not much, but I thought if you wanted we could share our first night of wedded bless here." He looked so concern as he pulled up a small road that had obviously been driven down several times recently.

I gasped in surprise at the small bungalow that we pulled in front of. It was quaint but fit into the island so well than anything else wouldn't have fit the theme of our surroundings. We walked to the front door and he opened it, before lifting me into his arms. I could only gaze around wide eyed, at the beauty inside.

It was simple, yes, but a small living area with kitchen, completely decorated met my eyes. Samson didn't give me much time to study it as he walked toward the back, opening another door. A queen sized bed, draped in white silk duvet appeared, and I grinned. "It's beautiful."

"I'm glad you like it. The guys came out a few weeks ago and installed everything and this is the first time I've seen it. Fortunately for them, they did good." He chuckled and lowered me to my feet. "Miles brought your bag in off the yacht, if you want to change."

"Do you think we could test the bed first? I mean, we need to find out if we can sleep on it tonight." From the moment we'd said our vows, all I could think about was making love to him.

"I think, Mrs. Harold that we can do whatever your sweet little heart desires."

That sexy smirk. I hope our guests weren't waiting impatiently for our return, because I had some serious need to love my husband at the moment. "What I desire, is you." Standing up on my tip toes I kissed him. His soft growl of approval told me he was on the same page.

He turned me around, and made quick work of my zipper. "This dress needs to go now, that is if you plan on keeping it." Showing me just how impatient he was, he slid it from my shoulders and it fell to the ground around my ankles.

The hell with the dress. I loved it but I loved him more. Kicking it aside, my hands moved to the buttons on his shirt, and I had him bare chested in seconds. My lips moved to his chest and I placed kisses down his six pack as I knelt before him. Undoing his belt, I slid it from his pants, and lowered his zipper. "This now belongs to me, Mr. Harold."

Shaking his head as I lowered his pants and underwear in one quick movement, he chuckled. "Whatever you say baby." That chuckle turned into a groan as I devoured him with my mouth, determined to consume all his passion.

He pulled me up and cupped my covered mound. "Just remember, that this belongs to me."

I leaned into the press of his hand and whimpered. "Prove it." I loved when we teased each other, but my emotions were overwhelmed from the ceremony and right now, I just wanted him deep inside.

He grinned wickedly, and ripped off the thin scrap of silk covering me. "Baby you should be really careful what you ask for." Pushing me back toward the bed, I fell back and he gave me no time to catch my breath. Spreading my legs wide, his head lowered and within seconds I was squirming in pleasure as he licked, suckled, and darted his tongue in my wet heat.

"Samson please. I don't want to wait any longer." I lifted my hips, grinding my core against his mouth.

"Your wish," he lifted his head, draped my legs over his shoulders, and drove home with one power thrust, "is my demand."

There was nothing tender about our lovemaking, he consumed my body with his power and I ate it all up, begging for more. I couldn't think, only feel as he drove into me making my body strain to reach that pinnacle of pleasure that remained just outside my grasp.

He was a man possessed as he continued to plunder, and I cried out loudly as the gates of passion finally broke free. "Fuck you feel amazing baby." He continued on, relentlessly until final he found his own world of bliss and filled me with his love.

Several minutes later our sweat-covered bodies separated and I laughed. "I guess walking is overrated."

He looked regretful for a moment, before he chuckled softly. "I guess I'll have to carry you around baby, because I'm never going to have any control where you're concerned." He kissed me softly and shook his head.

"I like it when you're out of control." Sliding from the bed, when all I really wanted to do was lay in it with him, I stood up. "I guess it's rude to keep them waiting?"

"If it were just the guys I'd say let them wait, but I'd hate for your parents to not like their new son-in-law." He found his feet and led me by the hand to the bathroom. It was surprisingly modern and I was glad we didn't have to use the outside shower like we did on our first visit to the island.

We bathed off quickly and I changed clothes. "Didn't Miles bring your bag?" He looked gorgeous in his now slightly wrinkled clothing, but I wanted him to be comfortable.

"It's in the closet but since as soon as we get them off our island I plan on making love to you all night, I don't see the point in changing."

Grinning at his thought process I decided to just go with the flow. I was wearing a cotton sundress, and slid on a pair of sandals. My hair was wet, so I combed it out and decided they'd just have to live with casual me. We quickly made our way back out to the golf cart, and I think it's safe to say both of us were thinking the faster we joined them, the sooner we could be alone again.

Hours later we finally had the guests back on the yacht and Samson and I drove them back to the mainland. Two beautiful weeks of bliss awaited us and I couldn't wait to get the honeymoon on.

CHAPTER EIGHT

Luck of Three

Returning to New York was somewhat of a disappointment. Normally I loved the bustling city and all the people but after living in paradise, I'd grown accustomed to having Samson all to myself. Leaving him to go to work while I packed up to move in to his mansion left me feeling depressed.

Brandy was moving in Rachel as I was trying to get all my things together. In some ways I was resentful that she would now have my best friend more than I would. They were joking about something inconsequential when I sat down in the floor and bawled like a baby. Definitely not like me at all.

Rachel joined me on the floor, pulling me into her arms. "Okay baby girl, spill it. What's going on with you? You've been moody as hell since you walked in the front door."

"Brandy's moving in with you, I'm moving in with Samson, my whole damn life is changing so fast that I haven't had time to catch my breath." I clung to her like a child needing comfort from her mother. Something was really fucking off with me.

I knew these feelings were irrational but my emotions were all over the place. Then a wave of nausea hit me so hard, I stood up and ran to the bathroom. Losing the contents of my stomach, I hugged the porcelain thrown tightly, crying while puking my guts out.

"Holy fucking shit! When was your last period?" Rachel was holding my hair back as I hurled again. The concern in her voice made me want to cry even more.

"My whole life is changing and you're worrying about my cycle?" Oh yeah, something was definitely off with me.

"Baby girl your life may be changing more than you think. Now when did you last get a visit from Mother Nature?"

"Well fuck, Rachel. I've had so much going on I really haven't thought about that." Then it hit me, what she was implying. I couldn't be pregnant. Could I? I was on the pill. Racking my brain I tried to remember the last time I'd bought tampons and I felt my world spin out of control, that was over two months ago! Instead of crying, I started hyperventilating.

"Brandy! Bring me a paper bag." I heard Rachel screaming as I tried not to pass out. I couldn't be pregnant, I just couldn't. Samson and I were going to spend the next year in wedded bliss, travel the world, and just enjoy each other like all newlyweds should. A baby would change everything.

I felt the bag being pressed over my mouth, and wondered what the hell Rachel was doing. "Breathe in deeply and slowly." She was caressing my hair with one hand and holding the bag to my mouth with the other.

"Should I call an ambulance?" Brandy was freaking out if the tone of her voice said anything and I wanted to laugh. Now that my heart wasn't racing and I could finally breathe again, I knew that I had to calm my shit down. Pushing away the bag, I pushed away from the toilet, my stomach settled somewhat.

"I don't need an ambulance, though Samson might if I find out we're going to have a baby." Slowly pushing to my feet I walked over to the sink, and mindlessly began brushing my teeth.

"Would you be an angel and run down to the drugstore for a pregnancy test?" Rachel sounded excited as she asked Brandy the question and I rinsed my mouth looking at her like she'd grown two heads.

Brandy nodded and ran off like someone lit a fire under her ass. Wiping my mouth with the back of my hand, I stared into my reflection. Me as a mother? Shaking my head, I knew it was probably just a bug I'd picked up while traveling. There was no way I could actually have a little life growing inside me. I wouldn't even know who the father was.

A loud, insistent knock on the door, pulled Rachel out of the bathroom, and I stared at my face, seeing how flushed it was. Leon and Leif's booming voices pulled me out of the daze I was in and I quickly pulled my hair up into a ponytail before walking out to meet them.

"Samson sent us over to help you pack up." Leif walked over and lifted me in his arms, and I felt my stomach revolt at the overwhelming scent of his cologne. I'd always loved that scent of his before, but today? Groaning I ran back to the restroom.

"Shit sweetheart, you sick." Kneeling down beside me at the toilet, I decided this was the most humiliating way to have a man see you.

"I think she's knocked up." Rachel was not known for her discretion but this was one time I'd wished she had her own mouth filter.

"Pregnant. Shut the fuck up." Leif joined the party in the bathroom and I wanted to smack the shit out of all of them.

"Could we have this conversation when I'm not puking my brains out?" Lifting my head I glared at them. Needing to strike out I turned my heated gaze to Leif. "You really have to stop wearing so much cologne." I knew it was a bitchy move but the fragrance was overwhelming.

"Sorry, sorry." Leif backed out of the room and I felt the queasiness recede. Feeling like I could stand again, I did with Leon's help. We walked back into the living room and I noticed Leif at the kitchen sink with wet paper towels, wiping at his neck.

I couldn't help it, it was funny. I started laughing. He was so sympathetic to my plight, immediately he attempted to rectify the situation. "Sorry love, I shouldn't have been so bitchy."

"Are you kidding me? I'll throw the damn bottle in the garbage when I get home. Are you okay? Do you need anything? I could make you some toast and hot tea?"

Shaking my head at his sweet, but unwarranted focus, I grinned. "It's probably just a stomach virus, Rachel is just worrying you for no reason." It had to be that, because I wasn't sure I was ready to give up my freedom for a child.

"We need to be sure." Leon pulled his cellphone out of his pocket and after five minutes of yelling I knew he'd called Samson. Those two always ended up in a testosterone match and he was usual level-headed with other people. He ended the call, and looked pointedly at me. "Samson's getting in touch with the doc now, he wants you at his place in fifteen."

"You really should have asked me before calling him." I was not happy. When all of this turned out to be a fluke, I was going to be pissed that he'd worried him for nothing.

"Be angry with me later, if I hadn't called him, he'd be jumping all our asses later for not getting him involved." Leon shrugged and I rolled my eyes at how he took control of the situation. This was my body, and only I should be making decisions about what anyone knew about it.

"I'm going to give in this time, but only because I want to know what the hell is going on. For future reference when it comes to me, I don't need you or anyone else making decisions for me. Capisce?"

Holding his hands up as if to fend me off, he grinned. "Calm down tiger, we'll talk about this after we find out if you've got a bun in the oven."

Rolling my eyes in exasperation, I grabbed my purse of the island bar counter. Brandy walked through the door breathlessly, and I could tell she'd ran her ass off to get me the kit. Her eyes widened when she saw the guys in the living room.

Leif was instantly in flirty man mood, and he winked at her. Again I rolled my eyes. Seeing Brandy blush was pretty hilarious, since she was usually so confident, and I grinned. "Leave her alone Leif." He stalked over toward her and I had to say something when she took a few steps back.

"Let's get this show on the road. Everyone coming?" Leon was glaring at Leif and I had no idea why he was getting so pissed off that Leif was being his normal flirty self. Another time, I could worry about that. Knowing Samson he'd be waiting impatiently for us to show up at his, correction our, house.

Brandy and Rachel joined us as we made it downstairs. I wasn't sure that all of them joining in on this little adventure was the best idea, but I was feeling exhausted and didn't want to deal with the argument if I asked them to stay behind.

Leon opened the passenger door for me and I slid inside. Leif got in the back with the two ladies. My stomach was a bundle of nerves as we drove. Leif's blatant come on lines with the ladies did make me laugh though. I stopped when I noticed how tightly Leon was grasping the steering wheel. Definitely trouble in paradise with those two, I thought.

Leif obviously didn't noticed since the laughter in the backseat didn't let up until we reached Samson's. Leon held the door open for me again as we arrived, and Leif had his arms draped over Brandy and Rachel's shoulders as we made it inside.

Just like I'd thought, Samson was waiting impatiently and held the door open until we were all in, before wrapping me in his arms. "I don't want you to worry about anything. If we're having a baby, then I'll take perfect care of you. You won't have to lift a finger, I'll treat you like a pampered princess."

He squeezed me tightly and I gasped. "Baby if you don't loosen your hold I'm going to puke down your shirt." Samson was being sweet, but sheesh, give a girl some breathing room. He let me go almost immediately and stepped back.

"Oh fuck, baby, did I hurt you? Do you need to sit down? I'll carry you to the couch." He moved to lift me into his arms and I took several steps back.

"Stop it!" I laughed softly at this side of him but I knew I needed to put my foot down. "We don't know anything yet, but even if I was pregnant, you wouldn't be treating me like some fragile little thing. Now let's calm our shit down until we have some answers."

Samson looked like he was about to come unhinged, but he nodded. We walked into his living room, and Leif fixed everyone refreshments. I asked for a pop with very little ice, hoping it would soothe my aching tummy.

Samson chugged down two fingers of scotch and then began pacing the room. I'd never seen him so out of control before. When the doorbell rang, he quickly walked away answering it. He came back with the physician that handled all the clubs physicals, Roxie Ferguson.

"Thanks so much for coming on such short notice Doc." Samson really liked Roxie, and I'd never asked how they'd met, but they seemed to be lifelong friends. In my frame of mind at the moment the thought made me extremely jealous. It didn't help that she was a gorgeous red-head that looked a little too damn sexy to be a physician. Doctors were supposed to be middle-aged men with glasses, I thought to myself, glaring.

"Hey there Zoey, Samson tells me we might have an extra wedding gift?" Her sweet demeanor made me feel guilty for thinking so badly about her. I calmed my shit down.

"I'm sure it's just a stomach bug, but since I have missed a few periods, I figure better safe than sorry." I refused to allow myself to think I was pregnant.

"Well let's do a preliminary test, and see how that goes." Pulling a urine kit out of her purse, she smiled warmly. "Where's the restroom?"

I don't know why it pleased me that she didn't know, except that if she didn't know where the bathroom was, she hadn't visited here before. Yes I was being a jealous bitch again. "Follow me." When everyone else stood up I held up a hand. "This isn't a peep show, we'll be back soon."

Dr. Ferguson followed me down the hall and explained how to use the kit. It was fairly simple and she left me in the bathroom to pee in the cup. Once I'd finished I allowed her in to do her thing. Five minutes later she called me and told me that the test was positive. She rambled off a dozen things that we would do next, but to be honest I only heard the word positive. Sitting down on the toilet I forced myself to take deep breaths so I wouldn't hyperventilate again.

"Do you want me to ask your husband to come back?" Her question bit through the haze in my mind and I nodded absently. Holy shit! I was going to be a mother!

Samson walked in the room looking like he was going to throw up. "Is everything okay? What did the doc say? She wouldn't tell me shit, said it wasn't her place." He was obviously not pleased with that since he expected people to do as he demanded.

"I'm pregnant." The words sort of rolled off my tongue, since I was still in shock.

He pulled me off the toilet and held me in his arms tenderly. "Baby that's great news. I always wanted kids."

"What if it's not yours?" I remember vaguely the doctor telling me that I could come in for an ultrasound to determine the date, but common sense told me if I'd missed two periods it could be any one of the guys.

"It's mine no matter who the father is baby. When we wanted our little group involved this question did come up Zoey. All of us, except Leon can have children, so it was bound to be a concern eventually."

"You talked about children?" It never came up in our conversations, so this was definitely news to me.

"Of course we did. No form of birth control is one hundred percent accurate, and eventually we all knew that we wanted a large family." He was stroking my hair, trying to soothe me, and I wasn't sure what to think about his confession.

"I didn't miss a pill." I needed him to know that I hadn't been careless. It was important to me.

"It was meant to be, baby. Stop worrying so much, it's not good for the little pop tart and it's definitely not good for you. You're going to be a great mother." He hugged me tightly before remembering how strong he was and loosening his hold.

"What if I'm not? I'm pretty selfish. I mean, I wanted you all to myself so we could travel and now I've screwed everything up." Sheesh. What was it with me and all the waterworks today, I was leaking again!

Samson smiled at me tenderly, and wiped away the fallen tears. "We've got an eternity to do those things' sweetheart. Now we just have someone new to share them with. Just wait, Zoey, you're going to love her like you've never loved anyone before."

"So you want a girl?" I was a little surprised by that. Samson was such a macho guy, I could see him wanting a son he could do all those manly things with.

"Son, daughter, I don't care. I just want a little person that's healthy and no matter what sex, we're going to spoil the little one rotten." He was smiling so big at that moment that I couldn't help but smile back. Samson would be a great father.

"Please. You are going to be such a control freak that our child will be lucky if let him scrape a knee." I giggled at that thought, thinking of how overprotective he could be when he really cherished something.

"I'm sure you'll put me in my place." He grinned and that sexy dimple in his chin stood out. "Let's go tell our friends the good news."

With Samson being so accepting, and obviously thrilled that we were going to be parents, how could I not be happy? From the way the guys, Brandy, and Rachel were so enthused, it was obviously the best thing that could ever have happened in their eyes.

Dr. Ferguson, excuse me, Roxie as she demanded I call her, stayed to celebrate with us over lunch. Samson began making all these plans about hiring a housekeeper, chef, and employees that he'd refused to have until he found out I was pregnant. The man was seriously in love with me, since he was willing to let his house be staffed for the first time ever.

CHAPTER NINE

Happy Endings

Finding out your pregnant is such exciting news, but dealing with nine months of hell, that can dampen the enthusiasm a bit. My ankles were swollen, my stomach looked like I was carrying a beach ball, and two months ago I'd been put on complete bed rest because I was carrying twins, and having trouble making it to my due date.

I had no lack of company during my confinement, since the guys also Rachel, Brandy, and Amber were always around. Amber and Miles were now exclusive and she beamed with confidence under his love. Miles was almost as overprotective with me as Samson was and I knew it drove his girlfriend nuts, but she took it in good grace, at least while they were here.

I was so tired of lying in bed or on a couch that I was counting down the moment until my little bundles of love arrived. We were so not having any more kids after these, I decided when I stood up to go to the restroom and basically peed myself.

Samson was working but Leif and Brandy were with me today. He refused to ever leave me in the house alone so they'd set up a schedule of who'd spend the day with me. I was mortified when urine began running down my leg. Then the pain hit and I would have hit the floor if Leif hadn't been there to catch me. If my fat ass could have doubled over, I would have, instead I just cried out.

"I think I pissed myself." I laughed in embarrassment, and my situation when the pain subsided. After months of tests, I had little mouth filter about my condition and spoke without giving a damn.

"Um baby, I don't think thanks urine." Brandy, glanced at Leif with a smile, "You're in labor."

"Fuck, shit, damn, hell. What do we do, call an ambulance, screw that, let's get to the car." Leif was freaking out and it would have been adorable if another pain didn't hit leaving me crying out in misery. He lifted my hugeness into his arms and began walking quickly toward the front door.

Obviously my water had broken and I knew that in my case that wasn't the scenario we wanted. They'd planned to induce next week. Leif helped me into the backseat, and Brandy took the keys from him since he was so freaked out, he couldn't even figure out what to do. I grinned as he slid in beside me and she drove.

"Okay, do your breathing exercises. Samson said you had to breathe and relax when the time came." He started taking deep breaths in and out and it was so comical that I giggled because I was fine, he was the one about to hyperventilate.

Brandy called Samson, letting him know we were on the way to the hospital as we drove. Yeah, yeah I know you're not supposed to talk on the phone and drive, but there are always exceptions. I was so glad she was with us today because I couldn't see the rest of them being so calm. She handled things like a pro, getting us to the hospital in one piece, and walking inside to inform someone we were in labor.

A young man come out with a wheelchair, and Leif glared at him as he situated me in it. "I got this." The look Leif gave him told him he better not argue and the man gauged his size deciding to lead the way instead of dealing with an irate person.

My contractions were coming every two minutes by the time we arrived, and the doctor had told me that being pregnant with twins sometimes sped up the labor. They had me in a birthing room so quickly I barely had time to catch my breath.

Samson, Miles and Leon walked in together and I could see the fear in their faces. "Guys, I'm fine. People have babies all the time." The moment I said that another contraction came and I cried out loudly. Fuck that shit hurt.

"Give her something for pain. Now!" Samson was screaming at the nurse as I tried to breathe through the contraction.

"Your wife wanted a natural childbirth, Mr. Harold." The nurse, thankfully had a sense of humor, or was just accustomed to dealing with irate men, because she just smiled.

"I don't give a damn what she wants, she is not to be in pain." Leon grabbed Samson as he stalked toward the nurse.

"Calm your shit down. Go hold your wife's hand and be useful." Glaring at him, Leon was giving his best you don't want to screw with me look.

Samson didn't even argue with him, he just walked over and squeezed my hand. "I'm so fucking sorry, I'll never let this shit happen to you again."

The contraction had ended, and I forced a smile even though I felt like beating the hell out of someone. "I'll be fine." I sure as hell wasn't getting pregnant again though because holy mother of pearl, this shit was really agonizing. It felt like someone had twisted all my stomach muscles up and then ripped them apart with each contraction.

Dr. Ferguson came in and did an internal exam. "You sure don't waste any time Zoey, you're eight centimeters dilated."

That bitch was smiling at me and I wanted to rip her hair out as the next contraction hit. For the next hour I may have threatened to have Samson's castrated and all men along with him as my body prepared to give birth. They seriously all deserved to meet a horrible death as pain wracked my internal organs. Men say that women are weak? Let them attempt having a baby, then we'll talk!

I felt the overwhelming need to push and gave a grunt of pain. Roxie moved between my legs again, and smiled widely. "Let's have some babies."

Samson began sweating profusely and grabbed my hand in a death grip. Rachel had arrived earlier and was now holding my other hand. The room was filled with all my favorite people as I began pushing, and brought two little miracles into the world. Kaitlin and Kaleb Harold.

Holding their little bodies in my arms made every ounce of pain I'd suffered worth it. Instantly, I was in love. Both of them had a head full of dark hair and wrinkled little pink bodies, and I knew as long as I'd lived, I'd never seen anything as beautiful as these two perfect little angels. I counted all their fingers and toes before the hospital staff took them away to do assessments.

I was exhausted, but happier than I'd ever been before. Resting in that bed, listening to the laughter and congratulations, I realized just how lucky I was. I'd come to Fantasy's Bar & Grill worrying how I was going to move forward after everything that had happened at the last law firm. Now here I was, married to one of the most beautiful men in the entire world, and mother to the most gorgeous children any woman could ever hope to have. Fantasy's had definitely made my fantasy come true.

ABOUT THE AUTHOR

Michelle lives in Alabama with her husband and four children. As a former singer/songwriter, she began writing after leaving a successful career in music to raise her family. Her love of romance began early in life when she used to "borrow" her grandmothers Harlequin romance novels. When she began penning her own books she wanted to take those happily-ever-stories and spice them up with contemporary elements.

Those who know her in real life say that she's Betty Crocker when it comes to her home life and a deviant diva when it comes to her work. There's a hidden sex goddess in all of us, and Michelle enjoys sharing her fantasies with readers who enjoy a little extra spice in their reading adventures.

Website: http://www.tearsofcrimson.com
Facebook: http://www.facebook.com/authormichellehughes
Twitter: http://www.twitter.com/MichelleHughes_

11696577R00192

Printed in Great Britain
by Amazon.co.uk, Ltd.,
Marston Gate.